A Pixie's Promise

Dianna Sanchez

DREAMING ROBOT PRESS

Las Vegas, New Mexico. USA

DREAMING ROBOT PRESS
Las Vegas, New Mexico

1 3 5 7 9 10 8 6 4 2

* * *

Publisher's Cataloging-in-Publication data
Names: Sanchez, Dianna, author.
Title: A Pixie's promise / Dianna Sanchez.
Series: The Enchanted Kitchen
Description: Las Vegas, NM: Dreaming Robot Press, 2018.
Identifiers: ISBN 978-1-940924-34-2 (pbk.) | 978-1-940924-36-6 (ebook) | LCCN 2018950161
Summary: Petunia struggles to find her own identity while fighting assumptions about her Pixie
heritage.
When an epidemic strikes she learns to stand for herself.
Subjects: LCSH Pixies--Fiction. | Family--Fiction. | Witches--Fiction. | Friendship--Fiction. |
Healing--
Fiction. | Fantasy fiction. | BISAC JUVENILE FICTION / Fantasy & Magic
Classification: LCSH PZ7.S1947675 Pi 2018| DDC [Fic]—dc23

Cover illustration by Nataliia Letiahina
Map by Oscar Paludi, Exoniensis

For my family:
You are an endless source of inspiration,
all ten bazillion of you.

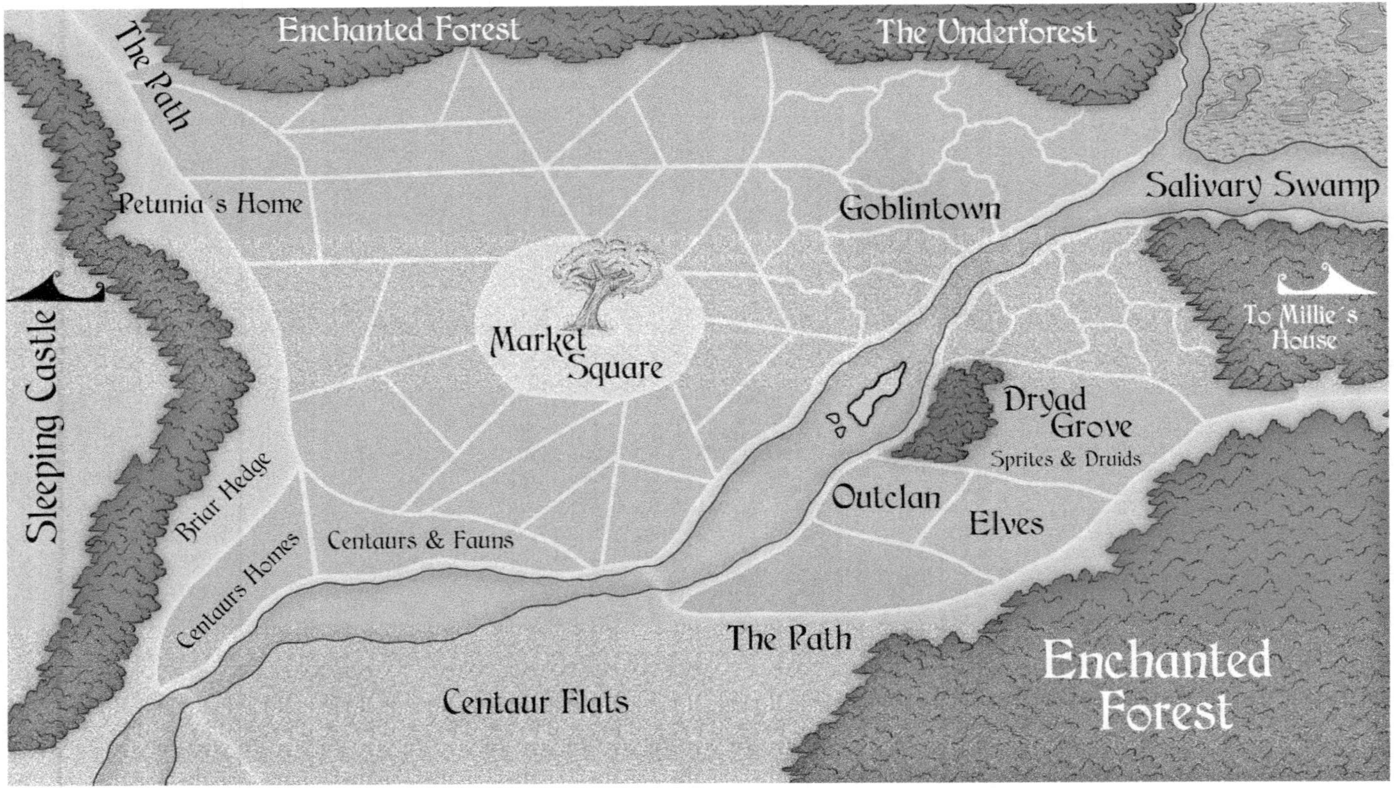
Enchanted Forest
The Underforest
The Path
Petunia´s Home
Goblintown
Salivary Swamp
Sleeping Castle
Market Square
To Millie´s House
Dryad Grove
Sprites & Druids
Outclan
Elves
Briar Hedge
Centaurs Homes
Centaurs & Fauns
The Path
Centaur Flats
Enchanted Forest

Contents

Recipes

 Chapter 1

The Problem with Pixies

Deep in the Enchanted Forest Realm, in the small village of Pixamitchie, in a home neatly woven into a gap in the briar hedge around the Sleeping Castle, a six-inch-tall, ten-year-old, blue-skinned pixie woke with the dawn, even though it was the first day of school vacation.

Today's the day! Petunia thought, and her eyes snapped open to her sister Daisy's curved yellow neck and tangled brown hair. Above them, leaves rustled in the branches and brambles of the briar hedge that her father had woven together to form the bedroom ceiling. The entire room swayed with the morning breeze, lulling Petunia, but she was so full of sizzling excitement that she couldn't possibly drift back to sleep. *Time to go!*

That didn't mean she should wake everyone else up. Gently, Petunia lifted a purple elbow off her stomach— Vetch's elbow, in fact—and turned her shoulder away so that Clover's green foot fell out of her armpit. Peaty was curled up behind her knees. She sat up carefully, put one knee over Vetch, and stuck her foot in a bare patch between him and Holly. Petunia picked her way among the sleeping forms of her sisters, brothers, and cousins, all sprawled across a single enormous mattress stuffed with dandelion fluff. Vetch was the eldest of them still living at home, then Holly, then Clover, and Petunia smack in the middle. At last, she reached the edge and stepped off gingerly, avoiding Primrose, who'd fallen off the bed again and was sleeping curled in a pale pink ball on the moss-covered floor. She paused to gaze at all fourteen of them for a moment, listening to the chorus of breaths and grumbles and soft snores.

I'm going away for ten whole days! she thought. *Ten days away from this, ten days of sleeping alone!* Not once in her life had Petunia slept in her own bed. To be able to stretch without whacking someone next to her, to sleep without being nudged or jostled or rolled over... what would it be like? Would she miss her sisters and brothers? Or would she finally get a full night's sleep?

And what would it be like, living in Millie's house with Millie's mother, the cranky witch Bogdana Noctmartis? Millie was Petunia's best friend, even though she was a human, and Millie had invited Petunia to stay at her house during vacation if she could just do Millie a small favor.

No one stirred behind Petunia as she tiptoed out into the hall, then sprinted for the bathroom. A short while later, she emerged clean and wearing her favorite daffodil dress and her everyday acorn cap, polished until it gleamed. Peaty was waiting for her just outside the bathroom door. He raised his dark brown arms for a hug. Petunia sighed and gathered him up, tousling his green curls, a few shades darker than her own hair. He was only five, after all.

"Why're you awake so early, Tunie?" Peaty asked.

Petunia rubbed noses with him, which made him giggle. "I'm sorry I woke you up, Peaty. I'm going to go stay at Millie's house during vacation while she's in the Logical Realm."

Peaty shuddered. "Scary. But if Millie's going away, why are you going to her house?"

"She needs someone to take care of Thea. You remember, the baby tree?"

Peaty nodded. They had visited Thea at Millie's house a few times. Peaty made a good playmate for Thea, even though she was still too young to walk or speak. "Why can't Millie's mum take care of the baby tree?"

"Can you imagine Bogdana doing that?"

Peaty screwed up his face, then reluctantly shook his head. "Too grumpy. But Tunie," he protested, "who will take care of me while you're gone?"

Petunia laughed. "Oh, nobody. Just Mum and Da and Holly and Vetch and Clover and everyone else. You've got a whole family to take care of you. Thea only has Millie. And me."

"I don't want you to go," he whined.

Petunia looked him in the eye. "Peaty, I made a promise."

His eyes grew wide. "A Pixie's Promise?" he asked.

She crossed her fingers behind her back. "Yes."

The little brown pixie nodded solemnly. "Okay, then you hafta do it. I gotta go potty."

Petunia let him slither out of her arms, and he darted into the bathroom. She suppressed a twinge of guilt as she packed a basket with her things: dresses, underwear, nightgown, dust catcher, comb, and of course, her reserve pouch of pixie dust. She hadn't made a Promise to Millie, she'd just agreed to help out. *But it feels like a promise,* Petunia thought.

A Pixie's Promise was serious business, a magically binding contract that would compel Petunia to do anything and everything she could to fulfill that Promise.

Pixies who failed or broke a Promise suffered terrible
consequences. One of Petunia's cousins had turned into a
mushroom when he failed in his Promise, and it had taken
several sorcerers to turn him back. Legend had it that some
pixies died trying to fulfill their Promises, though Petunia
had never heard of anyone who'd actually died.

Pixies who broke their Promises and survived were
almost always banished from pixie society. In practice,
pixies took great care not to Promise anything they couldn't
easily do. "Never make a Promise you aren't absolutely
certain you can keep," Petunia's mother often said.

So Petunia had made no Promise to Millie, and Millie
hadn't asked for one.

By the time Peaty came out of the bathroom, she was
done packing. "Come on," said Petunia, "let's get you
some breakfast."

They scrambled down the bramble stair to the kitchen.
Their mother, Cherry, was already up with the one-year-
old twins, Lilac and Lily, both howling in their high chairs
at the enormous round dining table, at least a foot across,
standing sturdily upon a great slab of slate their father
had dragged up there himself, magically strengthening the
briar canes supporting it. The walls were lined with open,
rectangular baskets full of dishes and foodstuffs. They had
been woven by Petunia's eldest brother, Fescue, who now
lived in Withywindle Village serving out his apprenticeship
with a master basket-maker.

A pot simmered and burbled upon the stove, which had
been hammered out of an old tin can and was stoked with
dry briar branches. Cherry kneaded the morning bread,
her normally pink cheeks flushed bright red with effort, the
muscles of her arms flexing smoothly. She pulled a pinch
of pink pixie dust from a nearby jar and sprinkled it over

the dough. Immediately it began to rise, doubling in size as Petunia watched.

Cherry spotted them. "Oh, good. Daisy, would you get the twins their oatmeal?"

"It's Petunia, Mum," growled Petunia. She hated that her mother never remembered her name. It made Petunia feel invisible. Just once, she wished her mother would remember, would actually *see* her.

Cherry waved a floury hand. "Yes, yes. Oatmeal, on the stove."

"I want some, too," Peaty piped up.

Petunia set down her basket, grabbed three acorn cap bowls from the cupboard, and filled them all with oatmeal. She set one down in front of Peaty, then one on each highchair. The twins dug in with both fists, and the howling stopped, leaving blissful silence. Petunia brought Peaty a spoon, then chopped up a raisin the size of her fist and sprinkled bits of it over his oatmeal. She grabbed a jug of milk from the icebox and poured him a glass.

Cherry looked up from shaping a fifth loaf of bread. "Holly, can you fill the twins' bottles while you're at it?"

"It's Petunia, Mum."

"Yes, yes." *Thump*, went another pile of dough on the floury table.

Petunia gritted her teeth. She knew she shouldn't let her mother get to her. She grabbed two bottles, filled them with milk, sprinkled them with a pinch of her blue pixie dust, then whispered a phrase of High Mystery: "*Lämpene*" The bottles heated nicely to the same temperature as her skin. She handed one to each of the twins.

"Mum," Petunia said, "remember when I told you I was going to help Millie during vacation?"

Cherry, hefting the baking sheets with their loaves into

the oven, just grunted.

"Well, that's today, so I'll be going now."

"Going where?" huffed Cherry, turning back to the next round of dough.

"To Millie's house."

Cherry frowned. "Milkweed? Who's that? Sounds seedy."

Petunia rolled her eyes. "Millie, Councilor Noctmartis's daughter."

"That witch!" Cherry snorted. "I swear, she keeps raising the price on your father's gout remedy."

As if conjured by the mention of him, Petunia's father hobbled into the kitchen, his right foot swollen nearly twice as large as his left. Where Cherry was broad and strong, Thorn was orange-skinned and slender, except for a full purple beard, a pot belly under his oak leaf tunic, and that gouty foot.

"Hi, Da," said Petunia. "Your foot's looking better."

"Aye, it'll be back to normal in no time, my girl." He peered at the stove. "Any bacon ready?"

"No bacon for you!" Cherry thwacked him on the shoulder with a wooden spoon. "D'you want that foot to swell up the size of a melon?"

"No, dear," Thorn said meekly.

"Bread'll be ready in twenty minutes. You can have oatmeal till then. And mind the twins."

Lilac burped, spattering Lily with oatmeal, who howled and threw oatmeal back.

"I don't want you to go," Peaty said suddenly. "Can't someone else help the baby tree?"

"Don't want who to go, my lad?" Thorn asked him, poking at the oatmeal dismally. He'd long since given up remembering everyone's names, so he just called all his children "my girl" or "my lad." In some ways, Petunia thought that was worse, as though he just didn't care who was who.

"I don't want Tunie to go!" And Peaty burst into tears.

"Well, my boy, you all have to go to school."

"No, Da, it's Endsday," Petunia reminded him, "and school vacation. We've got two weeks off."

"Two weeks? With all of you underfoot?" Thorn tried and failed to hide his dismay. "How will I get all my briar-weaving done?" Thorn's magical specialty was plant-taming, and he'd given their cozy apartment in the hedge improvements such as watertight outer walls and ceilings and running water reeds in the bathroom and kitchen.

"Well, I'm going to Millie's, so I won't be here," Petunia said.

"Good thinking, my girl," Thorn said. "She's the one makes those excellent scones, isn't she? Bring some back for us?"

Petunia sighed. "I'll be gone for ten days, but sure, when I come back, I'll bring you some."

Thorn patted her shoulder. "That's a good girl. And if you can," he leaned over and whispered in her ear, "bring some bacon, too."

"NO BACON!" roared Cherry, which caused both twins to join Peaty in wailing. "Don't you give him any, Primrose."

"It's *Petunia*, Mum!"

"Tunie, don't go!" Peaty shrieked.

Thorn glared at Cherry. "Bristles and brambles, Cherry! There they go again! They'll wake the whole neighborhood."

Cherry glared back. "So do something about it, you lump! I've got bread to make."

Thorn turned to Petunia. "You shut them up, my girl.

Go on!"

Petunia wished her sister Hydrangea were still here. She had an amazing talent for soothing babies, but she'd turned fifteen and married and lived on the other end of the hedge now. Petunia knew only a few tricks.

"Calm down, Peaty. Want to hear a joke?"

"No!" everyone yelled, even the twins.

"What did one wall say to the other wall?" Petunia asked, despite the fact that everyone had clapped their hands over their ears. "I'll meet you at the corner!"

Peaty and the twins redoubled their wailing. Thorn grimaced. "Didn't you say you were leaving?" he asked.

Petunia clenched her fists. "Yes, I did. Not that any of you except Peaty will even notice me being gone!"

Clover came pounding down the stairs. "Mad morning as usual," he said cheerfully. "What's for breakfast?"

"Oatmeal," said Petunia. "Look, I'm going. Watch Peaty for me?"

Clover shrugged. "Whatever. No bacon?"

Petunia seized her basket and rushed out of the kitchen as Cherry began roaring again.

Chapter 2

Grumbles in Goblintown

Petunia dashed down the twisting staircase, though she had to beat back encroaching briar tendrils. It was her father's job, among others, to coax them back daily, but with his gout, he'd been avoiding the stairs. She passed the home of her Aunt Clematis, Uncle Ash, and their dozen-or-so children, whom she could hear shouting and wailing just like her own family, then several feather-lined sparrowkin nests in a row, down to the ground floor landing beside Mr. Pricklesnout's burrow. The hedgehog poked his nose out as Petunia passed. "Rent's due next week!" he called to her.

"Mum knows," she called back.

Petunia dashed off into the village of Pixamitchie, hodgepodge home to dozens of races, from the tiny denizens of the hedge to centaurs, griffons, gargoyles, and one eccentric dragon, with goblins, gnomes, dwarves, humans, elves, brownies, dryads, and fauns in between. It made for some interesting architecture, with smallish apartments in stacks next to large, wooden barnlike structures for centaurs and stone towers for enchanters and gargoyles. Through it all wound the Path, wide enough that two horse-drawn wagons could pass going different directions.

As the magelight lampposts flickered and shut off above her, Petunia ran down streets and alleys, darting between wagons and barrows piled high with turnips, beets, cabbages, crocks of milk and cream, piles of wool, and tubs of stinking fish. A centaur nearly stepped on her, his hoof as large as her whole body. He pulled a cart of goats' milk cheeses, snorting at the clatter and clanging of a gnome tinker's cart hung with pots.

Emerging into the market square, Petunia skipped around the great spreading silver maple tree at its center and passed Bartleby's Bakery with its tempting smells of freshly baked rolls. Her stomach grumbled. She could have had oatmeal at home or waited for the bread, but she knew a far better breakfast awaited her at Millie's house. Ignoring her stomach, she waved at the constable, a dwarf wearing his official rose-colored uniform and jaunty beret, a wand in his fist and a rusty sword buckled at his side.

On the far side of the market square, Petunia skipped past Maud's Twillery Tailors (Odd Sizes Our Specialty) and took a short cut down an alley through Goblintown, where the ramshackle, haphazard homes were slapped together out of loose timber, fallen tree branches, reeds, and mud dredged out of the Salivary Swamp. Goblins tended to sleep in, so she was surprised when she came across a lone goblin, cornered by a gang of pixies, fairies, and sparrowkin, the feathers on their heads and backs raised aggressively.

That's odd, she thought. Goblins never traveled alone if they could help it. Stranger still: he seemed to be covered in small bumps ranging in color from nasty yellow to bright, moldy green against the dark olive green of his skin. The gang taunted him and threw clods of dirt and scraps of garbage at him, but instead of fighting back, he just hunched over and tried to scurry away. He glanced over his shoulder at her, and Petunia caught her breath.

It was Grumpkin.

If Grumpkin hadn't stolen Millie's hat on the first day of school, and Petunia hadn't helped get it back, she might never have gotten to know Millie at all. Grumpkin had made Millie's life miserable at first, but when he stole and ate Millie's lunch, he'd fallen under the charm spell Millie had accidentally put in her scones, and from then on, he'd begun helping her. Grumpkin had been their friend ever since, but at a price.

Without pausing to think, Petunia rushed forward and placed herself between Grumpkin and the other pixies. A rotten blueberry hit her in the knee. "Stop that!" she shouted.

"What're you defending him for?" cried a lemon-colored pixie boy. "After all the times he and his pals have beaten on all of us, you should be kicking him yourself."

"Yah, he sprained my wings!" called a fairy.

"He kicked me across the street!"

"He pinned me in an alley and dumped garbage on me!"

"Just like you're doing right now?" Petunia said.

The gang fell quiet for a moment. Then the yellow pixie said, "It's what he deserves."

"No one deserves this, Aspen," Petunia said.

Aspen cocked his head. "He's a miserable, worthless goblin. Why do you care?"

"Because this miserable worthless goblin helped me and my friends." She looked back at Grumpkin, who, despite being five times the size of any pixie or fairy, knew he was outnumbered and was trying his best to creep away. "Have you ever seen a goblin by himself? He lost his patron because he helped us, and I'm guessing he's being shunned by the other goblins now. Now here you are, punishing him more for doing a good and kind thing."

Aspen stepped right up to Petunia, scowling. "He's a goblin. Goblins are our enemies. Always have been. Now either you help us, or you get out of the way."

Petunia hesitated. These pixies were her friends. But so was Grumpkin. She put down her basket and put up her fists. "Or I beat every one of you first."

Aspen laughed at her. "You asked for it." He stepped forward and swung at her, and Petunia ducked, then kicked him in the shin. "Run!" she called to Grumpkin.

The other pixies and fairies began pelting her with the dirt and garbage they'd been hurling at Grumpkin. Petunia grabbed Aspen, dragging him in front of her. He stepped hard on her foot, and she let go, howling. Several more pixies piled on, punching and slapping and kicking.

It was unlike any fight she'd ever been in. Usually, Petunia could use her small size and speed as an advantage, darting in to punch a knee or twist an ear, then dancing away. Fighting pixies and fairies her size meant she had no advantage, and there were so many more of them than her. She tried to curl into a ball, protecting her head and stomach, and the others piled on top of her. Petunia groaned under their weight and squealed when someone pinched her ear, right at the tender pointed tip. Then, abruptly, the load lightened. Grumpkin had begun plucking pixies and fairies off the pile and tossing them across the alley in all directions.

Petunia gave Aspen a good knee in the ribs, and he let go of her ear, gasping. She scrambled back to her feet. "Go home!" she yelled at them all. "Don't you have anything better to do during vacation?"

Bruised and grumbling, they scattered, Aspen glaring as he staggered away.

"Are you all right?" Petunia asked Grumpkin.

"I've been worse," he said. "Thanks for the help. I was worried they'd ruin Mam's medicine." He held up a small bottle.

Petunia cocked her head at him. "Looks like you could use some of that yourself."

He shrugged. "She's much worse than I am." He hesitated, then said, "Have you seen Cretacia lately?"

Petunia jumped. "What, here? She's back?" Grumpkin used to work for Cretacia, Millie's obnoxious cousin, who loved tormenting Millie for her lack of magical skill. When Cretacia had threatened the newborn Thea, Grumpkin had found the courage to stand up to her and protect Thea. Cretacia had gotten in terrible trouble and fled rather than face the justice of the Enchanted Forest Council.

"I don't know," Grumpkin said. "But my sister's been acting strangely, not just from being sick, and she said something that made me think Cretacia might be back in the Underforest."

A chill went right down Petunia's spine. "I haven't heard a thing about Cretacia for weeks, and believe me, we've been checking. I'll tell Millie about it, okay?"

Grumpkin nodded. "And will you tell me if you hear anything?"

"Of course," Petunia said.

Grumpkin gave her a small, shy smile. It changed his whole face, softening it into something almost pleasant. Maybe with practice, and if he weren't covered in bumps.

"Hope you and your mum feel better soon," Petunia said. "If that potion doesn't work, you should ask Bogdana for help."

His face fell. "She won't sell to goblins."

"Oh. Sorry."

He shrugged. "That's how it is." He shuffled away and disappeared into the warren of goblin homes.

She watched him go with a sinking feeling. Cretacia, back from wherever she'd disappeared to? Petunia had to tell Millie. Bending to retrieve her basket, she looked herself over and sighed. Her best daffodil dress had torn in several places and was smeared with dirt and potato peels. So much for looking her best. Picking up the basket, she headed for Millie's house.

Chapter 3

Bargaining Over Breakfast

Petunia felt strange, hurrying down the Path when school was out, especially after having the sort of brawl she tended to get into at school. Then, just over a small hill, she caught the faint scent of baking. Petunia paused to take a deep breath: scones, bacon, poached eggs. Millie never went halfway. Petunia laughed and hurried on around the bend to Millie's house.

It could not possibly be anything but a witch's house. Petunia knew from first-hand experience that it was haunted. The entire structure leaned theatrically to the east. Every single chimney was crooked. The paint peeling off the clapboards might once have been black, but it had faded to a nondescript grey. Weeds choked the yard, and nightshade straggled and draped itself all over the grey picket fence. Ragged curtains covered every grimy window except one: the bright, clean, open window above the kitchen sink. Petunia could just spy a poofy white hat bobbing inside.

She ran up to the kitchen gate and climbed a nightshade vine right to the top. "Millie!" she called.

The hat disappeared, and a moment later, Millie burst out the kitchen door, her blonde hair flying beneath her enchanted chef's hat, apron strings streaming behind her, clogs clomping as she ran down to the gate.

"Hi, Petunia!" Millie called. "Don't worry, I had Mother change the wards for you. Now you can come and go as you please."

Millie held out her hand, and Petunia leaped into it, expecting to be pushed back by the invisible wards that shielded Bogdana's property, but she slipped right through to land in Millie's palm, dancing with excitement. "I'm here! I'm here! How's Thea this morning?"

"Let's go see." Millie lifted Petunia up to her shoulder and strode out into the weedy backyard. A space had been cleared of weeds just under the shade of a spreading elm tree, and in its center, a sapling no more than twice Petunia's height had been planted. "Good morning, Thea. Good morning, Mx. Elm," Millie called out.

The sapling shook delicately and waved a single leaf at them. The elm above them rustled her own greeting.

"Mix Elm?" Petunia asked, confused.

"Oh, it's something Sagara told me," Millie explained. "A lot of trees like elms aren't just male or female, they're both at the same time. Sagara says the elves have special words for people who are both, but I can't remember them, so I came up with Mx., which is both Mr. and Ms. put together."

"What about Master Quercius and Thea?" Petunia asked.

Millie nodded. "Them, too, only Master Quercius prefers to use male titles and pronouns, and he says Thea prefers female."

"Huh," Petunia said. "Is that okay with you, Thea? I need to know because I'm going to stay with you for ten whole days!" She vaulted off of Millie's shoulder to the ground and ran up to hug Thea. Thea wrapped a couple of low leaves around her and shook as though she were giggling.

Thea was no ordinary tree. The Enchanted Forest School that Petunia and Millie attended took place in the branches of an enormous, intelligent, and magical oak tree, a dodonos named Quercius. Dodonoi were extremely rare—there were only four in the whole Enchanted Forest Realm before Thea came along.

Millie had been sent off to the Enchanted Forest School because every spell she tried at home went horribly wrong. At school, Millie had accidentally transformed a green bean into a cacao bean, and because it had sprouted so close to Quercius, it became a dodonas, an intelligent, magical tree: Thea. One day, Thea would walk and talk and even attend school, learning to use her magic. But for now, she was still just a baby and needed care and protection.

Millie picked up a nearby watering can. "Time for breakfast, Thea. Some nice compost tea for you."

"What's compost tea?" Petunia asked.

"Come and look," Millie said, leading her over to a water barrel and pulling off the lid. Petunia leaped up to the lip of the barrel and peered inside at the murky, brownish water, very like strong tea and smelling of musty earth. "I made this by putting finished compost in a cheesecloth bag and letting it steep. It's full of nutrients that will help Thea grow."

"Like milk for a baby," Petunia said.

Millie nodded. "Exactly. Master Quercius taught me how to do it. There should be enough here to last until I come back." She placed the watering can under the barrel's spigot and filled it up. "There. Now let's go feed Thea."

Petunia jumped down and ran back over to the little dodonas.

"Watch out, Petunia, unless you think you need a shower this morning," Millie said.

Petunia dashed away. "What do you call a dirty pixie?" she asked.

"I have no idea," Millie said, sprinkling the soil around Thea with compost tea.

"P-icky!" Petunia said.

The elm tree groaned, but Thea bent nearly to the ground, shaking with laughter. Millie just shook her head. "You can do better than that," Millie said.

"Bring me back some joke books from the Logical Realm," Petunia said. "I need new material."

Millie looked at Petunia critically. "Actually, you do look like you need a shower. Did you get in a fight or fall down a hill or something?"

Petunia glanced down at her daffodil dress, dirty, bruised, and torn, smeared with blueberry stains. "Oh, yeah," she said, feeling embarrassed. "I helped Grumpkin out on the way here. He was getting pelted by a gang in Goblintown. He was all alone, and he looked kinda sick, so I had to defend him."

"Well, that was nice of you, but you can't have breakfast with Mother looking like that," Millie told her.

"No worries," Petunia said. She took a pinch of pixie dust from the pouch at her waist and sprinkled it over herself, saying, "*Puhdista.*" The dirt and stains disappeared; the tears in her dress sealed up. She looked almost as fresh as she had when she'd stepped out her front door, though the daffodil skirt now seemed... blurry, as though someone had painted it over, filling in the texture of the flower. "Now, how about some breakfast for me?" she asked. "It's hard to make jokes on an empty stomach!"

Millie laughed. "Come on, then. Mother won't be up for

another hour at least. You can eat all the scones you like."

Petunia didn't need to be told twice. She ran for the open kitchen door. *Bump.*

"Ow," she said, rubbing her head. Her acorn cap had fallen off, and she could feel a slight lump rising on her forehead.

Millie gasped. "Oh, darkness. I'm sorry, Petunia. Mother must not have changed the house wards." She knelt down next to Petunia and peered at her head. "Are you okay?"

Petunia nodded, though that made her head hurt more. "It's okay, Millie."

Millie's frown deepened. "I'm tempted to wake Mother up right now and yell at her, but I don't think that will help." She shrugged. "Well, if you can't come in to breakfast, breakfast will have to come to you."

The young witch stood up, a scowl of concentration on her face. She raised her hands and intoned, "Tablecloth, *tänne.*"

From inside the house, Petunia heard a faint clinking.

"Come on," Millie muttered, backing away from the door. The tablecloth, laden with dishes, tea, and food, floated out the door and followed Millie into the yard. She led it over to Thea's clearing. "*Paikka,*" she said, lowering her palms.

The tablecloth settled on the freshly turned earth. Not a single teacup had tipped over.

"There!" Millie said with satisfaction. "It's a perfect morning for breakfast in the garden, don't you think, Petunia?"

Eyeing the enormous pile of scones, Petunia said, "Absolutely!"

They sat on the tablecloth and dug in. Petunia had three chocolate chip scones, a poached egg, two slices of bacon, and three cups of chamomile tea. Millie watched in amazement. "Where does it all go? That food is bigger than you are! It can't possibly all fit in your stomach."

"I convert it into pixie dust," Petunia told her. "That's how we store extra energy."

"Oh," Millie said, looking impressed. "That's rather clever. It explains why you're ravenous all the time, and it explains how pixie dust gets its power."

"Speaking of power," Petunia said, "that was a first-rate levitation spell. Your magic is really improving. It's hard to believe that just three months ago you couldn't cast a single spell."

"Thanks! Baba Luci taught me levitation." Millie sighed. "I'm still so far behind, though. And going away for ten days isn't going to help. Ten days of no magic at all." She shook her head. "The Logical Realm is so weird!"

Of the many Realms of existence—the Enchanted Forest, Atlantis, Elysium, the Dragon Realm, and many, many more—only one Realm lacked magic: the Logical Realm, where humans used technology instead. Millie had recently discovered that her father, Dean, lived there and, with a little help from Petunia, her brother Max, and their friend Sagara, she had gone to visit him in his home city of Salem, where he was a chef in a restaurant.

"I bet it will help your cooking," Petunia said. "Your dad's going to teach you so much. I can hardly wait to try all your new recipes!"

Millie grinned. "That is going to be soooo much fun. And I'll finally get to know my father." She hugged herself, and Petunia wasn't sure if it was from happiness or fear. Maybe a little of both.

"Ludmilla?" came a grumpy voice from the kitchen. "What happened to breakfast?"

"Ah, Mother's up." Millie glanced at Petunia. "Are you sure you want to deal with her for ten whole days?"

Petunia squared her shoulders. "Of course! She's not so much worse than my mum."

"Your mum is unlikely to turn you into a toad."

"Pfff," Petunia said. "Then Bogdana would have to do all the work of caring for Thea. Don't you worry, I can handle her."

"Ludmilla!" came a plaintive wail from the kitchen. "I must have tea!"

"Wait here," Millie said. She rose, dusted the scone crumbs from her apron, and marched into the house.

Petunia caught snatches of their conversation, particularly as their voices grew louder and angrier.

"Rude!" said Millie.

"Not in my house!" said Bogdana.

"Promised!" cried Millie.

"All my secrets!" yelled Bogdana.

"BABA LUCI."

Silence fell. For a moment, creeping doubt took hold of Petunia. Could she manage without her best friend for ten days? Could she live with Millie's cranky witch of a mother?

"Oh, very well," said Bogdana. She chanted some words in High Mystery, then poked her head out the kitchen door. Petunia gasped. She'd never seen Bogdana without her witch's hat on. Her hair was... rather pretty, when it wasn't tangled into a horrible mess. "Come in, you nuisance. We need to chat."

Swallowing hard, Petunia hopped up and headed for the door. Behind her, the tablecloth rose and followed. Bogdana stepped back from the door, and the tablecloth passed over Petunia's head to settle on the dining room table. With a dramatic sigh, Bogdana sank into a chair at the table and began heaping breakfast onto her plate. Horace, their house ghost, quietly drifted in through the wall, took a seat as far from Bogdana as possible, and, giving Petunia a wink, began helping himself to breakfast.

"It seems my daughter has promised that you may stay in her room while she is gone," Bogdana said between bites. "I don't know what possessed her to make this offer, but apparently I am bound to honor it. However," she put down her knife and pointed a bony finger at Petunia, "there are rules by which you will abide while you are in this house."

"Mother," Millie began, but Petunia shook her head.

"It's all right, Millie," she said. "This is your mum's house, and it's only right that I follow her rules."

Millie crossed her arms. "As long as they're reasonable rules."

"Of course they're reasonable," Bogdana huffed. "First, you are forbidden to enter the basement. That is my private workshop."

Petunia nodded. "Yes'm."

"Second, you may not touch any of my potions, salves, or tinctures unless I give you my permission." Bogdana glowered at her. "I will know if you do."

"Yes'm."

"Third, you will prepare our meals and clean up afterward."

Millie surged to her feet. "Mother! Petunia is our guest!"

"I thought you said you'd already prepared meals for ten days. All she needs to do is cancel your suspension spells and set the table."

"Well, yes," Millie admitted.

Bogdana turned to Petunia. "And don't tell me you, a

pixie, don't know a first-rate cleaning spell."

"Of course I do," Petunia said, thinking of her dress.

"Well, then, it should be no great burden."

"It's rude, Mother," Millie began, but Petunia waved her to silence.

"It's all right, I don't mind being useful," she said. "I have chores like this at home, so it's no different."

"Good." Bogdana drummed her fingers on the table, considering. "Fourth, you will look after yourself and stay out of my way. And, finally, you will perform all the care the dodonas requires."

Petunia laughed. "That's the whole reason I'm here."

Bogdana snorted. "Very well. You may stay."

"Hurray!" Petunia cried. She started forward to hug Bogdana, but at the witch's icy glare, Petunia turned and hugged Millie instead.

"Come on," said Millie. "I'll show you my room."

 Chapter 4

Friendships and Farewells

Petunia followed Millie upstairs, leaping up, step by crooked step, to the attic.

"It's huge," she whispered, wide-eyed, taking in the four-poster bed, the chest of drawers, the rag rug on the floor, and the little attic window.

Millie shrugged. "It's okay. It suits me well enough. I've changed the sheets for you. I put a box under the bed for you to keep your things in. The bathroom is on the second floor."

Petunia leaped up onto the bed and jumped up and down on the black patchwork quilt. "It's amazing, Millie!"

"Really?"

"Are you kidding?" Petunia said. "For the first time ever, I'll get to sleep without an elbow in my ear or a knee in my ribs. I'll have this whole bed all to myself!"

Millie cocked her head, smiling. "I should have you over more often." She pulled out a large carpetbag. "Let's see... dresses, underwear, stockings, aprons, spare clogs, my toothbrush, my journal, my recipe box, that elvish cookbook Dad wanted... What am I forgetting?"

"I'm surprised you're not taking your whole kitchen," Petunia said.

Millie grinned. "Dad has two! One at his restaurant and one at home. You should see all his equipment! Gas stoves, automatic mixers, deep fryers, microwave ovens, and all these special tools. And he's going to teach me to use them all! Soufflés! Fondant! Beef Wellington! Macarons!" Millie bounced up and down on the bed with excitement, tumbling Petunia like a crouton in a salad.

Petunia laughed out loud. "It sounds wonderful. Delicious! I wish I could go with you."

Millie stopped bouncing. "You know that's not a good idea. We were very lucky last time we went to the Logical Realm, when I transformed you into a human. Baba Luci explained to me everything that could go wrong, and it makes me sick, just thinking about it. I could have killed you!" Her lip trembled.

Petunia ran over and hugged Millie's arm. "It's all right. Nothing happened. And this is why you're studying with Baba Luci, right? How's that going?"

"What, studying with the most powerful witch in the Enchanted Forest, who maintains the balance of good and evil, who also happens to be my grandmother?" Millie shrugged. "About how you'd expect. It's intimidating and very hard, but Baba Luci is a much better teacher than Mother. Oh, but don't tell Mother that!"

Petunia rolled her eyes. "ANYONE would be a better teacher." Millie's mother had been so mortified that Millie was a kitchen witch, Bogdana had put a magical block on the kitchen to force Millie to learn other, more fashionable forms of magic. The result: Millie's talent kept manifesting anyway, ruining any spell she attempted, so that she and her mother both came to believe that she was hopeless at magic. It had been Baba Luci's idea that Millie start attending the Enchanted Forest School, and when Baba

Luci found out what Bogdana had done, she'd taken over Millie's training as a witch.

Happy shouts echoed from downstairs.

"Ludmilla!" came Bogdana's voice from downstairs. "Your brother and your little elf friend are here. Kindly keep them out of my hair until it's time to go."

Max came pounding up the stairs, his brown hair sticking out in every direction from under his purple wizard's cap, a scone clutched in each hand. Nine years old, he was actually Millie's half-brother: same mother, but his father was a wizard, Alfonso Salazar, member of the Enchanted Forest Council, who had moved from the Logical Realm once he learned he could do magic. "Millie!" Max shouted. "We're going, we're going! Oh, hi, Petunia."

"Hiya, Max!" Petunia waved.

Sagara stomped up the stairs behind him, dressed as usual in jeans and a T-shirt, not even bothering with elf robes or braids in her ash-blonde hair. "Your mom is super grouchy today, Millie."

"That's my fault," Petunia said.

Millie put her hands on her hips. "It is NOT your fault. You're doing us a huge favor, Petunia. Mother's just being pushy."

"You're taking care of Thea, right?" Max asked.

Petunia nodded. "Easy peasy. She's so much fun to play with."

"I'd be more worried about Bogdana," Sagara said.

"Aw, she won't even notice I'm here," Petunia said.

Max spluttered, spitting scone crumbs everywhere. "Are you kidding? Mother notices everything. 'Don't you ever comb your hair? Can't you greet me properly? Doesn't your father teach you any manners?'" He paused to swallow. "I sure hope my grandparents aren't like that."

"If they're like your dad, I'm sure they'll be lovely," Millie said.

"Well, even if they aren't, it's going to be an interesting trip," Max said. "We're going to ride in an airplane—you remember, those giant metal flying machines?—to a city with millions of humans in it and buildings as tall as mountains. It's called New York, but also Brooklyn, which still confuses me."

Petunia felt her eyes go round. "Millions of humans? In one city? It must be enormous."

"No, it's on an island," Max said, "with lots of huge bridges. And it has these machines that burrow underground and carry humans from place to place."

Sagara frowned. "If it's an island, wouldn't the burrows flood with seawater?"

Max shrugged. "I guess I'll find out. Maybe the machines swim, too? Anyway, then we're going on another airplane very far away to a much bigger island called Puerto Rico. That's where my grandparents are from. They want me to meet all my cousins."

"Bleh," said Petunia. "I have too many cousins. You could just have some of mine."

"Mine, too," said Sagara.

"And you already have a bazillion cousins here," Millie pointed out.

"Like Cretacia? No, thank you," Max retorted.

"Oh, that reminds me!" Petunia said. "I met Grumpkin on the way here, and he asked if I'd seen Cretacia lately. He thinks she's back in the Enchanted Forest."

"What?" Millie leaped to her feet. "Where? Oh, darkness, we can't leave now! What if she comes after Thea again!"

"Relax," said Sagara. "The Enchanted Forest Council has

been continuously scrying for her since she left. If she is here, they'll spot her and bring her in immediately.

Max nodded, his wizard's cap waggling back and forth. "My dad says they check for her every day, and so does the Coven and Master Quercius. There's no way she could make it in here undetected. And even if she does, Mother and Petunia are here to protect Thea."

"That's right," Petunia asserted, crossing her arms. "Besides, Grumpkin didn't say he'd actually seen Cretacia, just that his sister was acting weird, and he thought Cretacia might have something to do with it."

"Well..." Millie said.

"You shouldn't let Cretacia ruin your vacation when she's not even here," Sagara pointed out. "Don't you want to go see your dad?"

Millie sank onto the bed. "More than anything. I have so many questions." She smiled at Sagara. "I bet you have a lot planned with your mother, too."

"We're going to a forest," Sagara replied, her voice filled with scorn, "in some place called New Hampshire. Like we don't have any forests here. No, we have to go help my stupid brother save an endangered species and bring it here. The Northern Bog Lemming. What a thrilling vacation."

"Oh, come on, Sagara," Max said. "You'll get to spend ten whole days with your mother! That's worth a few lemmings, surely?"

Sagara cracked half a smile. "Well, she did say she was going to bring her laptop and let me explore the Internet. That's like a whole library and city and theater and, oh, a whole Realm just of ideas. And it's all made up of numbers." Her hands twitched, reaching for an invisible keyboard.

Listening to them, Petunia began to feel left out. All her friends were going off to have adventures, and she'd be stuck here, alone, with Bogdana. Her vacation was starting to sound much less interesting.

Max glanced at her. "On the other hand, I kinda wish I was staying here. Ten whole days of Millie's cooking would be amazing."

Millie grinned. "It was a little challenging, getting all those meals ready for Petunia and Horace and Mother, but kind of fun. I made all my specialties, plus a few new recipes I'd been meaning to try. I hope you like them."

A grin spread across Petunia's face. "I know everything will be fantastic!" she told Millie. "And I get this whole bed to myself. This is going to be my best vacation ever."

"Yup, the only bad thing is that we'll have to go back to school in ten days," said Max.

"Oh, did I tell you what happened in Master Tertius's enchanting class yesterday?" Sagara asked.

They gossiped about school and their families, and Petunia thought that vacation would be perfect if it could be just like this, with all of them together the entire time, when Horace the house ghost glided up through the floor.

"Millie, I think lunch is ready," he told them, rattling his chains in excitement.

"Whoops," Millie said. "Time flies."

"Like tablecloths!" Petunia quipped, and they both laughed while Max and Sagara looked confused.

"Was that another of your bad jokes?" Sagara asked. Petunia stuck out her tongue at the elf girl.

"Thanks, Horace. Please tell Mother I'll be right down. I've got something special prepared," Millie said, grabbing her carpetbag. "You can have the leftovers for dinner, Petunia."

Max sniffed and suddenly went cross-eyed. "Is that... roast goose?"

"Yup," Millie said. "Come on down and have some!"
Max needed no persuading. He leaped to his feet and
hurtled down the stairs with Sagara following behind him,
trying to look like she didn't care as she almost ran down the
crooked steps. Petunia jumped from the bed onto Millie's
shoulder, and they went down the stairs together, Millie
giving last minute instructions. "All the rest of your meals
are prepared and waiting for you in the pantry. The release
phrase for the suspension spell is 'Open sesame seeds.'"

"What does that mean?" Petunia said.

"It's traditional in the Logical Realm to say that when
you want to open things. I have no idea why," Millie told
her. "Anyway, all your meals are made. All you need to
do is feed Thea her compost tea in the morning and play
with her until lunchtime, when she takes her nap. In
the afternoon, take her the scrying bowl for lessons with
Master Quercius. Then pick up the bowl after dinner and
say good night to Thea. If you run into any trouble, scry
Baba Luci. She'll help you straighten out Bogdana."

"Millie, you told me all this already," Petunia said.
"Don't worry so much. Everything will be fine."

They went down to the dining room where Bogdana was
waiting impatiently and Max's dad, Alfonso Salazar, looked
like he was trying very hard not to drool. Uncharacteristically,
Bogdana's hair was smoothly brushed under her great black
witch's hat, and Alfonso was wearing a Red Sox sweatshirt and
jeans instead of his usual wizard's robes. Horace hovered beside
him. Petunia hopped down to the table, which Millie must
have set that morning before Petunia arrived.

Millie went into the kitchen and grabbed some hot pads.
Opening the oven, she pulled out a roast goose, stuffed
with bread and chestnuts, then a dish of sweet potatoes and
another of maple-roasted brussels sprouts. She delivered

these to the dining room table, along with a tossed salad, a basket of fresh, warm rolls, and a dish full of lingonberry jam to go with the goose.

"There we are," Millie said. "Mother, would you like to carve?"

Bogdana pointed a finger at the goose. "*Paloittele tämä hanhi*," she intoned in High Mystery. Instantly, the goose came apart in perfect slices. "You may be seated," Bogdana said to everyone else.

They scrambled to sit at the table, except Petunia, who sat on the table itself at a plate next to Millie's. "May I have a drumstick?" she asked Millie.

"Me, too!" Max cried.

"Of course," Millie replied, handing Petunia a drumstick about the same size as her, then handed the other to Max.

They stuffed themselves, and when they were done, there was still a quarter of a goose left and leftovers of everything else. Alfonso kept sneaking glances at Millie with a look of mild astonishment. Finally, he said, "Do you think you could teach Max to cook like this?"

Millie blinked. "I have no idea. I've never tried teaching other people to cook."

Petunia clapped her hands. "What a good idea! I want to learn, too. You could start a cooking school. What do you think, Sagara? Want to enroll?"

"Teach me to make elf cakes, and I'll be your slave forever," Sagara said in her usual sarcastic voice, but Petunia thought she might mean it.

"Not in this house," Bogdana declared. At all their downcast faces, she said, "It would be far too disruptive to my work. Find some other kitchen."

"How about our kitchen?" Max asked. "Dad, what do you think?"

"Millie is welcome in my kitchen anytime," Alfonso said, suppressing a burp.

"Ludmilla has a great many demands on her time as it is," Bogdana retorted, her long warty nose in the air. "Between school, private lessons with Baba Luci, and caring for Thea, I'm sure teaching all of you is the last thing she needs. Besides," she said, pushing away from the table, "it's time to go, if we are to arrive at the Portal at our scheduled departure time."

They rose from the table, gathering bags and baskets and parcels, Petunia leaping up to Millie's shoulder as usual. Bogdana picked up her broomstick from beside the kitchen door and strode impatiently out to the yard. Alfonso led Max and Sagara out to his huge magic carpet, where their packed bags lay piled in the center. He sat down in front, and Max and Sagara sat behind the luggage.

Bogdana bestrode her broomstick. "Come on, stop dawdling!" she called to Millie.

Petunia gave Millie's ear a little hug. "Good luck!" she whispered, then jumped down. Millie sat on the broom behind Bogdana.

"I expect you will have cleaned up after breakfast and lunch by the time I get back," Millie's mother told Petunia.

Petunia gulped. Breakfast *and* lunch dishes? "Yes, of course." Millie was frowning at her mother, so Petunia added, "Don't worry, Millie. It's only ten days. What could happen?"

Bogdana kicked off and zoomed into the sky, with Millie clutching her carpetbag while also trying to wave goodbye.

"Bye, Petunia! See you in ten days!" Max cried as the magic carpet rose into the air and flew after Bogdana and Millie. Petunia waved and waved until they were out of sight and her arm was sore and she was all alone. Petunia was never alone, not for an instant, and she paused, trying to figure out how she felt. Isolated. Left out. Annoyed. She was on vacation, and Bogdana was treating her like a servant.

"Dishes smishes," she said to herself. "I'm gonna go play with Thea."

# Chapter 5

A Sudden Sneeze

Sunlight streamed through the small window at the far end of the attic as Petunia awoke. She stretched luxuriously under the black quilt and sighed. Getting to sleep without all the squirming of her siblings had been surprisingly hard. She was so used to all the whispering and grumbling and snores that all the silence seemed to ring in her ears. But once Petunia finally drifted off, she had never slept so well in her life. Part of her wanted to lie in Millie's bed all day long, but she also felt energized, ready to jump up and tackle the day's challenges.

Which were pretty small: get breakfast ready, clean up afterward, water Thea and play with her, set up the scrying bowl for her lesson with Quercius that afternoon, and then Petunia's time was her own. She and Horace had shoved aside the dirty lunch dishes and eaten leftover goose for dinner all alone. Cleaning everything up had been a snap with a handful of pixie dust. Bogdana had returned well after sundown, nibbled a leftover scone, and gone to bed.

Petunia had no idea what she would do with herself. At home, she'd be helping to feed her younger siblings, getting Peaty dressed, shopping for her mother, and cleaning up any number of messes. This really was the best vacation Petunia had ever had.

She sat up, kicked off the covers, and leaped down to the floor. Rummaging in the box of her things, Petunia pulled out her dust catcher and laid it out on the floor. Woven from unicorn hair (highly magic-resistant) and coated with a special mixture to make it just a little slick, the dust catcher lay flat and shimmering on the rag rug. Seizing her comb, Petunia sat in the middle of the dust catcher and carefully, thoroughly combed through her hair, shaking all the pixie dust she'd generated during the night onto it. The air crackled with static and magical potential as she combed. It seemed to take forever to comb all the dust out. She'd eaten so much of Millie's delicious food yesterday that she'd generated more than twice her usual amount of pixie dust.

When she was finished, she stood up, shook herself all over, and stepped off the cover, which was now coated in a thick layer of blue dust. With the ease of long practice, she flipped the edges of the cover over to collect the dust on one end. Pulling out her pixie dust pouch, she attached it to the end of the cover and tipped the day's dust in until it bulged. Then she folded the dust catcher and tucked it away. Briefly, she wondered who was helping Peaty with his dust catcher that morning.

Selecting a dress made of daisy leaves and petals, Petunia slipped off her nightgown and got dressed. She put on her acorn cap and headed out of the attic to the stairs. The slanted stairs amused her, and she spent a good five minutes skipping up and down them before she arrived in the kitchen.

Horace came gliding out of the pantry. "Good morning, Petunia," he said, rattling his chains in greeting. "Did you sleep well?"

"Better than I've ever slept before!" Petunia said. Her stomach rumbled, and Horace laughed.

"Time for breakfast, I think," he said. "Millie's been cooking extra food for a week so that you and Bogdana will have plenty while she's away. And she wouldn't let me have any of it." Horace pouted. "But you can get it ready now, right?"

"Right!" Petunia confirmed. "Let me put the kettle on for tea and set the table, and then I'll get breakfast out."

She opened the firebox and found it cold. Tossing in a couple of logs, she added a pinch of pixie dust and whispered, "*Syty*," the word in High Mystery that lit fires. The logs flickered and caught. Leaping up to the top of the big cast iron stove, Petunia checked the kettle. It was only half full after last night's dinner, so Petunia picked it up over her head, leaped to the kitchen table, and from there to the sink.

Horace whistled. "You're strong!"

"Of course," Petunia said. "All pixies are strong. I can lift ten times my own weight, and I'm not even full grown. My uncle Ash can beat goblins at wrestling." She opened the top of the kettle and pumped water into it, then carried it back to the oven. The surface was already heating up, and she danced upon it gingerly as she set the kettle on the burner, then leaped back to the table. "I'm going to have to put down a hot pad."

"Or you could wear shoes," Horace pointed out.

Petunia stuck out her tongue at him. "Pixies never wear shoes! We need to feel the earth beneath our feet. I hated wearing those clogs when I was a human in the Logical Realm. They're so heavy!"

Then she paused. Yesterday, Millie had set up breakfast and lunch, and Petunia had just left everything out for dinner.

Today, though, Petunia wanted to make a good impression and have everything ready when Bogdana woke up. But she'd never set a human-sized table before. Of course, she could use pixie dust to levitate everything out, but if she did that for three meals every day, and then the cleaning afterward, she might run out of pixie dust, even with all the extra she was generating. And besides that, it felt like cheating. But how was she going to get everything out on the table?

Rolling up her daisy-petal sleeves, she opened the china cabinet door and leaped up to the shelf with the teapots. Selecting one, she lifted it over her head, like the kettle, then leaped down to the table. But she'd forgotten the lid, which spun off in midair and shattered on the floor.

"Oh, dear," said Horace, glancing nervously up the stairs.

Petunia set down the teapot and looked at the lid. "Oops. Don't worry, Horace. I can fix it." She jumped down to the floor, collecting up all the fragments. Beneath the china cabinet, she spied a hole in the floorboard. *Mice?* she wondered. But then she had gathered up all the tiny shards of porcelain. Heaping them together on the floor, she sprinkled a tiny pinch of pixie dust over the fragments, and said, "*Yhdisty.*" The fragments drew themselves together and became a whole lid again. Petunia picked it up and examined it. If you looked hard, you could just see the hairline cracks in the lid. Hopefully, Bogdana wouldn't notice.

"Nice job!" Horace told her.

She fetched chamomile from the spice and herb rack and shook a good quantity into the teapot. Then Petunia leaped back to the china cabinet and, one by one, pulled out human-sized plates and cups for herself, Bogdana, and Horace, along with a pixie-sized cup Millie kept just for her. Petunia jumped them over to the table and laid them out, then went back for silverware and napkins.

The kettle steamed and began to whistle, so Petunia nabbed a hot pad, threw it onto the stove, and leaped onto it. Then she realized that she had no idea how she could pour the water into the teapot, when the bottom of the kettle was too hot to handle. With a shrug, Petunia tossed a pinch of pixie dust onto the kettle and said, "*Nouse.*"

The kettle rose into the air. Petunia pointed it over to the teapot, and it floated over and poured steaming water into the pot. She waved it back over to the oven and set it on the side rack. Leaping back to the table, she put the newly mended lid on the teapot, then turned her attention to the pantry.

"I wonder what Millie made us for breakfast today?" she said as she jumped down to the floor and headed for the pantry door.

"They're all labeled," Horace said. "Come and see!" He glided through the pantry door ahead of her. Petunia grabbed the bottom of the door and pulled it open, then gasped.

There, laid out on the counter, were piles of brown paper packages glittering faintly from the preservation spells laid upon them. Each one was labeled in Millie's neat handwriting. The pantry was Horace's favorite part of the house to haunt. He must have been staring at them for days.

"Here, Petunia," he said, pointing to the package nearest the door. "This one's breakfast."

Petunia jumped up to the counter and found the one labeled, "First Onesday Breakfast." She picked up the package, grunting a bit. Millie was pushing the limit of Petunia's strength, which could only mean that it was packed with delicious things. She wrestled it over to the kitchen table and set it down beside the teapot, Horace hovering anxiously over her the whole way.

"Ready, Horace?" Petunia asked.

"Oh, yes. Please hurry, I'm famished!" the ghost replied.

Petunia laughed. Only Millie could make food that both living beings and spirits could eat; it was one of her magical talents, along with transformation. Petunia tapped the package twice and said, "Open sesame seeds!"

The glitter of magic faded away, and the twine holding the package together untied itself so that the paper fell open, revealing a stack of fresh crepes, whipped cream, steaming hot scrambled eggs, sautéed mushrooms, and fried ham. Atop the crepes lay a small note. Petunia picked it off the crepes and read it aloud to Horace.

Dear Petunia and Horace,

I hope you enjoy this first breakfast. Crepes are Mother's favorite, and they should put her in a good mood today. It's possible that she will eat them all, so just in case she does, here is the recipe. They're pretty easy to make. The essential ingredient is the powdered sugar, which gives them their lovely slightly crispy edges. Make sure you beat them well with a whisk so the sugar blends completely!

3/4 cup flour
1/2 teaspoon salt
1 teaspoon double-acting baking powder
2 tablespoons powdered sugar
2 eggs
2/3 cup milk
1/3 cup water
1/2 teaspoon vanilla

Sift together the dry ingredients. In a separate bowl, scramble the eggs, add the remaining ingredients, and beat together. Pour into the dry ingredients and whisk together. Don't worry about a few lumps, they'll dissolve when you cook them. Heat a skillet and grease it with butter. With the medium ladle, pour about half the ladle into the skillet and then use the bottom of the ladle to smooth the batter out into a pancake. Wait until the top is no longer gleaming with moisture and the edges are just starting to come up, then flip the crepe and lightly brown the other side. Remove and repeat until you're out of batter.

I recommend that you try them with some of my jams and jellies. I particularly like the apricot jam and the raspberry blueberry rhubarb preserves. If you prefer a savory crepe, there are several nice cheeses in the icebox. I like the sharp cheddar with eggs and ham.

I wonder what I'll be eating for breakfast while you're eating my crepes? What new and interesting things will my father introduce me to? I'm so excited, but also a little scared. What if I'm not a good enough cook? What if I disappoint my dad? What if I don't like what he cooks for me? And what if I can't really cook without my magic? I wish you were coming with me. Max and Sagara will be in the Logical Realm, too, but Max is going to visit his grandparents, and Sagara will be with her mom and brother, so I don't think I'll see much of them.

But I'll be with Dad, and I think that will be wonderful. Also, I want to try out his crepe pan.

Hope you're enjoying each other's company. Please remember to water Thea and play games with her and tell her I miss her, just like I miss you.

Hugs,
Millie

"Oh, good grief," Petunia said. She had rolled her eyes so much during this, she was a little dizzy. As if Millie would ever be terrible at cooking, as if anyone would hate her food. "If her dad doesn't like her cooking, he's an idiot."

"He'll love it," Horace said. "I remember Dean. He's just like Millie in so many ways, and just as obsessed with food."

Petunia squinted at Horace. "You knew Millie's dad?"

"Of course. He came here several times before Millie was born, and a couple of times after."

Petunia put her fists on her hips. "And did you ever tell Millie this? I bet she'd like to know more about her dad."

Horace ducked his head and faded so much, he was almost invisible. "Bogdana made me promise never to speak of him to Millie."

"And for good reason," said Bogdana, rubbing her eyes as she wandered into the kitchen, "which is none of your business. You set up breakfast, good. Is the tea ready?" Petunia noticed that her hair was back to its normal tangled, witchy mess under her witch's hat.

"Should be," Petunia said.

"Then do me the courtesy of being silent as we eat." Bogdana seated herself and took three crepes, which she arranged around her plate and began filling. "Go fetch the jams, pixie. Make yourself useful."

"Hmph," Petunia snorted, but she jumped over to the cabinet and climbed up to the shelf with the jams and preserves. "Apricot or strawberry rhubarb?" she asked.

"Marmalade," Bogdana replied.

In my house, we say please, Petunia thought, but she just shrugged. Witches don't need manners. She was feeling pretty confident by now, so she hoisted a jar of marmalade onto one shoulder and the apricot jam on the other, then leaped for the table. Mid-leap, she felt her grip on the jar slip down the glass. She tried to catch at the lid, but the marmalade jar went spinning off to crash on the floor, splattering the room with orange goop.

"Idiot pixie!" Bogdana cried. "Look what you've done!"

Petunia set down the apricot jam with great care. "Sorry! I can fix it."

"You will not," Bogdana said. "You'll botch it. I don't want glass shards in my marmalade." The witch got up and bustled over to the smashed jar. She hummed to herself for a moment, then intoned, *"Kuten kerran olit, niin oletkin."*

It was like watching the jar shatter, but in reverse. All the drops of marmalade flew back together as the shards of glass reassembled themselves, and the lid screwed itself back on. Bogdana plucked it up from the floor and stomped back to her seat. "That's how it's done," she muttered. Then, looking at the stricken pixie, she said, "Well, go on, eat. I don't see how you can pour the tea, so I'll do it."

Petunia didn't much feel like eating, but the rising aroma of crepes convinced her stomach. She took the apricot jam over to her seat. Seizing a crepe, she dragged it onto her plate and slathered it with apricot jam.

Bogdana poured the tea. When she got to Petunia's cup, she frowned. "How am I supposed to fill that thimble without spilling all over the table?"

"Well, usually," Petunia explained, "Millie pours her own tea and then lets me scoop out my own before we drink."

"You're not drinking from my cup," Bogdana declared.

"It's okay," Petunia said. "That's why I set out a normal cup for myself, too."

Bogdana snorted. "As you wish." She filled the extra cup.

Petunia took her cup, which was, in fact, a porcelain thimble with a handle attached, and dipped out a good big scoop for herself. Horace slurped from his own cup.

They settled into eating, filling crepe after crepe with delicious things. Petunia ate three whole crepes plus an extra slice of ham. Horace ate four, and Bogdana ate six. *Millie's right,* Petunia thought. *The apricot jam is splendid, especially with whipped cream. It's like eating sunshine.* A pang of loneliness went through Petunia. Just then, she really missed Millie.

Eventually, the eggs disappeared, along with the ham and the whipped cream. There were two lone crepes left, which Bogdana put on her plate with the remaining mushrooms. Rising, she announced, "I'll just take these for a midmorning snack while I work. I shall be in my workshop. Clean up as quietly as possible so that you do not disturb me. And try not to break anything else." She swept out of the kitchen and down the stairs to the basement.

Petunia surveyed the wreckage of their meal. "Slugs and bugs. This is almost as bad as when the twins have a food fight with Peaty."

"I'd help you if I could," Horace said.

Petunia laughed. "It's all right, Horace. I'm a pixie, after all. But I'd better not risk breaking anything else." Opening her pouch wide, she took a good handful of pixie dust and blew it all over the table. The air glittered and glistened with it as it fell on food and plates alike. "*Siivoa!*" she cried.

All the jar lids leaped onto the jars and screwed themselves shut. The food disappeared from all the dishes, and the dishes floated away to their places. The napkins also turned spotless, folded themselves, and returned to their drawer. The teapot flew out the kitchen window, dumped the tea leaves on the compost heap, and returned to its proper shelf, sparkling clean. The crumbs marched themselves off the table like a line of ants, to leap into the compost as well, leaving the table surface tidy as could be. All that was left was the faint glimmer of leftover pixie dust, which dissipated into the air.

"There," said Petunia with satisfaction. "Now I'm off to feed Thea..."

"AAAAA-CHOO!!!!!!" The floor shook with the force of Bogdana's sneeze.

Horace jumped right through the table. "Great rattling bones! I've never heard Bogdana sneeze like that before."

"Maybe she's making a sneezing curse," Petunia said.

"Maybe," Horace said, looking doubtfully at the stairs. "I hope so."

Petunia hopped down from the table. "Anyway, Thea's waiting. Time to go tree-sit."

Chapter 6

Dances with Trees

Petunia pushed open the kitchen door and stepped outside into a gorgeous summer morning. The blue sky and bright sunlight made even the peeling gray paint on the house look nice. Petunia filled the watering can, hoisted it over her head, and listened to its happy sloshing as she paraded over to Thea.

"Good morning, Thea," the pixie called out. "Here comes breakfast!"

The little tree wriggled all over, waving her leaves in greeting. The elm leaned over protectively, keeping her shaded as cacao trees prefer. "Good morning to you, too, Mx. Elm," Petunia called.

Petunia tipped the watering can over, sprinkling Thea and the ground around her with caramel-colored compost tea. Thea shook her leaves and scrubbed along her bark, turning and bending to get the tea over every inch of her. When the soil around Thea was good and wet but not muddy, Petunia set the watering can down.

"I've got the whole morning to play with you," Petunia told her. "What would you like to do?"

Thea wrapped two leaves around the middle of her trunk and wobbled back and forth as though she were laughing.

"Jokes? You want me to tell you jokes?"

The dodonas nodded her crown emphatically.

"Wow. No one actually asks me to tell them jokes." Petunia remembered the first day Millie came to school, when the little witch had laughed at her jokes. It filled Petunia with a warm, happy feeling. She sat down on a dry patch of grass. "Okay, here goes. What do you call a goblin with good manners?" She paused, and Thea leaned forward to hear. "A snoblin!"

Thea shook with silent laughter while the elm tree groaned.

"What do you call a messy goblin? A sloblin!"

Thea clapped her leaves and gestured for more.

Petunia grinned. "What do you call a goblin thief? A roblin! What do you call a large group of goblins? A moblin! What do you call a goblin that has melted? A bloblin! What do you call a goblin diplomat? A hobnoblin!"

Petunia had to stop because she was laughing so hard at Thea. The dodonas had bent all the way over and was slapping the ground with her leaves, shaking with helpless laughter. A single leaf broke off and drifted to the ground. The elm pointed an accusing branch at Petunia.

"Okay, okay, I'll give her a break," Petunia said, wiping tears from her eyes. "But it is so much fun to be able to say all of them without someone telling me to shut up." She let herself fall over backwards and lay on the grass, looking up through the elm's leaves at the clouds floating by overhead. "This is so wonderful. If Millie were here, too, it would be the best day ever."

Millie would have loved those jokes, then chided her to be kinder to goblins. Petunia hoped she was having a good time in the Logical Realm. Had she slept well in a strange bed, too? Was someone there telling her Logical jokes?

Thea straightened up again and began swaying back and forth.

"You want to dance?" Petunia asked.

Thea nodded her crown.

"Okay, let's play Ring Around the Runestone. I'll sing it for you." Petunia scrambled to her feet and began skipping around the dodonas, singing, "Ring around the Runestone, sing a song of sea foam, splashes, splashes, we all dive down!" Petunia dove at the ground, tucking her head and rolling at the last moment. Thea, who had wiggled and swayed along, leaned over and smacked the ground with her crown leaves. Straightening up, she clapped her leaves together for more.

"Again? Okay, here we go!"

Petunia spent the morning singing and playing all the games she played with Peaty, while the sun slowly rose until it was high overhead.

"PIXIE!" roared a voice from the kitchen door. "Where is my lunch?"

"Oops!" Petunia, who had been amusing Thea by putting her feet behind her head, untwisted herself and got up. "Gotta go, Thea, but I'll be back this afternoon with the scrying bowl so you can have your lesson with Master Quercius. Bye, now!"

Thea bobbed and waved. Millie said she usually napped at noontime, and the dodonas did look a little droopy. Petunia patted her trunk before sprinting for the house.

Bogdana waited inside, tapping her foot impatiently. "I expect my lunch promptly at noon. Did Millie not explain this?"

"No, no, she did," Petunia agreed. "I just lost track of time playing with Thea."

Bogdana snorted. "I cannot fathom what possible interest

you could have in an infant tree. This evening, I expect a prompt meal at six o'clock, and not one minute later."

Petunia wanted to stick her tongue out at Bogdana and tell her to get her own dinner, but she curtsied instead. "Yes'm, I'll pay more attention to the time. Sorry."

Bogdana looked down her long, crooked nose. "And?"

"And what?"

"AND WHERE'S MY LUNCH?"

Petunia jumped, then rushed over to the pantry. She used a pinch of pixie dust to levitate the lunch package to the table, another pinch to set the table, and a third to instantly heat the tea kettle.

"There!" she said with satisfaction. "All ready."

"ACHOOOO!" said Bogdana, then she wiped her nose on her tattered lace sleeve. "Hmph. Must be coming down with a cold. I'll just take a cure." She swept into the parlor where she kept her potions for sale.

Petunia took advantage of this to jump up onto the table, open Millie's package, and swipe the note, hiding it under her plate. Then she turned to the food, inhaling deeply. Millie had made croissants, the magnificent, buttery, flaky, light rolls that Petunia wanted to burrow right into, but they had already been sliced in half. Beside them were two crocks, one of chicken salad and one of smoked eel salad, both smelling of fresh fruits and dill. A shaved beet and fennel salad filled a third crock, and there was a plate of assorted sliced cheeses. For dessert, raspberry rhubarb crumble and vanilla ice cream.

Bogdana returned, dropping an empty potion bottle into her pocket. "Ah, croissants!" she exclaimed, sitting in a chair and grabbing a croissant in each fist.

"Horace, lunch!" Petunia called.

Horace drifted out from behind a cupboard to Petunia's

side. "Is she done yelling?" he whispered.

Petunia nodded, so Horace hovered above his own seat and began spooning beets and fennel onto his plate.

They ate in silence, and Petunia tried to enjoy her food, but she kept wondering about Millie's note. She bolted through her chicken salad sandwich with a slice of nice havarti cheese while Bogdana took her time, smacking her lips and fixing one sandwich after another. By the time they got to the crumble, the ice cream was half-melted, though still delicious, and Petunia was ready to scream with frustration. Finally, Bogdana pushed back from the table and wiped her raspberry-smeared lips on her other sleeve.

"I trust that I do not have to remind you to clean up," she said to Petunia.

"No, ma'am."

"Very well. I shall be in my workshop. Dinner had better be on time." Bogdana stomped out of the room and down the stairs.

"At last!" Petunia exclaimed, dragging the note from under her plate.

Horace floated through the table to look over her shoulder. "I was wondering what happened to the note." He glanced over it. "Oh, good thing you hid it."

> *Dear Petunia (and Horace),*
> *I'm guessing by now that you've learned that while Mother tends to sleep in mornings, she's very punctual about lunch. I'll try to remember to warn you about that, but I think there's a good chance I'll forget in all the bustling about on Endsday, so I'm apologizing in advance (sort of).*
>
> *I made an extra-yummy lunch, just in case Mother was in a bad mood. Did you try the smoked eel salad,*

*Petunia? It's one of Mother's favorites, made from our
very own swamp eels, but you can make it with any
smoked fish: trout, mackerel, herring, salmon. The
secret to its deliciousness isn't actually the fish, it's the
fresh herbs. You can substitute dried herbs, but it's just
not the same. Otherwise, it's quite easy to make.*

> *6 ounces smoked fish*
> *1/4 red onion or 1/2 shallot or 1 scallion, finely
> chopped*
> *1/2 apple, diced*
> *1-2 teaspoons capers*
> *2-3 pickle or cucumber slices, diced*
> *2 tablespoons raisins or dried cranberries or 5-6
> grapes, quartered*
> *2 tablespoons chopped walnuts, pecans, or almonds*
> *1/4 cup mayonnaise*
> *Fresh dill, thyme, and rosemary, finely chopped*
> *Salt and pepper to taste*

*Place the fish in a bowl. With two forks, shred the
fish into small pieces. Combine with the remaining
ingredients and stir until well mixed. You can adjust
the amount of mayonnaise to taste.*

*It's good in croissants, but I also like it open-face
on a slice of bread with a slice of tomato and a slice of
mild cheddar or swiss on top, lightly toasted.*

Petunia checked to see if there was any left over.
There wasn't. Bogdana had eaten it all and scraped
the crock clean with a piece of croissant.

*Did you have a good morning with Thea? Did you
feed her the compost tea? I hope you remembered that
she likes it when you sing songs to her. She's a good
dancer for someone with no feet (yet). Once you're done*

cleaning up after lunch, please bring out the scrying
bowl and call Master Quercius for Thea's lesson. That
gives you a free afternoon to do as you please! Horace
is a good chess partner if you get bored, and there are a
few books in my room you could try.

I hope you're having a good time (as much as
Mother will allow). I'm sure I'm missing you both
fiercely right now. Just eight days to go!

See you soon,
Millie

Petunia sighed. She did miss Millie. It would be so
much more fun staying here with her. Petunia wouldn't
have to cope with Bogdana directly, she wouldn't have to
do all the chores by herself, and they could both play with
Thea. She and Millie could practice their magic together.
Maybe Millie would even teach her how to cook.

"I miss her, too," said Horace. "Chess does sound like
fun. Do you play?"

"Nope, never have," said Petunia.

Horace smiled and rattled his chains. "I could teach you
then!"

Petunia considered. "Maybe later. Horace, does this
house have mice?"

"A long time ago, but not since I've been here," Horace
replied, puffing out his chest with pride. "It's one of my
jobs to scare them out."

"Must be a hard job, given how yummy Millie's food is.
But you're good at it." Petunia glanced around. "I've never
seen any mice, and I've been here lots of times."

"Millie doesn't allow them in the kitchen," Horace said,
"and she had me do a cleaning before you came."

Petunia grinned to herself. "Good to know. Now, time

to clean up and take the scrying bowl out to Thea."

"Okay," said Horace, losing interest. "If you want to play chess, meet me in the parlor." He drifted away.

Petunia scraped a last bit of crumble out of its baking dish and popped it into her mouth. She took another handful of pixie dust from her pouch and used it once more to tidy the kitchen. "At this rate," she grumbled, "I'll be out of dust by bedtime."

Below her, Bogdana let loose a series of earth-shaking sneezes. Petunia was certain the house was leaning just a little more to the left when the witch finally ceased. Hastily, she went to the cupboard to get the scrying bowl. Filling it halfway with clean, clear water, she headed out the door to the back yard.

Thea was motionless, her leaves wafting gently in the breeze. Above her, the elm rustled a soft, treeish song.

"Hello, Mx. Elm," Petunia said, setting the scrying bowl down before Thea. "It's time for Thea's lesson with Quercius."

The elm rustled and changed the song to something more lively. Thea also rustled, then snapped her leaves wide.

"Hiya, Thea! Have a nice nap?" Petunia asked.

Thea stretched her branches one way, then the other. Petunia could almost hear her yawn.

"Ready for your lesson with Master Quercius?"

That brought Thea all the way awake. She nodded eagerly.

The water in the scrying bowl had grown still, making the bowl a mirror in the shade of the elm. Petunia touched its rim and said, "*Anna minun puhua Quercius.*"

The reflection of Thea shifted, becoming an image of a great oak tree. The image focused on its trunk, where knots revealed themselves as eyes, a slash in the bark a

mouth, framed by a mossy beard. Like Thea, Quercius
was a dodonos—in some sense, he was Thea's father. But
a busy school full of young, rowdy students was no place
for a sapling like Thea. Until she grew eyes and a mouth
and legs, she needed to be carefully protected, and Millie,
who was responsible for Thea's creation, had agreed to care
for her. Quercius had once been able to walk about the
Enchanted Forest and many other Realms besides, but he
was quite old and firmly rooted in place now. So instead of
visiting Thea, he scryed her each day.

"Greetings, my dear Thea. Are you well today?"

Thea nodded emphatically and murmured something in
tree speech.

"I am glad to hear it," Quercius replied. "And greetings
also to you, Petunia. How are you enjoying your stay with
Councilor Noctmartis?"

Petunia grinned at the caretaker of the Enchanted
Forest School, in whose branches she had learned
reading, history, arithmancy, and many other forms of
magic. "The bed is comfy, and the food is amazing. I
love playing with Thea, too. She laughs at all my jokes."
The pixie gave him a sly grin. "It's too bad you're not a
pear tree, Master Quercius."

"Oh?" said Quercius. "And why is that?"

"Because then you would be Thea's pear-ent!"

Thea quivered all over with laughter, clapping her leaves
together merrily, as Quercius stifled a groan.

"I see you are keeping her amused. Thank you for caring
for Thea while Millie is away. I am indebted to you."

Petunia blushed. "Nonsense. Thea is my friend, too. I'm
just helping a friend."

"Then thank you for being a good friend to my
daughter."

"Happy to help," Petunia replied.

"Would you like to participate in the lesson? I am teaching Thea the maple dialect of tree speech, which is quite interesting..."

Petunia rocked back on her heels. Learning? During vacation?

"Sorry, Master Quercius," she said hastily, "but Horace invited me to play a game of chess."

Quercius smiled and winked at her. "Next time, perhaps. Have a good game, Petunia."

"Thank you, Master Quercius. Bye, Thea!"

The little tree waved to Petunia, and she dashed back to the house, feeling just a little guilty. She had better things to do than play chess.

Chapter 7

Waltzes Through Walls

Entering the kitchen, Petunia glanced carefully around. Horace was nowhere to be seen, and Bogdana was still in the basement. Quick as a pixie, she darted under the china cabinet and into the mouse hole.

It smelled musty inside, disused and perhaps a bit moldy. Deep and dark, too dark for her to see. Petunia took off her acorn cap, touched the tip of its stem, and whispered, "*Hehku.*"

The stem began to glow softly, just enough for her to peer into the gloom. She was inside the wall, wood timbers reaching up high above her, lath and plaster on the inside wall, long wooden planks on the outside. Old, dusty cobwebs stretched between them as far as she could see. On the rough timber that formed the floor, old bits of plaster and clumps of dust and lint clustered along the walls and in the corners. Ahead of her, mice had gnawed a hole in the timber, just large enough for her to crawl through. It looked well-worn but old and was coated with a fine layer of dust. Petunia scrambled through and went exploring.

Though she'd been around houses her entire life, Petunia had spent little time in any of them. She recalled that her eccentric spinster Aunt Linden lived in a faun's closet for most of her life, but rambling about inside these walls, Petunia doubted her aunt had restricted herself to just the closet. From inside the walls, Petunia could go anywhere in the house.

She popped out inside one of the pantry cupboards, then dove back into the walls and circumnavigated the first floor. Finding an abandoned chimney, probably the original kitchen hearth, she climbed up to the second floor and peeped in on all the bedrooms. Locked with heavy padlocks on the door, Bogdana's room was off limits, but Petunia found a hole in the wall, perhaps where a picture had once hung, and climbed up a timber to it, clinging to an outcropping of plaster. Peeking through, she began giggling furiously. Bogdana had painted the room an embarrassing rosy shade of pink and slept in a four-poster canopy bed with frilly white lace curtains and lots of cute, frilly pillows.

"WHAT ARE YOU DOING HERE?"

Petunia screeched with fright, lost her grip on the plaster and would have plummeted to the floor if Horace had not wrapped his misty form around her and slowed her fall.

"Horace! You nearly scared me to death!" Petunia cried.

The ghost still swirled about her. "You're not supposed to be here!" he wailed.

"No one said I couldn't," Petunia pointed out. "Bogdana just said I couldn't go in her workshop or disturb her."

"This is my space! No one comes here except me."

Petunia frowned at the seething, misty form. She couldn't even make out his head right now, he was so agitated. "That sounds lonely," she told him. "Haven't you ever wanted a friend to play with here?"

Horace slowed a bit. "Well," he admitted, "it is lonely sometimes."

"I bet it's really lonely when everyone else is away."

"Yeah," he said in a small voice. Slowly, his form coalesced until he was about the same size as Petunia. He was so condensed, he almost seemed solid, and for the first time, Petunia could clearly see his face: a human boy with a small, upturned nose, a sprinkling of freckles, ears that stuck out from his head, and closely cropped hair. He wore a long nightshirt and, like her, was barefooted.

Horace is a child? Petunia thought. She'd always imagined him as a doddering old man. "Wow," she said, "you look a lot different when you're small."

He grinned at her. "I like to make myself bigger. Then I'm scarier, don't you think?"

"Definitely," she agreed, nodding. "I didn't know you could change your size."

"Sure! I can get even tinier." He demonstrated, shrinking to the size of an acorn, so compact he gleamed like a large pearl. "Or I can fill the whole house!" And he expanded outward until he was so thin, she couldn't see him at all, yet Petunia could still, ever so faintly, feel the chill of his presence.

"Come back!" she called.

"BOO!" he yelled behind her, and Petunia jumped about a foot. She spun around and found Horace, shrunk back to her size and doubled over, laughing.

Petunia put her fists on her hips. "You are entirely too good at being a ghost."

"I should be," he retorted. "I've been one for hundreds of years."

For just a moment, Petunia saw the years piled on years in his face. His body was a boy's, but his eyes looked so old. Then he grinned, and his eyes twinkled at her.

"Come on, let me show you around," Horace said, and

he shot away through the walls.

Horace showed her his collection of old mice nests, which he'd nudged into an odd space beneath the stairs on the second floor. He showed her the chink in the abandoned chimney where they could spy on the bats that roosted there. He took her to the walled-up closet that still held a forgotten pair of old leather gloves, cracked and dry and gnawed by mice. He showed her his hoard of lost objects, small things he could slowly poke through mouse holes and chinks into a space the size of a bread box: a cat's eye marble, a faded red ribbon, a baby shoe that Horace told her had been Millie's, a broken necklace chain, a whole, hollow robin's egg. Under his direction, Petunia arranged them all neatly, coiling the chain and folding up the ribbon, nesting the egg inside the shoe.

"Come on," Horace invited, and Petunia followed him up through the walls. He led her right out onto to the roof, where she could clamber out from under a loose shingle. They sat together on the ridge of the roof, looking out at the Enchanted Forest all around them like a rolling green sea, the Salivary Swamp to the west, and the Path winding its way between the trees. In the sunlight, Horace was all but invisible

"I come here a lot," Horace said. "When I want to be alone or to think about things."

"It's beautiful," Petunia breathed. "Thank you, Horace. Thanks for showing me around and helping me with things and sharing your treasures with me. This is one of the best days ever."

Horace looked surprised, then he smiled. "Yeah, for me, too."

The sun was getting low over the trees. Petunia stood up. "I'd better go set the table for dinner," she said, heading for the loose shingle. Then she stopped. "What's that?"

A dwarf had emerged from around the bend in the Path, pushing a wheelbarrow in which another dwarf lay unconscious. And covered with yellowish-green spots.

"Looks like a customer," Horace said. "We'd better get downstairs."

Petunia nodded and squeezed back under the loose shingle. Horace led her down through the walls to the hollow space behind the pantry, his favorite lurking space, where he retreated whenever Millie and Bogdana argued. As Petunia followed him along the timber supporting the floor, a glimmer of light caught her eye. Automatically, she pressed her face to a crack between the stones of the basement wall and gasped.

She could see into Bogdana's workshop, and it was the most wonderful place she had ever seen.

Millie had described this room in terms of deepest loathing: dark, dank, filled with strange and even noxious smells, cluttered with the paraphernalia of a potion witch's trade. Petunia could sort of see why. Every surface and corner and niche had something strange and fascinating in it. Long workbenches lined two walls. A third was lined with cabinets and cubby holes packed full of equipment and ingredients. Petunia counted at least eight glass jars full of eyes of different sizes, some dried and some suspended in greenish liquid.

The wall opposite the door had a wide fireplace with several iron hooks and moveable bars set in the stones above the banked flames. Bundled herbs wrapped in cheesecloth hung from the ceiling rafters, along with strings of bulbs and dried fruits, several sleeping bats, and a complete stuffed kelpie bigger than any she'd spied in the Salivary Swamp.

Petunia loved it.

In the center of the room, Bogdana stood before a work table with small cauldron suspended over a brazier, its coals glowing orange. She picked up a vial, unstopped it, and carefully dripped one, two, three drops into her brew. The witch muttered something in High Mystery and stirred the cauldron with even, measured strokes as the brew within it turned an orange just a shade lighter than the coals. Sighing, Bogdana set down the spoon and dropped into an overstuffed armchair, mopping her brow. She rested for a moment, then went to a cabinet and began loading empty vials into a basket.

"Hey!" Horace hissed in her ear. "You're not supposed to go in there!"

"I'm not in there," Petunia pointed out. "I am very definitely outside the workshop, and I'm not disturbing her."

Bogdana frowned and looked up, and both Horace and Petunia fell silent. Petunia wondered if Horace could hold his breath. Bogdana shook her head and went back to her vials.

"We should go," Horace insisted.

"In a minute," Petunia whispered back, fascinated. She felt as though her chest were expanding, as though she could breathe, really breathe for the first time ever. Certainty filled her: Petunia would get into that room, no matter what.

The doorbell rang.

 Chapter 8

The Spickle Pickle

"Oh, darkness," Bogdana swore and began hauling herself out of the chair.

"Quick!" Horace whispered, zipping away.

They darted through the walls to the mouse hole and out into the kitchen. Petunia ran to the parlor window, where she could see the dwarves at the front door. Horace hovered at her shoulder. She heard the heavy basement door creak open. The witch stomped up the stairs and through the kitchen into the parlor, where she spied Petunia waiting.

"It seems I have a customer," Bogdana growled.

"Two," said Petunia. "I saw them coming up the Path. A dwarf pushing another dwarf who's covered in these weird spots."

Bogdana's scowl of annoyance changed to a frown of concern. "Spots, you say? Hmm."

Petunia followed as Bogdana opened the front door. The spotted dwarf sat slumped on her doorstep, while the other dwarf panted and mopped his head with a handkerchief.

"Excuse me, Councilor," the sweaty dwarf said. "My brother's terrible sick. Can you help?"

Bogdana sniffed. "Did you not ask Rosmerta the Apothecary for help?"

"Aye, I did," said the dwarf. "She said it was a curse and gave us an antidote, but it did no good."

"That," said Bogdana, glaring down her nose at him, "is because Rosmerta is an idiot, even for a brownie. This is no curse. Your brother has spickle pox."

The dwarf gasped. "I was pretty sure it was some kind of pox. It's all over Goblintown. But spickle pox? Are you sure?"

"Quite sure. You are likely infected as well. It's highly contagious."

The dwarf's red cheeks turned pale. "Oh, no," he whispered. "And what about my children?"

"If you live in one home together, them, too." Bogdana smiled. "But have no fear. I have a small supply of cures. Once taken, they render you immune to spickle pox. You had better come in." She closed her eyes and said, "*Katoa!*"

The infected dwarf slumping in the doorway fell over into the parlor as the ward holding him outside dispersed. Petunia had to jump back to avoid being squashed by him.

"Place him on the couch," Bogdana said. "I will get the cure. Petunia, see that they do not leave the parlor. I will not have my home further contaminated." She headed for the kitchen, muttering under her breath. Petunia could feel the tingle of magic in her wake.

The pale dwarf picked up his spotted brother and gently laid him out on the couch.

"How long has he been like this?" Petunia asked.

"Three days. You're one of Thorn's lot, aren't you?"

Petunia leaped up onto the arm of the couch. "Yup, I'm Petunia." She peered down at the infected dwarf. He really did look just like Grumpkin.

"I'm Tarn. This un's Berto. What's a pixie doing here? Is your family well?"

"Oh, they're fine," Petunia assured him. "I'm here

helping out Bogdana's daughter, Millie. She's gone to visit her father, and I'm tending Thea while she's gone."

"Ah, the young dodonas," Tarn said, tipping his cap to her. "What a blessing upon the Forest. It's good that you're caring for her."

Petunia blushed and ducked her head. "She's my friend. Of course I'd help her."

Bogdana returned with a small covered basket. Opening it, she revealed about twenty vials of glowing orange liquid. "Here we are. Now, the matter of payment. I would say an umbre wyrm's egg would cover two vials, wouldn't you?"

Tarn grabbed his cap with both hands and nearly tore it in two. "An umbre wyrm's egg? Are you mad? Do you know how hard they are to find?"

"Well, the cure is rather difficult to make, and the ingredients are pricey." Bogdana sighed. "Oh, all right. I'll throw in cures for your children as well."

"I've got no umbre wyrm eggs!" Tarn cried. "It'd take me weeks to get them."

"Oh," said Bogdana. "What a pity."

"Isn't there something else I could offer?" Tarn asked desperately.

"Hmm," said Bogdana, tapping her nose with her finger. "Well, do you have a good source of sulphur?"

Tarn sagged with relief. "Oh, aye, that I do. My cousin, Rondal trades in it, mined from under the Mountain."

"What about tourmalines?"

"Aye, the same cousin."

Bogdana sat down in the chair next to him. "Excellent. I should like to draw up a contract with you, then. I shall need approximately two tonnes of sulphur and eleven stone of tourmalines. In exchange, I shall supply you with as many vials of cure as your family requires, Rondal included."

Tarn stuck out his hand. "It's a deal. I'll scry him as soon as you've given Berto his cure."

Bogdana eyed him, then took a vial and drank it herself. "Can't be too careful," she said. Gingerly, she took his hand and shook it. A shake was as good as a signed contract for dwarves. The witch handed Tarn two more vials. "Take your own first, then give the second to your brother." As Tarn uncapped his vial, Bogdana handed another to Petunia. "You've been exposed. You need to drink this as well."

Petunia had been a little worried about that very problem. She took the vial, which was half her size, uncapped it, and drank it down. It tasted of oranges and vinegar, with the faint fizz of magic. She almost gagged, it was so nasty. "Does Horace need one?"

Horace laughed. "Ghosts don't catch diseases, since we're already dead."

Tarn coughed loudly, then opened Berto's mouth and poured the contents of the vial down his throat. Berto stirred, the first time Petunia had seen him move on his own, and then his entire body seemed to relax. As she watched, the yellow-green bumps began to fade.

"Rockslides!" cried Tarn. "You've done it."

Bogdana nodded. "The pox is gone, but he'll be quite weak for several days. He needs rest and plenty of fluids. You might feel a little weak yourself for a day or so. Your children, if they're infected, will sleep more deeply for a few days as well. How many children?"

"Three," Tarn said.

Bogdana handed him four vials. "Three for the children, and a fourth for Rondal. The sooner he can get me the sulphur and tourmalines, the better. Now, rest here a bit before you head home. Petunia, come help me make some tea for our customer, if you please."

Petunia glanced at her in surprise. Bogdana had never been polite to her before. "Um, sure," she said. "Good luck, Tarn." The pixie jumped down from the couch and followed Bogdana into the kitchen.

Bogdana was actually filling the kettle herself. "Light the oven," she told Petunia.

Petunia opened the firebox and poked the coals with a bit of kindling until they caught again. She blew a pinch of pixie dust onto them, and they roared to life. She tossed on another log and closed the firebox.

"Now listen," Bodgana said, intently, and then she stopped. Her nose wrinkled, her eyes rolled back, and she let loose a terrible sneeze that knocked her back against the sink.

"Wow, that was a doozy!" Petunia said. "Are you sure you're not coming down with this pox?"

Bogdana shook her head, irritated. "No, no, spickle pox does not affect the sinuses. It saps the magical energy of its victim while simultaneously attacking the nervous system. Untreated, it can leave a patient paralyzed and bereft of magical talent. A terrible fate, but particularly bad for those races who depend upon magic to exist."

A cold hand wrapped itself around Petunia's heart. "Like us pixies," she whispered.

"Pixies, fairies, centaurs, sprites, dryads, even dragons, though they are more resistant than most, relying more heavily on spirit energy than magical energy. For the others, spickle pox means almost certain death. It's a terrible disease." Bogdana sat in her chair. "We haven't seen spickle pox in the Enchanted Forest for over a hundred years, but there's an outbreak in Vanaheim right now. That's why I have some of the cure ready to hand. I was going to ship it there, for a tidy profit, I might add. Now I will have to get the local outbreak under control first."

"Goblintown," Petunia whispered, thinking of Grumpkin. "He said it's all over Goblintown."

Bogdana stared down her nose at Petunia. "Yes. There will be more customers, many more. If we are lucky, I can keep the outbreak confined to Pixamitchie. I must scry the constable immediately to close the city to travel, though that will be difficult in Goblintown. Meanwhile, I will require your assistance."

"Of course!" said Petunia, thinking of her family, who would need dozens of vials if they caught the pox. "How can I help?"

"For now, keep the kettle on and make tea available to customers. You may sell the vials. The standard rate is four dragon scales or seven roc feathers or something of equivalent value."

Petunia's jaw dropped. "But that's much less expensive than an umbre wyrm's egg!"

"Yes, but I needed that contract. Both sulphur and tourmaline dust are essential ingredients in the cure, and I am nearly out. The sooner we get that supply, the better. The value of the six vials I gave him is fairly close, and I expect him to wrangle one or two more out of me on delivery."

"Oh," Petunia said. "I see. That was pretty clever."

Bogdana gave her a tight smile. "Pay attention, pixie. You may learn something." She gave another small sneeze, then pulled herself to her feet. "Stupid cold. I don't know why my cold cure potion isn't working. Well, no time now. I must complete the batch of cure I was making before I was interrupted and brew more after that.

"I will leave the front door wards open for now, but I've placed a new ward on all doors from the parlor to the rest of the house. You tend to our customers and let me know when we run out of cure potions. Oh, and I had better get more vials from the storeroom..." She headed for the basement stairs, muttering to herself.

Horace, back to his usual indistinct size, glided up. "See, she's not as awful as she pretends to be."

"Huh. I guess not."

The kettle began to sing, so Petunia magicked it off the stove, set up a tea tray with plenty of cups, put some good mint in the teapot, used pixie dust to fill it with hot water, and carried it out to Tarn.

Berto's eyes were open. "What happened?" he was saying.

"Easy now, Berto, you're all right. I brought you to the witch's place, an' she cured you."

Petunia set the tray down on the coffee table. "Tea will be ready in a minute. Feeling better, Berto?"

"I feel like I've been trampled by ogres," Berto gasped out.

Tarn stroked his face. "Not to worry," he said. "You'll be weak a few days, but then you'll be right as rain." He turned to Petunia. "Miss Petunia, if you have a scrying mirror about, I can call on Rondal while we wait for the tea."

"Oh, it's out back with Thea," Petunia told him. "I'm sure Master Quercius won't mind if I interrupt the lesson. He'll want to know about the spickle pox anyway. Wait here, I'll be right back."

Petunia ran out to the backyard, where Thea, Quercius, and the elm tree were all rustling pleasantly at each other. "Excuse me!" she called out. "I'm sorry to interrupt, but we need the scrying bowl. There's been an outbreak of spickle pox in Pixamitchie."

Quercius frowned. "That is grave news, indeed. Has Councilor Noctmartis alerted the Enchanted Forest Council?"

Petunia bit her lip. "I don't think so. She's busy brewing

cures. But she said she'd talk to the constable about closing the village to travelers."

"That's a good thought. Please remind her to contact the Council as well. Thea, our lesson was nearly done anyway. We shall resume tomorrow, my dear. Petunia, good luck." Quercius faded from view.

"Bye!" Petunia called. "Sorry, Thea. Very busy. Gotta go. Hopefully, I can play with you some more later."

Thea bowed to her and waved several leaves cheerfully.

"Thanks!" Petunia hoisted the bowl onto her head and ran it into the house, setting it down beside the tea tray. "Here you are, Tarn. You talk while I pour tea."

Tarn scryed his cousin while Petunia used more pixie dust to pour the tea, levitating a cup to Berto, who took a small sip.

"Oh, that's good," he sighed. "I feel as though I've drunk nothing for a week." He sat up a bit and took the cup himself, sipping again.

"Good, Rondal, thanks. Yes, the sooner the better. All right, see you tomorrow." Tarn ran his fingers through the water, breaking the connection. "There, all set. Rondal will be here tomorrow with the witch's supplies."

"Oh, thank you," Petunia said. "I'll tell her when she comes up to supper."

Tarn glanced at his brother. "Look at you, sitting up! Are you ready to go home?"

"I'd rest easier in my own bed," Berto admitted.

"Well, then, we'll take up no more of your time," Tarn said.

The doorbell rang. Petunia looked at Tarn, then ran to open the door. A centaur stood there with a wagon behind him. He looked surprised to see a pixie at the door.

"Excuse me," he said. "Is Councilor Noctmartis available?"

"Let me guess," Petunia said. "Yellowy-green spots?"

The centaur nodded.

"And the apothecary can't help?"

He nodded behind him. "She's in the cart, along with her family."

Petunia rubbed her head. "Oh, slugs and bugs. Okay, it's spickle pox, we have the cure, four dragon scales, seven roc feathers, or something of equivalent value."

The centaur nodded. "Rosmerta told me to bring her jar of dragon scales. She said they were good tender for potion-makers." He opened the jar and counted out twenty scales. "Five, please."

Petunia took the scales. "Got room for one more going back?" She nodded her head at the dwarves.

The centaur nodded.

"Good. Tarn, can you help me carry the vials? It'll be faster than me bringing them one at a time."

Tarn helped Petunia distribute the vials to the four brownies lying in the wagon. Rosmerta was the worst off, barely breathing. The centaur took the fifth vial and swallowed it before helping pour Rosmerta's cure down her throat.

Petunia repeated Bogdana's instructions and then politely offered the centaur a cup of tea as Tarn loaded Berto into the wagon. He shook his mane. "I had best get back. This will get worse before it gets better."

"Tell the constable not to let people into or out of the village," Petunia said, remembering Quercius's message.

"He's sick, too."

"Frogs and bogs." She grabbed a vial and gave it to the centaur. "Here, for the constable. I think we're going to need him up and healthy as soon as possible."

The centaur bowed his head. "I will deliver it as soon as I've taken these folk home. Thank you."

"Quite welcome!" Petunia said. "Good luck!"

They turned to leave, Tarn pushing his now-empty wheelbarrow, and passed a limping dryad making her way up the path. Every leaf of her head was covered with spickle pox.

Panic seized Petunia. What if Thea got sick? She grabbed a vial, ran out to the back yard, and poured the contents over Thea's roots. Thea reacted violently, shaking and curling her leaves in disgust.

"Sorry, Thea!" Petunia cried, hugging the little tree. "This medicine will keep you from getting sick. Would you like some more compost tea to wash it down?"

Thea nodded emphatically, so Petunia got the watering can and gave Thea a good long drink.

The doorbell rang.

"Gotta go, Thea, but I'll be back soon!" Petunia called, dashing back into the house.

Chapter 9

A Helping Hand

Bogdana was right. Along with Rondal and his shipment of sulphur and tourmalines the following morning, three more customers arrived at their door just after breakfast. And four more by lunch. Over the next three days, they saw a steadily increasing stream of customers. At first, Petunia was able to go out and play with Thea in the morning as she was supposed to, running in only when she saw customers coming up the Path. But by her fifth day in Millie's house, the stream came in so thickly that she barely had time to give Thea her compost tea. The rest of the day she spent coping with customers while Bogdana brewed cures as fast as she could in the basement.

At breakfast the next Onesday (eggs benedict, hash browns, fruit salad, yogurt, and granola with freshly squeezed orange juice), Millie's note read:

> *Dear Petunia (and dear Horace!),*
> *By now, Mother should be hitting peak grouchiness, because she's realized you're actually a nice, helpful, pleasant person, and she doesn't want to admit it. Don't worry, she'll come around today, probably after lunch. I know it's hard, but just stick with it. And remember*

that, even though she's a curmudgeon, Mother really is a clever person, so listen to her. Behind all the grouchiness, she usually knows what she's talking about.

Just in case you run out of granola, here's my favorite recipe. It's quite easy, and we have plenty of ingredients.

10 cups rolled oats
3/4 cup sesame seeds
1/2 cup sunflower seeds (shelled)
2 cups raw almonds, roughly chopped
1 cup shredded unsweetened coconut
1/2 teaspoon salt
1-1/2 tablespoon ground cinnamon
3/4 cup canola oil
1 cup maple syrup
1-1/2 tablespoons vanilla extract
1-1/2 teaspoons almond extract
1/4 cup raisins or dried cranberries

Preheat the oven to 250 degrees F. That's a low heat. Place the two racks in the top of the oven.

Combine the oats, sesame seeds, sunflower seeds, almonds, coconut, salt, and cinnamon in the largest bowl you can find. Stir until the contents are uniformly mixed. In a separate bowl, whisk together the oil, maple syrup, vanilla, and almond extract to make a uniform syrup. Pour this over the dry ingredients and stir until everything is coated.

Line two big baking sheets with parchment paper. Spread the granola in an even layer on each pan. Put them in the oven and set the timer for 30 minutes. Swap the trays, and when you do, put the fronts to the back so it cooks evenly. Set the timer for another 30 minutes. Rotate the trays again, and bake them for 30 more minutes, (a total of 90 minutes altogether). Put out the fire in the oven and leave the granola in there overnight or for at least 6 hours. When it's fully cooked, sprinkle with the raisins or cranberries (or both!) and store in a big jar or crock with a tight lid.

Love and hugs,
Millie

"It's true," Horace said. "Bogdana can be harsh, but she's usually fair."

The doorbell rang. "Oh, here we go again," Petunia said, snatching a bite of poached egg and hollandaise sauce. Bogdana had placed a full basket of her latest batch of potions in the parlor, which Petunia had been doggedly selling for roc feathers, dragon scales, and other assorted trade goods. The customer at the door, a prickly thistle sprite, offered her a pound of high quality dark chocolate, which Petunia immediately accepted on Millie's behalf, and an envelope addressed to Bogdana.

"Millie's not home?" the speckled sprite asked as she accepted her cure. "Oh, that's too bad. I was hoping for one of her goodies."

"Try the cookie jar," Horace suggested. "Millie always keeps some extra treats in there." He led Petunia over to the cookie jar in the kitchen, and sure enough, it was full to the brim with oatmeal raisin cookies. "She keeps them for when her brother visits," the ghost explained.

"Of course!" Petunia said. "They're Max's favorite. Well, I'm sure he won't begrudge our customers a few cookies." She toted the cookie jar out to the parlor and handed one to the sprite.

"What do you call a thief who robs a bakery?" Petunia

asked. "A crook-ie!"

The sprite laughed and munched her cookie. "Now I'm sure to get well," the sprite grinned at her, her spickle pox already fading.

The doorbell rang, and Petunia opened it to a pair of familiar dwarves.

"Tarn! Berto! What are you doing back here?"

Tarn lifted Berto out of the wheelbarrow and shoved his way in angrily. "Berto's not getting better. I want him cured up proper, or I want a refund." He laid Berto down on the sofa.

Petunia hopped up onto the arm of the sofa. "What's the problem? His spots are gone. How're you feeling, Berto?"

With effort, Berto opened his eyes. "Tired," he whispered. "So, so tired."

Petunia frowned. "Well, Bogdana did say he'd be tired for a while."

"It's been four days, an' no improvement," Tarn growled.

"Huh, that's weird," Petunia said. "How are *you* feeling? And what about your kids?"

Tarn took off his cap and scratched his head. "We're all fine, s'truth. As the witch said, I did get a bit knackered for a day or two, and all the children slept late, but we none of us got the pox. Them cures worked, but Berto's was defective."

"That doesn't make sense. They were all from the same batch," Petunia said. "There must be something else going on."

Tarn's frown deepened. "I want to talk to the witch."

"She's still sleeping." At Tarn's reddening face, Petunia added, "She was up most of the night brewing more potions. I'm trying to let her get some rest. Here, have some of Millie's cookies while you wait, and I'll fetch some tea." She handed them each a cookie. Berto began nibbling it, but Tarn dashed his to the ground.

"I'll see the witch right now!"

An ear-splitting sneeze erupted from the kitchen.

"Why is breakfast cold?" Bogdana croaked, peering into the parlor.

Petunia stared at her. Her skin, normally a shade of green somewhere between avocado and mold, was instead pink so pale it was nearly white. Dark circles ringed her eyes, which were bloodshot, and her large, crooked, warty nose was red at the nostrils. Her hair, rather than artfully tangled into a black cloud around her head, was now matted and more brown than black. She clutched a gray knitted shawl about her shoulders with one hand and a handkerchief with the other.

Abruptly, Bogdana flung her head back, then threw it forward into the handkerchief. "AAAAACHOOOOOOOO!!!"

"Rockslides," whispered Tarn, his cap in his hands.

"Slugs and bugs," Petunia said. "That cold's getting worse."

"Nonsense," Bogdana said irritably. "I'm just tired."

"You look terrible," Petunia told her frankly.

Bogdana straightened in her seat. "Do I really?" She allowed herself a thin smile, primping her matted hair. "Well, thank you. Now, why is breakfast cold?"

"I set it out an hour ago. You slept in later than usual."

Bogdana picked up the envelope. "And what's this?"

"It was on the doorstep this morning."

"Hmph," Bogdana opened it, snorted, crumpled the letter, and tossed it into the stove. Cheered, she heaped some food on her plate. Bogdana pointed at the food and began to say, "*Lämpene,*" but halfway through, she sneezed again, and the hollandaise sauce caught fire.

"*Katoa!*" Petunia yelled, putting the fire out.

Bogdana glared balefully at her and the hollandaise both, then said, "Actually, I just want oatmeal."

"Um, sure," Petunia said. "You just deal with these customers, and I'll make you some."

Bogdana glared down at Tarn. "You, again? What now? I've no time to take petty complaints."

Petunia darted into the kitchen. Oatmeal was one thing Petunia could cook herself. She got a saucepan, filled it with water, and put it on the stove to boil. Then she slapped her forehead. "I forgot to water Thea! I'll be right back."

She dashed out the kitchen door, grabbed the watering can, and hurried over to Thea, who was looking a little droopy and listless.

"Thea, I'm so sorry. Here you go!" She poured the compost tea over the little dodonas. Thea shook herself and stretched her leaves under the shower.

The elm rustled angrily above them. "I know," Petunia told her, "I'm late. It's on account of the spickle pox. So many people are sick."

The elm stilled her branches and drooped sadly.

Thea, however, had perked up. She clapped her leaves together expectantly.

"I'm sorry, Thea. I don't think I can play today. I need to help Bogdana." She hesitated. "But I'll tell you one quick joke, okay?"

The little tree bobbed happily.

"What's a ghost's favorite pie? BOO-berry!"

The little tree shook with silent laughter. Petunia knew a ton of ghost jokes. She would have to try them out on Horace.

"Okay, I have to go. I'll be back this afternoon with

the scrying bowl for your lesson with Quercius." Petunia
hugged Thea. She glanced at the Path, and to her
surprise, she saw Tarn and Berto walking away. Berto
looked a little worn down but much better than before.
She waved at them, and they waved back, Tarn a little
sheepishly. The sprite followed, skipping along the Path.
Must not have been a very bad case, Petunia thought,
puzzled. Passing them coming up the Path came a family
of gnomes in a goat-drawn cart. Sighing, Petunia ran
back to the house.

The pot was boiling on the stove. Petunia dumped in
oats and salt, then moved it back off the heat a bit. She
hopped up on a nearby canister and began stirring with a
long wooden spoon.

"Is that oatmeal ready?" Bogdana growled at Petunia as
she entered the kitchen.

Oatmeal usually took a good hour to cook. Petunia took
a pinch of pixie dust and dropped it in the pot, whispering,
"*Nopeasti.*" The oatmeal softened and swelled, absorbing all
the water in an instant.

"Just done," Petunia told her. "Help yourself!"

Bogdana took down a bowl from the cupboard and
spooned in the oatmeal while Petunia fetched milk from
the icebox. The witch sat heavily at the table, sprinkling the
oatmeal with sugar and raisins. The doorbell rang.

"Go and deal with that," the witch said, and she began
shoveling in the oatmeal.

"Um, sure," Petunia said. She hurried into the parlor as
a gnome couple stumbled in, carrying their three children.
She pulled two vials from the basket, balanced one on each
hip, and brought them over to the gnome father. "That'll
be twenty dragon scales or thirty-five roc feathers, please."

A massive sneeze sounded from the kitchen, followed by

a sharp crack. Petunia glanced over and saw that Bogdana's oatmeal bowl had cracked in half, spilling oatmeal all over the table. The witch pushed herself up from the table. "Wasn't all that hungry anyway."

The gnome father began pulling feathers from a satchel. Bogdana peered at them, then squawked, "Those aren't roc feathers! They're golden goose feathers! How dare you try to cheat me! AAAAHHHH-CHOOOOOOOOOOO!"

The poor gnome burst into tears. "Please," he said, "I've got nothing else. My whole family is so sick. Please, can't you spare a few vials?"

Bogdana's eyes narrowed. "If you have a golden goose, then I'll take your next three eggs in payment."

"But that's our rent! Where will we live?"

"At least you'll be alive. I'm certain you will think of something."

Shaking and sobbing, the gnome agreed.

"I will draw up a contract," said Bogdana.

Petunia got angry. "That's cruel! You can't cost them their rent! How are they supposed to get better without a home? Why can't you just give them the cures?"

Bogdana fixed her with a steely gaze. "SILENCE. You are a guest in this house, and if you wish to remain, you will respect me and my business practices. ACHOO!"

The gnome mother said bitterly, "You should be charging the goblins. They're the ones brought the spickle pox in the first place, the nasty, filthy things."

"Hush, now, Maeve," said the gnome father. "We don't want more trouble."

The doorbell rang, and Bogdana shuffled across the parlor to get it, letting a fairy flit in.

Bogdana groaned. "How many?"

"Fifteen," twittered the fairy, then fell to the floor and

lay still.

With surprising tenderness, Bogdana scooped her up and lay her on a pillow. Turning to the gnome, she said, "If you take this fairy and her vials back with you, I will reduce your debt by one goose egg."

The gnome nodded gratefully. Bodgana gave the fairy a cure, then packed all the remaining vials in a basket for the gnome to take along. The fairy fluttered and opened her eyes.

"The cure?"

Bogdana nodded. "You've had it, and I've packed the rest for you."

"Ah," said the fairy. "Then consider this your Favor repaid."

Petunia gasped. Bogdana had owed a fairy a Favor? Fairy Favors were nearly as rare as Pixie Promises.

"Thank you," said Bogdana, words Petunia never expected to hear from the witch.

Bogdana pulled open a desk drawer and drew out parchment, ink, and quill. She wrote out the contract on the coffee table, then handed the quill to the gnome. He signed with a shaking hand.

"Petunia, give them the cures."

Petunia doled out vials to the gnome family, helping the younger children to drink them down.

She helped the gnome and his family outside to their cart, and Bogdana followed, placing the fairy, pillow and all, gently in the cart along with the basket of vials. They watched as the gnome father led the goat back up the Path, his head bowed in despair.

Fists clenched in anger, Petunia followed Bogdana back inside the house. The witch sat down on the sofa, and suddenly, Petunia could see the utter fatigue permeating

Bogdana. Slowly, for emphasis, Bogdana said, "We are out of cures."

"What?" Petunia said. "But you were up most of the night making them!"

Bogdana glared at her. "I can only brew so much at a time."

"B-but, all those poor people! They'll be paralyzed or die!" Petunia protested.

Horace glided up. "You need help," he told Bogdana. "Call on your sisters, or Baba Luci."

"My mother has already mobilized the other potion witches in the Enchanted Forest. The spickle pox has spread beyond Pixamitchie."

"How far?" Petunia asked.

"Last time I scryed her, she said the pox has reached from Eastmarch to the Dragon Vale. The elves very sensibly closed the borders of the Sylvan Vale and quarantined the few who succumbed to the illness, and the dwarves of the Iron Mountains have done the same. But everywhere else..."

Petunia covered her mouth with her hands. "Those fairies, where did they come from?" The upper levels of the briar hedge she lived in were occupied almost entirely by fairy families. Had it spread to the hedge? Was her family in danger?

"None of your business," Bogdana snapped at her.

"What about an apprentice witch?" Horace asked. "Get one of your nieces over to help you brew."

Bogdana snorted. "What, and have them spying around my house, reporting back to my sisters? Not on your death."

Petunia would have given her eyeteeth to be one of Bogdana's nieces right about then. She wanted so badly to get into that workshop and explore all its nooks and crannies.

"If only..." she muttered.

Horace turned to her. "If only what?"

"Well," Petunia said slowly. "If I were a witch, I could help."

Horace condensed a bit, just enough for Petunia to see his boy-face give her a sly grin. Then he said, "Who says you have to be a witch?"

"ACHOO!" Bogdana snuffled and pinched the bridge of her nose. "What are you suggesting, Horace?"

Hope swelled inside Petunia. If she didn't need to be a witch. "What about me?" she cried. "I've been studying potion-making in school. I could help you!"

Chapter 10

A Pixie's Promise

Bogdana looked down that long, crooked nose at her. "A pixie? Making anything more complicated than oatmeal? Ridiculous."

"I can so brew potions. If Millie were here, she'd tell you."

"Tell *me*," Bogdana grated out. "Have you ever brewed a potion without using pixie dust?"

Oops. "Well, no," Petunia admitted.

"Just as I thought," Bogdana said with a satisfied snort. "You're lazy, like all pixies."

Petunia clenched her fists. "I am not lazy. I'll prove it. Put me to work."

"Why not?" Horace said. "Give her a simple task, something she can't mess up. She doesn't have to brew potions, just help you with some of the preparation."

"Hmm, maybe." Bogdana considered. "How do I know you won't betray me? How do I know you're not a spy, here to steal the recipe for your father's gout medicine?"

"I wouldn't do that," Petunia protested. "You can trust me."

"Why?" Bogdana asked her. "I hardly know you. All I know about you is that you're Millie's friend, which in my opinion shows dubious taste, and your father eats too much fat. I have absolutely no reason to trust you."

Petunia could see her opportunity slipping away. She wanted to get into that workshop so badly, it made her reckless. "I could make a Promise," she blurted out. "I could Promise never to reveal your secrets."

Bogdana looked thoughtful. "That... would be acceptable. A Pixie's Promise is binding. Yes, that will do nicely." She leaned forward. "Promise me that you will tell no one of anything that you see or hear or do in my workshop, and you may assist me."

Petunia felt a sudden pit in her stomach. Promises were dangerous. She thought it over, but she couldn't see any harm in it. It was a well-phrased Promise, limited in scope. If things got weird or difficult, she could always just leave the workshop. But Petunia was determined to stay and learn everything she could.

"All right," she said. "I Promise that I will tell no one of anything I see, hear, or do while I assist you in your workshop."

Immediately, Petunia felt the Promise take hold, a tingling and tightening of her skin. She shivered.

Bogdana gave her a large, toothy smile. "Good. Clean up after breakfast and then meet me in the workroom." She levered herself up from the sofa and removed another sheet of parchment from the desk. With the ink and quill, she wrote out a notice in large letters, blew on it, then took it across the room and stuck it to the outside of the front door. Closing the door, she locked it firmly. "Be quick," she told Petunia. "We have a lot of work to do." She poured herself a cup of tea and took it down the basement stairs with her.

Petunia went to the kitchen and looked over the table.

"Better have a full breakfast first," Horace told her. "You never know how long Bogdana will keep you down there."

Petunia agreed, though she could hardly think about food, with the tingling of the Promise on her skin and the lure of the workshop. She sat down and began stuffing herself with cold eggs, hash browns, and fruit. Horace ate more sedately next to her.

The doorbell rang.

"Don't answer that!" Bogdana called up the stairs.

It rang several more times, then someone began pounding on the door.

The delicious hash browns stopped tasting quite so good, and Petunia had to fight to swallow. Eventually, after a few sharp kicks to the door, the knocking ceased altogether.

"This is awful," Horace moaned beside her. He pushed his plate away.

Petunia nodded. She didn't much feel like telling ghost jokes now. "Time to get to work." In a twinkling and a liberal application of pixie dust, she cleaned up breakfast, storing the leftovers in the icebox just in case she needed to feed up a customer or two, once they had cures again. Then Petunia rolled up her iris-petal sleeves and marched herself down the basement stairs.

Behind her, Horace whispered, "Good luck."

Peeping through the crack in the wall had not prepared Petunia for entering Bogdana's workshop. The smells rolled over her: musty, spicy, acrid, sweet, vinegary, coppery, and things so strange she could not name them. Her bare feet slid on a stone floor worn smooth, almost buttery under her feet. From below, rather than above, Petunia could see all the cabinets and storage containers scattered about the room, including a glass tank containing several live, scuttling scorpions. The persistent residual tingle of magic raised all the fine hairs on her arms and legs, different from the tingle of pixie dust, somehow: purposeful, intent.

In the center of the room, Bogdana was setting up the brazier on the battered work table. "Stop gawking and come here," she snapped at Petunia.

The pixie crossed the slate floor and jumped up onto the table. The residual magic in it was so strong, it made her toes curl for a moment.

"Pixies are strong for their size, so you should have no trouble crushing these tourmalines. That will save me ages in preparing cures." Bogdana pushed a large stone mortar and pestle over to Petunia, then poured in several large multicolored crystals, like three-sided prisms that had trapped their rainbows. "They need to be powder-fine, like sugar."

"Sure as sure," Petunia said. She hopped up to the rim of the mortar, hugged the pestle with both arms, and began pounding the tourmalines. To her surprise, they fractured easily, splitting along the layers of crystal. Before long, she got into a rhythm, pounding it slowly but surely into sparkling sand.

Bogdana peered into the mortar and gave a grunt of approval. "Good. Let me empty that, and you can get busy grinding more."

Petunia hopped down so that Bogdana could tip the tourmaline powder into a jar, then refill the mortar with more crystals, which Petunia then pounded into powder as well. As she pounded, she watched Bogdana work. Carefully, meticulously, the witch laid out and prepared her ingredients. Bogdana measured out sulphur by the cupful, then blended it with a black powder. Iron? Ash? Petunia sniffed. No, something herbal.

"What's the black stuff?" she asked.

Bogdana blinked in surprise. "Black mugwort, dried and powdered."

"Why use it?"

"Mugwort has healing properties, particularly against parasites, but black mugwort is also effective against boils and skin ailments."

"Ah, that makes sense," Petunia said. "And the sulphur?"

"A general antibiotic," Bogdana muttered, stirring.

"And the tourmaline?"

Bogdana put down her spoon with a huff. "Why are you asking me all these questions? Millie never asks."

Petunia shrugged. "It's interesting. I've never seen anyone make a potion this complicated. I'm trying to understand how it all fits together."

Bogdana stared at her, and for a moment, Petunia thought she had made the weary witch angry. And then she realized that Bogdana was goggling at her in surprised disbelief.

"*Interesting,*" the witch repeated. She picked up the spoon again. "I can't be distracted by all your questions," Bogdana told her curtly, "but if you can keep from interrupting, I will explain what I do as I go. Will that suffice?"

"Oh, yes," Petunia said.

For the next hour, as Petunia pounded away, Bogdana explained each of the components of the potion, how the sulphur boosted the effect of the mugwort, how the tourmaline powder acted as a conduit for magical power within the nervous system, why purified mineral oil was essential as the liquid suspension for these powders so that it would not react with the scorpion venom (which explained the tank of scorpions on the floor). How just three drops of precious lunar eclipse dew would render the venom harmless to the patient but deadly to the pox. How the orange flavoring made it taste better. The precise brewing temperature for the first stage of the potion, and how to tell you'd reached it.

The three phrases of High Mystery required to combine the ingredients at each of the three stages of manufacture.

At each stage, Bogdana demonstrated her technique, and Petunia watched in fascination. She did all that, keeping the proper temperature, timing the drop of dew, chanting the strange words of High Mystery, without pixie dust to ensure it worked. When the potion in the cauldron turned the characteristic orange hue of the cure, Petunia exclaimed, "That's amazing!"

Bogdana glanced at her out of the corner of her eye as she fetched a fresh batch of vials. "Really?"

"Really!"

"Hmm," said the witch. "Well, hopefully, this batch will go faster without you asking questions." She began ladling the potion into the vials.

Petunia was silent for a moment, then she said, "You could teach me."

Bogdana stopped. "I could what?"

"You could teach me how to make the potions. That way, we could work in shifts, and you wouldn't get so tired."

Bogdana turned to her. "You want to learn how to make the cure."

Petunia nodded. "Sure, why not?"

Setting down the ladle and the vial she was holding, Bogdana fixed Petunia with a bloodshot stare. "This is an advanced potion, not for novices. It would take you weeks of training just to make some of the components."

"I've had tons of training," Petunia insisted. "I've been studying potions at school for years."

Bogdana raised an eyebrow. "Then why learn to make this one?"

"Well," said Petunia, twisting her hands in the hem of her dress, "because I want to help."

The other eyebrow went up. "And?" Bogdana prompted.

"And... and it's so much better than the stupid potions we make in school! This one is complicated and intricate. It has all these different parts, and they all interact with each other and work together and combine to make something new, something more than just all those parts. It's sort of like a really good joke, with the leader and the punchline, only... only more. Much, much more."

"I see," Bogdana said. "Tell me, what is the most complicated potion you've completed?"

"A sleeping potion," Petunia told her.

"Hmph, basic, simple," Bogdana told her. "And if you used pixie dust to do it, sloppy and inconsistent."

"I don't need pixie dust!" cried Petunia, balling her fists. "Didn't I just grind all these tourmalines for you?"

Bogdana nodded. "But that was a simple task. The temptation to use pixie dust is strong, especially for a potion as complex and delicate as this one. But pixie dust introduces inaccuracies. There's no consistency. You'd get widely varying dosages, or it might not work at all."

"Then I won't use it," Petunia insisted. "I can make potions without pixie dust."

Bogdana rested her chin in one hand, tapping her long, warty nose thoughtfully. "Well, I suppose I can test you on some of the simpler aspects of potion-making."

"And if I pass your test, you'll teach me this one?"

Bogdana frowned, then yawned broadly. "We'll see. Right now, I need you to take these vials upstairs and get back to selling them. This evening, after dinner, we can begin."

Chapter 11

Toil and Trouble

They brought the new batch of cures upstairs. There was a line of people waiting outside the front door, so Bogdana sold the twenty cures she'd just made while Petunia brewed the tea. Her head spun. She'd never known magic could be so complicated and, well, beautiful. It was like a tapestry, all interwoven of different strands creating one whole piece. Could she really do everything Bogdana had done? What if she messed up, like Millie used to? Bogdana might get angry at her or throw her out or turn her into a toad. Worse yet, she might blow up the workshop, and then what would happen to all the people who needed cures?

But at the same time, Petunia couldn't stop thinking about it, how one ingredient fitted into another, how they all connected for a single purpose. She wanted to try it.

By the time the tea was ready, they'd sold out again, to groans and sobbing and angry shouts outside. Bogdana slammed the door on the remaining customers. "Ungrateful wretches," she said, shoving dragon scales and roc feathers into her pockets. "Now, let's have that tea."

Petunia sat down on her empty spool and sipped her chamomile. Her arms ached from all the pounding, but she scarcely noticed, her head was spinning so.

"How did you learn all that?" she asked Bogdana.

"Hmm?" said the witch, putting down her cup. "All what?"

"Potion-making."

Bogdana chuckled. "Well, I learned, grudgingly, from my mother."

"You didn't want to learn potions?" Petunia prompted.

The witch leaned back in her chair. "I wanted to beat my sisters. Hepsibat creates golems. Ospecia has the power of transmutation. Ingratia turned out to be a first-rate fire witch. And Suspicia's the best illusionist we've had in our family in three generations." Bogdana let out a long, bitter sigh. "They were all so flashy and powerful. I wanted to be like them. I wanted to outdo them all! But my talent lay in potions. Boring, stodgy potions. Oh, how they lorded that over me, how they rubbed it in every chance they got.

"My mother knew very early on where my talent lay, but I fought her on it, tooth and nail. I tried everything: shapeshifting, planewalking, thaumaturgy, hydromancy. And Mother let me until I strayed into necromancy." Bogdana paused. "The less said about that, the better."

Petunia shuddered. Of all the forms of magic, necromancy—power over the dead—was utterly forbidden in the Enchanted Forest, and for good reason. Necromancy slowly eroded the soul of the user and drained the life force out of the surrounding area.

"Baba Luci put her foot down, made me swear never to engage in necromancy again, and then forced me into her laboratory where, by darkness, I learned my potions." Bogdana refilled her cup and took a large gulp.

Petunia had never thought of her brothers and sisters as competitors like this. It was hard enough just getting noticed. What if they were all better at magic than she was?

Or fighting? Or jokes? It would be so much worse than just being forgotten.

"So you never wanted to be a potions witch," she said.

Bogdana glared down her nose at Petunia. "Well, what do you want to be?"

"I, I don't know," Petunia stammered. "I've never thought about it."

Bogdana closed her eyes. "Pixies," she intoned. "You're lazy, the lot of you. None of you thinks ahead about anything because you always have your dust to do the hard work for you. What does your father do?"

"He's a plant-shaper," Petunia declared.

"Huh. At least he has some profession. And your mother?"

Petunia realized she had no idea. "Bakes bread and makes dinner, mostly."

Bogdana nodded in confirmation. "Most pixies never bother to find their talent, you know. They just wander through life, day to day, with no thought to the future."

"They do not!" Petunia cried defiantly. "They work as hard as anyone! Think it's easy, having a dozen babies? You've only had two, and you only take care of Millie! That's a whole job in itself, the cooking and cleaning and laundry and marketing and sewing and mending. Imagine finding time to do anything beyond that!" A pang of homesickness struck her. For one instant, she wanted a slice of her mother's bland bread more than anything, even one of Millie's triple chocolate brownies.

"I do imagine," Bogdana said. "I imagine a great deal, which is why I've chosen this life, such as it is. Even dull, boring potions are more interesting than a life of service to your own children." She pushed herself to her feet. "Come, pixie. Let us see if there is more to you than your pixie dust."

They went back down to the workshop. "Okay!" Petunia cried. "What do I do first?"

"Hmm. You can start on purifying water," Bogdana decided.

"What?" Petunia exclaimed. "But that's boring!"

Bogdana glared down her nose at her. "Lazy pixie, always shirking chores. Do you want to learn or not?"

Petunia grimaced. "Fine. Purifying stupid water."

"It is NOT stupid," Bogdana bellowed at her. "Purified water is an extremely important ingredient in every potion-maker's workshop. The first thing you must do before you begin making any potion is to cleanse your cauldron." Bogdana took the cauldron over to a sink and rinsed it out with water from a silver ewer. "This specially purified water nullifies any magical effect that might linger in the cauldron. Failure to clean your equipment can result in a dangerous buildup of magical residue."

"Oh, and then boom," Petunia said with sudden understanding. "I think that happened to Mum's bread pans once."

Bogdana rolled her eyes. "Pixies," she muttered. "Come to the sink, and I will teach you the incantation. The water must be held in a silver vessel to prevent outside contamination."

Petunia ran over and jumped up to the sink. It had its own hand pump, just like the one in the kitchen. Bogdana set the empty ewer down under the spout.

"Fill the ewer with water. Deep water from a well is always best, but you can use fresh rainwater or clear, running water from a stream in a pinch."

"Okay," Petunia said. She seized the handle and began pumping, shoving her entire body up and down. It wasn't hard; Bogdana kept her pump in good working order, and it moved smoothly, drawing the water from deep beneath them.

"Enough," Bogdana called out. "Now come take the ewer."

Petunia let go of the pump handle and ran over, taking the ewer by the neck with both hands.

"You must swirl it clockwise three times as you recite the purification incantation," Bogdana told her. "Go ahead and practice that to get the feel of it. A smooth, easy motion makes the spell easier."

Petunia tried, and on the first swing, she sloshed a good amount out of the ewer. But after a few swings, she got the hang of it, producing a nice, easy swirl.

"Not bad," said Bogdana grudgingly. "Stop a moment, and I will teach you the incantation."

Petunia stopped swirling and set the ewer down.

"Listen carefully to the pronunciation," Bogdana said, "and repeat after me: *Puhdista tämä vesi.*"

Petunia repeated the phrase as precisely as she could, but Bogdana stamped her foot and said, "Terrible! Who taught you to speak High Mystery? Your intonation lacks the proper vibrancy. Now, listen, and watch my mouth as I speak it."

Petunia managed not to roll her eyes. She'd never needed to get the High Mystery right before, but she dutifully repeated after Bogdana several times until the witch declared her passable.

"Now," the witch instructed, "begin swirling as you speak the incantation, and will your magic through your words, into the water. And NO PIXIE DUST."

Petunia nodded, her hands sweaty. She rarely cast spells without pixie dust, and her mouth turned dry. What if it didn't work? What if Bogdana was right, and she couldn't work magic without it? She reached out to grasp the ewer, but with her sweaty palms, the ewer slipped right out of her grasp and spilled the water into the sink.

Bogdana put her hand over her eyes. "Refill it, quickly. Remember, there are people in need of this cure waiting outside."

Petunia cringed with shame. She was beginning to see how hard this must have been for Millie. But then she straightened her spine, jumped into the sink, righted the ewer, and jumped out to work the pump again. Wiping her hands on her iris petal skirt, she took up the ewer again. "Okay, I'm ready," she told Bogdana.

"Well, then, go on and do it!"

Petunia began swirling. As she did, she reached into herself, to that inner reserve of magic all pixies have, and tried to push it out through the words she spoke: "*Puhdista tämä vesi.*" A faint tingling ran through her arms, but it fizzled out before it reached her fingertips.

Bogdana snorted. "Is that the best you can do?"

Petunia gritted her teeth. Swirling mightily, she shouted, "*Puhdista tämä vesi!*" This time, magic surged down her arms and into the ewer, causing it to glow for a moment. "Yes!" she cried, filled with the heady rush of triumph.

"Hmph, adequate," Bogdana said. "You used more magic than strictly necessary for such a simple spell, but you'll get better at it over time. From now on, it will be your chore to cleanse the cauldron after each batch of cure I make and to replenish the purified water as needed."

"Okay!" Petunia agreed. "What next?"

"Next, we light the brazier." Bogdana picked up the cauldron, took it to her work table. Tipping the ash in the brazier's pan into an ash pail, she put it back, then placed three fresh coals in the brazier. "I have seen you call fire, so this shouldn't be hard. Come, let's see you do it."

"Sure," Petunia said, hopping over to the table. Without

thinking, she began to reach for her pixie dust pouch.

"NO PIXIE DUST!" Bogdana roared.

Petunia snatched her hand away. "Sorry, habit," she said nervously. She'd just have to concentrate hard, like she did in school. Pointing at the coals, Petunia said, "*Syty.*" A little spark flickered on the coals and then died.

Bogdana snickered.

Petunia flushed a bright purple. "*Syty. Syty. Syty!*" But the coals refused to light.

"Just as I thought," Bogdana said with satisfaction. "Pixies are useless."

Clenching her fists, Petunia yelled, "*SYTY!*" The coals burst into flames.

"Well," drawled Bogdana. "You do have some power in you."

"Yes, I do," Petunia grated out, trying to hide her relief. For a moment, she'd thought the coals were going to explode. "Now what?"

"Now? Tourmalines, pixie. Get grinding."

"WHAT?" Petunia yelled. "I just proved I can do magic without pixie dust."

Bogdana, putting the cauldron atop the brazier, did not even glance at Petunia. "What you proved," said the witch, "is that you have power, but no control. You've let the pixie dust do that for you all your life. Now you have to learn to do it for yourself. When you can perform these very simple spells smoothly and easily, then we can progress to more complex steps."

Petunia thought about the almost-exploding coals and then considered what that could have done to a cauldron full of cures. Slowly, she nodded. "Fine." Hopping up onto the mortar, she hugged the pestle and resumed pounding, more determined than ever to learn to make the cure.

Chapter 12

Worst Vacation Ever

Petunia woke up in Millie's bed aching from head to
toe. Despite the wonderful comfort of Millie's bed, Petunia
wished a few of her brothers and sisters were there. She
needed someone to complain to. Of course, they'd laugh
at her and tease her for working with a witch, but Peaty
would hug her, and Holly would rub her sore feet, and
Clover would go out and pick a fresh flower and turn it
into a beautiful new dress, just to make her smile. And
then he'd dunk her in the next mud puddle they came to,
of course. She missed all that. She missed how simple her
life had been just a few days ago.

For the past two days, Bogdana had given her
increasingly difficult tasks to do. Once Petunia could easily
and reliably purify water, Bogdana had taught her to purify
mineral oil, which was much trickier to swirl and which
had to be stored in a magically protected crystal decanter.

Then Bogdana taught her how to harvest black
mugwort—the odd stuff growing on one wall that Petunia
had assumed was dead moss—and the dehydration spell
necessary to dry it so that Petunia could grind it into powder.
Mugwort was fiendishly hard to dry properly. On her first
try, it just sort of withered. Then Petunia made the mistake

of trying the spell again on the withered mugwort, and it
vaporized, filling the air with a choking mugwort haze that
Bogdana had dissipated with a pre-set ventilation spell. On
the fifth try, Petunia got it just right, and she spent the next
two hours rebuilding their stock of black mugwort powder.

On Threesday, Bogdana ran out of scorpion venom and
taught Petunia how to milk the scorpions. The trick of it
was to cast an illusion spell on the collection jar so that
they would sting it, then freeze them in place while their
venom dripped into the jar. Petunia had no trouble with
the freeze spell, having used it hundreds of times during
recess playing Hide and Leap, but she had never been
good at illusions. It took her half a day of practicing on a
chipped teacup to make it look convincingly like a hungry
rat. And then, once the venom was collected, it was back to
purifying and pounding tourmalines.

Between all this, Petunia was still caring for Thea and
setting the table and feeding everyone and dashing upstairs
with finished cures to sell to customers. Yesterday, a strange
tall fellow came to the door, looking like an elf except
with skin and hair as gray as stone, in darker gray robes,
and perfectly healthy. In heavily accented Canto, he'd told
her he was from Vanaheim and had come to collect the
cures Bogdana had promised. She told him that they were
out of cures and he'd just have to wait like everyone else.
Affronted, he'd stalked off down the Path. When Petunia
mentioned it to Bogdana, she just shrugged and sent
Petunia back to pounding.

Petunia felt as though all she did was run from one task
to another, all day long. She seldom even sat down to eat,
just shoved Millie's delicious food in while running from
one place to another. With Bogdana, she brewed potions
long into the night each night.

But they went faster. With Bogdana freed from all the small side tasks of potion-making, she was able to make twice as many cures as before. By the end of Threesday, Petunia had begun measuring the ingredients for her, the sulfur and the orange juice (which she squeezed by hand) and the mineral oil and the mugwort, so that all Bogdana had to do was assemble them in the correct order and with the correct incantations. Petunia had pounded and stirred until she thought her arms would fall off. This morning, she actually checked to make certain they hadn't.

This is not the vacation I had in mind, she thought. *And I can't even tell my family because they'll all laugh and say I told you so.* She realized that none of them would understand why she was doing any of this. She could tell them she was doing it to help out the folks of Pixamitchie, and Clover would say that people should look out for their own selves, and it wasn't her problem. She could tell them it was because she was deeply worried about Bogdana, who looked more sick and wasted with each passing day. She still sneezed, frequently, especially at mealtimes, but yesterday, it came out as a terrible raspy choking cough, and she wheezed all the time. But Petunia's mother would say that was the witch's problem, and any witch not capable of curing herself wasn't worth working for.

Petunia could tell them the truth, that the more she learned about potions, the more she loved it, every last bit of it. The pounding and the grinding, not so much, but gaining control of her magic, and learning the why of each component, and how putting them together made them greater than they were by themselves. She wanted to know more, so much more, all of it. She wanted a workshop of her very own, filled with amazing things that she could make and combine and enchant and create.

But she could hear her father's voice saying, *M'girl, there's no such thing as a potion pixie. It's just not done. And even if you could make the potions, no one would take you seriously. Best just leave such things to witches.*

And she could hear Bogdana saying, *A pixie? With her own practice? Ridiculous.*

Petunia ground her teeth. She WOULD do it. She would learn everything there was to know about potions, no matter what anyone said.

Groaning but determined, Petunia dragged herself out of bed, combed the pixie dust out of her hair, and dressed for the day. Down in the kitchen, she collapsed on the table, head cradled by her arms.

Horace glided out of the pantry. "Great rattling bones," he said. "You look terrible. Bogdana is working you too hard."

"She is not," Petunia mumbled. "People need those cures. I should do more. She should let me do more."

"You do any more, and you'll wear yourself down to nothing," Horace told her. "Don't let Bogdana bully you."

Petunia lifted her head and looked at him. "I know, Horace, and thank you for worrying about me, but she's really not. I'm actually enjoying this."

"Ha!" Horace scoffed.

"No, it's true," Petunia insisted. "Potions class in school is soooo tedious and boring. Potion-making with Bogdana is fascinating: the properties of the components, the way they interact, how she uses magic to kind of nudge them into working just the way she wants them to. I'd never paid attention before to how magic works. Why bother, when I can just use pixie dust?"

Horace stared at her. "Really? I don't think anyone has ever admitted to enjoying working with Bogdana. Well, not for a long, long time, anyway."

Petunia shrugged. "There's a joke in there somewhere, I think. What do you get when you cross a witch and a pixie? Pitch?"

Horace groaned.

"You're right, that was terrible, even for me. Well, it'll come to me eventually." Petunia shook her head. "First, I need some breakfast, only I'm too tired to move."

"Use magic," Horace said.

"Absolutely," Petunia replied. She took a large pinch of pixie dust, flung it into the air, and croaked, "*Tänne.*"

That day's breakfast package pushed its way through the pantry door, floated over to the kitchen table, and settled in front of Petunia.

"Open sesame seeds," she muttered, and the package unfolded, releasing the marvelous eggy scent of thick french toast stuffed with strawberry preserves and crème fraîche, crispy wedges of fried potatoes, and fat sausages, still sizzling, accompanied by a bottle of the Sylvan Vale's finest maple syrup and a carafe of orange juice.

Petunia plucked out Millie's note and began to read, Horace peering over her shoulder.

> *Dear Horace and Petunia,*
> *I made these especially for you, Horace. I know much you love stuffed french toast, but please leave some for Mother and Petunia. Just in case you can't restrain yourself, here's the recipe.*
> *8 slices of bread (for extra flavor, use an eggy bread like brioche or challah)*
> *2 eggs*
> *1/4 cup milk*
> *1/2 teaspoon vanilla*
> *Salt and pepper to taste*

Butter for the pan
Strawberry or raspberry preserves
Crème fraîche or cream cheese
Powdered sugar

Heat a skillet on medium heat and grease it with butter. Combine the eggs, milk, vanilla, salt and pepper in a flat dish and scramble well. Dip the bread into the batter on both sides, then place it in the pan and brown on both sides.

When all the slices have been cooked, take two slices. Spread preserves on one slice and creme fraiche on the other. Press together into a sandwich and slice diagonally. Sprinkle with powdered sugar and serve with maple syrup.

Both Petunia and Horace burst into laughter. There was enough french toast piled on that platter to feed them and half the morning's customers that day.

The maple syrup was a present from Sagara, and it really is the best maple syrup I've ever had. I hope you enjoy it. I wonder if they have maple syrup in the Logical Realm. We saw maples in Salem, so I'm guessing they do, but you never know. What if making maple syrup requires magic? What would life be like without maple syrup or maple sugar or maple candy? Oh, I'm missing the Enchanted Forest already, and I haven't even left!

But this is the ninth day of vacation, so I'll be home tomorrow. I hope everything has been going smoothly. If I find maple syrup in the Logical Realm, I'll bring some back for comparison.

See you soon,
Millie

"Millie," Petunia whispered. "Millie would understand." Relief flooded through her. Millie would help her learn potions, and she could help out with all the patients coming in, and she would know what to do about Bogdana.

"All right, time for breakfast," she said, much cheered. Petunia used pixie dust to set the table and pixie dust to make the tea and pixie dust to serve herself and Horace. Then they both dug in, and for several long minutes, Petunia and the ghost ate in contented silence. She cocked her head at him. "I'm glad you're here. I haven't seen much of you lately."

"Sorry about that," said Horace. "I'm not allowed in the workshop, you know."

"Yes, but I never see you when I'm tending to customers either."

Horace squirmed and went cloudier. "I don't want to scare them."

"Ha! You love scaring people."

"Well, it's cruel to scare sick people, don't you think?"

"Most of them are too sick to know you're there." Petunia took a good look at him, starting to edge away from the table, despite the lure of breakfast. "What's really going on, Horace?"

Horace slid under the table, hiding. From beneath, his hollow voice echoed up to her. "They make me nervous."

Petunia blinked. "What? How could a bunch of sick people make you nervous? You can't get sick; you're already dead, remember?"

"I think," Horace said, "I think they make me remember. I remember lying there like that, so weak and so thirsty."

Oh, thought Petunia. *Oh, poor Horace.* "Is this... do you think this is how you died?"

"It was so long ago, I don't really remember," he said, rising back up through the table. "But yes, something like this."

"I'm sorry, Horace," Petunia said sincerely. "I'd hide in the pantry, too."

Horace huffed. "I'm not hiding! I just... I don't like being around so many sick people."

The doorbell rang. Horace zipped away through the pantry door. From the second floor came a series of thunderous sneezes in response.

"I'll get it!" Petunia called up the stairs. She jumped down from the table and ran to open the door.

A green pixie boy stood there, covered from head to toe in pox.

"Clover!" Petunia exclaimed.

"Petunia!" Clover cried, and then he collapsed into her arms.

Petunia dragged him over to the sofa and tossed him up. "Clover, what happened? How are Mum and Da? How's Peaty?"

"What happened to you?" he said. "You disappeared! We were going to search, but then Holly got sick. We all thought you were dead!"

"Oh, slugs and bugs," Petunia said. "Doesn't anyone ever pay attention? I told Mum and Da where I was going, and I told you to look after Peaty. You have been, haven't you?"

Clover groaned. "Peaty's the worst off. He hasn't woken up in two days."

The orange juice soured in Petunia's stomach. "Why didn't you come for the cure before then? Surely you knew Bogdana had it."

"Too expensive," Clover muttered. "You know we can't afford it."

Petunia blinked. Four dragon scales or seven roc feathers,

multiplied by fifteen pixies... it would bankrupt her parents. She shook herself. "Well, I've surely earned your cures by working here." She fetched a vial, unstoppered it, and held it to Clover's lips. "Drink."

Clover sputtered and coughed, then lay back on the sofa.

"You rest," Petunia told him. "When you're better, I'll pack up a basket of cures for you to take home."

"You will... ACHOOO!" Bogdana stumbled down the stairs and into the parlor. "You will not. I do not give away cures."

Petunia gaped. Bodgana's skin had turned deathly pale, with red scaly patches here and there. Her eyes were sunken, her fingers bonier than ever. She clutched a black shawl around her shoulders with one hand and clung to the wall with the other. The witch could barely stand.

"Sit down before you fall down!" Petunia cried.

Bogdana sneezed again, her entire body shaking, then sneezed four more times in rapid succession. "I will not—ACHOO!—be given orders—ACHOO!—in my own home."

Horace glided over nervously. "Bogdana, you're sick. I think you have the pox."

"Non—ACHOO!—sense. My symptoms are completely different. ACHOO!"

"Well, whatever you have," Horace said, "It's getting worse. You should go back to bed."

Bogdana tried to shoo him away and nearly toppled over. "I have work to do. Potions to make. And I must oversee this wretched pixie to make certain she doesn't ruin me." She tried to reach the breakfast table, but halfway there, Bogdana folded in half and crumpled to the floor.

Petunia rushed over to her. "Horns and thorns! Horace is right, Bogdana. You are really sick."

"Jus' tired," Bogdana mumbled. "Be fine inna minute."

"Good grief," Clover commented, propping himself up on one elbow. "If the witch can't cure herself, what good are her potions?"

Petunia frowned up at him. "You're feeling better, aren't you? Your pox is gone, isn't it?"

Clover looked himself over with surprise. "Well, so it is. Then why doesn't the cure work on her?"

"She's got something else," Petunia said, shaking her head. "I don't know what."

"Tea," Bogdana moaned. "I want tea."

"We should get her back into bed," Horace said.

Petunia frowned. "I'm strong, but I'm not that strong."

"Then what should we do?" Horace said, wringing his hands and rattling his chains.

Petunia cocked her head. "I'll use pixie dust to float her back to bed. But first things first."

Petunia dashed into the kitchen and picked out a basket. She took it to the parlor and began stuffing cures into it. "Clover, are Uncle Ash and Aunt Clematis sick, too?"

"Everyone in the hedge is sick," he replied.

Petunia's shoulders sagged. "All right, I'll send you with thirty cures."

"You will do no such thing," Bogdana croaked out. "You're stealing from me."

"Stealing? Ha!" Petunia retorted. "I helped you make all those cures, and what have you paid me for it. Nothing!"

Clover peered at her. "You're really doing that? Helping her make those cures?"

"Fool pixie," Bogdana spat out. "You never asked for compensation. That's hardly my fault."

"Well, I'm asking now," Petunia said. "You give my family the cures they need, or I won't help you anymore."

Bogdana cackled, a horrible, wheezing laugh that turned into a deep, racking cough. "Think it's so easy? Think you can just walk away? Do that, and your whole family dies."

"Ha! And just what do you think Millie will think of that when she gets home tomorrow?" Petunia retorted.

Bogdana grimaced. "Millie will do as I say."

"Or she'll just stay in the Logical Realm with her father."

"That's—ACHOO!—tomorrow, pixie. What about today? What about your little Peaty?"

Petunia grimaced. "I'll just take these cures, and we'll call it even."

"Can you do that?" Bogdana whispered. "Just walk away? Really?"

Petunia bit her lip. She had learned so much, and she loved working with Bogdana. But her family needed her. Grimly, she picked up the basket. "Yes," she said.

"No," said Bogdana. "*Sulje!*"

Petunia felt the ward slam closed behind her.

"No one leaves this house with my property," Bogdana whispered.

Chapter 13

A Visitor from Vanaheim

Petunia set down the basket and marched over to Bogdana where she lay. "You miserable witch. After all I've done for you! Cooked and cleaned and everything! Can't you just be nice for once in your life?"

"Nice—ACHOO!!!—is just letting people walk all over you."

Petunia considered. What did she have to offer Bogdana, something no one else could give her? *Ah, of course.* Petunia pulled her reserve pouch of pixie dust off her belt.

"See this?" she told Bogdana. "This is full of nice fresh pixie dust. I know you need it, and I know it's very hard to come by, because we're all told from the time we learn to crawl never to give away our pixie dust, because otherwise we'd never hear the end of it." She smiled ironically. "People just walk all over you. So we only give it to non-pixies in dire need."

"Tunie, you can't!" Clover yelled. "Mum would have a fit."

Petunia turned to him. "Can you think of a better definition of dire need than the entire family dying?"

Clover shut his mouth.

"Right," said Petunia, turning back to Bogdana. "I know

that you need pixie dust. It's a component for Portal travel, isn't it?"

Bogdana's eyes locked onto the pouch. "Among other things," she rasped out.

"So, then," said Petunia. "I'll give you one pouch of pixie dust in exchange for the remaining cures."

"Hah," said Bogdana. "One pouch every week for the next six months."

"One pouch per month for the next three months," Petunia countered.

"One pouch every two weeks for the next four months," said Bogdana.

"For the next three months," Petunia said.

"Deal," said Bogdana. "You may have the potions. *Katoa*." The door ward came back down.

"Aw, horns and thorns," said Clover, tears rolling down his face. "You didn't have to do that, Tunie."

Petunia shrugged. "C'mon, I'll just make more. Besides," she said, looking over her shoulder at Bogdana, "I'm discovering I don't really need it. Now, you should eat something. People have been coming back thinking they're still sick, when all they need is feeding up."

She went to the kitchen and brought him back a plate of french toast, then packed up the basket of vials while Clover devoured it. "There, take these back home and give them to everyone. They should recover quickly, just like you did. And remember: eat!"

Clover nodded. "Righto, Petunia. I'll tell everyone."

Petunia lingered in the door, watching Clover trudge away, the basket perched on his head. She'd never seen him cry before. Thirteen years old, too. If she were going home with him, she would have teased him mercilessly for it. A gaggle of gargoyles passed Clover, heading for the house.

For a breathless moment, she thought they might try to steal Clover's basket, but then she saw that none of them could fly. They could barely drag their stone feet along the Path. Wearily, she waved at them to come in.

"Tea," Bogdana croaked behind her.

Horace glided out of the kitchen, looking pale even for a ghost. "Are you okay?" he asked Petunia.

Petunia clenched her fists. She was not okay. She wanted to run out the door after Clover and go take care of her family. But Bogdana was sick, and people were dying. She just had to hold out until Millie got home. "I'm fine," she lied to Horace. "Now what should we do about Bogdana?"

They studied the weary witch. Haggling with Petunia seemed to have taken the last of her strength. Bogdana could barely open her eyes.

"I should scry Baba Luci," Petunia said aloud. "She can figure out what's wrong with you."

"Oh, that's a good idea," said Horace. "I should have thought of it."

"Nooooo—ACHOO!" Bogdana said. "No, I forbid it."

Petunia went back to her and lay a hand on her forehead. It was burning hot to the touch. "You've got a fever, you're sneezing like a leprechaun in a roomful of pepper, and your skin is starting to flake off. You need help."

"ACHOO! I will figure it out myself," Bogdana said, "and you will not breathe a word of my illness to anyone. Not Baba Luci, not Quercius, no one."

Petunia frowned. "That's stupid. Baba Luci's your mum and the most powerful witch in the Forest. She's exactly the right person to call."

"No, no, no," Bogdana cried, thrashing back and forth. "If word got out, if my sisters learn of my illness, I'll never hear the end of it. They'll mock me to the end of my days."

"Better that you're alive to hear it," Petunia retorted. "I'll go get the scrying bowl."

Bogdana reached out and grabbed Petunia in her bony fingers and squeezed so tightly that the pixie could scarcely breathe.

"Hear me now, wretched pixie—ACHOO! If you breathe a word of this to anyone, I will ban you from my house, and you will never see either my workshop or Millie again. Understand?"

"Yes!" Petunia squeaked out.

"Promise me," Bogdana said. "Promise me you will tell no one of my illness." She shook Petunia like a doll.

"A Pixie's Promise?" Petunia gasped.

"A Pixie's Promise, or you go, for good."

Petunia's head was spinning. She knew she shouldn't agree, that she should go fetch Baba Luci. She knew that Promising would be dangerous. But she couldn't leave now, not when everyone needed her, not when she was just starting to understand potion-making. And she couldn't lose Millie.

"I Promise," she whispered. "I Promise I will tell no one that you are sick."

Bogdana released her, but Petunia still felt squeezed, the strength of her Promise winding and tightening around her. She doubled over and gasped for breath.

"Now—ACHOO!—I would like some tea, and I would like to go to bed."

Petunia brought her own cup to Bogdana, but the witch was seized by a terrible sneezing fit and could drink none of it.

The gargoyles arrived at the door, took one look at Bogdana, and left.

Bogdana snorted. "Just as well. Your family took all the

cures we had left. We must brew more."

"Bogdana, you can't," Horace protested. "You can't even walk."

Bogdana began levering herself up. "I *will* walk. I will...." Her eyes rolled back in her head, and she collapsed, unconscious.

"All right, then, bed for you," Petunia said. She took a good-sized pinch and sprinkled it on Bogdana, then floated her back up the stairs to her bedroom, along with her tea.

"Didn't you just trade that pixie dust to Bogdana?" Horace asked.

Petunia grinned at him. "I said 'a pouch,' not 'this pouch.' And Bogdana never specified when she'd start collecting them. Watching her haggle with all these customers has taught me a thing or two."

Horace chucked, then he laughed all the way up the stairs. They got to Bogdana's door, and Petunia said, "Oh, slugs and bugs. How will we get her door open?"

"Oops," said Horace. "I have no idea."

"Oh, fine," Petunia said. "I'll put her in Millie's bed. I can sleep on the couch."

They escorted Bogdana up to the attic. Together, Horace and Petunia wrestled the quilt back, laid Bogdana on the bed, and then covered her again.

"Could you stay here and keep an eye on her?" Petunia asked Horace.

"Good idea, if boring," Horace said.

"I'll bring up your chess set and some tea," Petunia promised.

The ghost shrugged. "All right."

Petunia ran down, loaded the chess set, the teapot, two teacups, and some leftover french toast onto a tray, then floated it up the stairs. "I'll be down in the workshop," she told Horace.

"Wait, what?" Horace said. "Why would you do that?"

Petunia faced him grimly. "We're out of cures. Bogdana's si—" The Promise stopped her. Even though Horace knew perfectly well how sick Bogdana was, she couldn't tell him. She couldn't tell anyone. "Bogdana's indisposed," she said. "Someone has to make more cures."

"She taught you how?" Horace said.

Petunia twisted her hair. "Well, she's explained how to do it, and I've seen her make at least two dozen batches. I think I can do it."

"Nooooooo," Horace moaned and rattled his chains. "This is a bad idea, Petunia. What if something goes wrong? What if you blow up her workshop? She'll never forgive you. She might even prosecute you!"

"Well, look on the bright side," said Petunia. "If I blow up the workshop, I can't possibly do anything else, and I can finally get some rest."

"I want nothing to do with this," Horace said, shrinking and hiding under the bed.

"Fine," said Petunia. "Just stay with Bogdana. I need to go water Thea and then get busy brewing."

Not waiting for his answer, she plunged down the stairs, out the kitchen door, and straight to Thea. She flung her arms around Thea's trunk and burst into tears. The little tree wrapped several leaves around Petunia.

"Oh, Thea, what have I done?" Petunia wailed. "I've made another Promise to Bogdana, and she's horrible, and she's... she's... ARRRRGH!!! I can't tell you because she made me Promise!"

The elm above them rustled angrily. Thea stroked Petunia's head.

"I don't know how to help Bogdana," she said instead. "She won't let me call anyone. I don't know what to do."

What if Bogdana dies? she thought. *She's Millie's mother. She might be a terrible mother, but Millie would still be devastated.*

And I'll never learn any more potions.

"Ahem."

Petunia pushed away from Thea to look at the person standing just beyond the kitchen gate. He was tall with elvish features and wearing long gray robes decorated with runes, but his skin was covered with fine brown fur, like a faun's, and deer's antlers sprouted from his head, parting his long, tan hair. He smiled down at her.

"Excuse me," he said. "Is this the residence of Councilor Noctmartis?"

Petunia wiped her eyes and nodded. "Yes. I'm her assistant, Petunia. Is there something I can help you with? You don't look sick."

He chuckled amiably. "I did not know the Councilor had taken an apprentice. What an... interesting choice. No, I am not sick. We Vanir are immune to mortal diseases. However, many of the lesser creatures of my Realm are quite ill with the spickle pox. Two weeks ago, I ordered a batch of cures from your mistress, but they have not been delivered. My attempts to scry have been ignored, my letter was not answered, and my page was turned away. I have come in person to collect my order."

"Oh," Petunia said, recalling the gray-skinned fellow. He'd worn similar if less elaborate robes. "I'm terribly sorry, but we're out of cures just now. If you'd care to wait in the parlor, I can bring you the next batch."

The Vanir stiffened. "Out? Do you mean that there have been cures available, but you have sold them before fulfilling my order?"

"Um, well, yes," Petunia said. "A lot of people here are sick. It's an epidemic."

He raised an eyebrow at that. "An epidemic? Really?" He smiled a bit before he could catch himself, then looked down at her sternly. "Regardless, my order was placed weeks ago, and it should have been fulfilled as soon as possible. My stock... that is, the people of my Realm are suffering greatly. Many of them hover near death. I must have those cures immediately."

Petunia bobbed a curtsy at him and said, "I'll get brewing just as soon as I've watered Thea here. It'll take an hour or so."

"That is unacceptable," said the Vanir. "I wish to speak to your mistress. Now."

"I'm very sorry," Petunia told him, "but she's, um, very busy at the moment and cannot be disturbed."

At this, the Vanir flew into a rage. "Do you have any idea who I am? I am Ospak, Master of the Hunt, minister to Queen Vidgis of Vanaheim! A slight upon me is a slight upon Her Majesty! You will fetch your mistress this instant!"

"I'll tell her you're here," Petunia said soothingly, "just as soon as I've watered Thea."

"No! You will go now, or I will fetch her myself!" Ospak reached for the kitchen gate, and sparks flew off his hands, the ward pushing him back. He threw back his head and bellowed in rage, then pushed harder.

Swiftly, Petunia ran for the watering can and filled it with compost tea. The barrel was nearly empty, but of course, Millie would be home the next day to make more. Petunia sprinkled the tea over Thea, who was shaking all over with fear. "Don't worry. No one can get through

Bogdana's wards. I'll tell Bogdana, and she'll make him go away."

There was a mighty crack from above them, and a large branch dropped from the elm. Ospak danced aside just in time to avoid being crushed by it. The elm moaned and thrashed its remaining branches at him.

"You will regret this," he snarled.

Something in Petunia snapped. "No, I won't," she yelled back at him. "That's just what you deserve, trying to attack us like that! I told you that you could wait in the parlor, and I told you I'd give you our next batch of cures, and that's the best I can do. If you don't like it, you can leave."

The Vanir stared down at her, and Petunia felt chilled to her very core. "Very well," he said, and he stalked off straight into the forest. *That* gave Petunia the deep shivers. The Path was enchanted to keep travelers safe, but the Forest, the deep, dark woods where Ospak vanished, was full of dark magic and terrible beasts. He must have been quite strong to go in there without a second thought.

"I sure hope that's the last we've seen of him," Petunia said.

Thea nodded in agreement, and Mx. Elm rustled her approval. Petunia gave Thea a last hug. "I'll be back with the scrying bowl after lunch. See you later, Thea, and don't worry."

Thea hugged her back. Petunia turned and marched herself back into the house.

 Chapter 14

Pixie Potions

Petunia stood at the top of the basement stairs, trying to gather the nerve to enter Bogdana's workshop alone. *I can do this,* she thought. *I've learned how to do magic without pixie dust. I've learned how to control my magic. And I've seen Bogdana do it over and over again. What could go wrong?* Petunia laughed to herself. *Well, just everything.* She shook herself, straightened her shoulders, and marched herself down the steps and into the workshop.

Temptation nearly overcame her. *Bogdana's in bed,* she thought. *I can look into any cabinet, read any grimoire, tinker around with anything.* She spread her arms, taking it all in, imagining that this was her workshop, her equipment, her business.

Hmph, she thought. *I'd have more windows and better light. And a nice rug so I don't have to stand on a cold stone floor. And my own apprentice.* Putting her nose in the air, one finger poised to waggle, she intoned in her best Bogdana voice, "First, we must wash the cauldron!" And Petunia got busy.

"Okay, clean the cauldron, check," she muttered to herself she worked. "Now light the brazier. *Syty!* Now, do I have enough tourmaline powder? Check. Mineral oil,

check. Mugwort, check. Phooey, I'm out of orange juice."
Petunia paused to squeeze some fresh juice. Then she
measured and laid out all the ingredients, just as she had
for Bogdana, then pushed over the canister she stood on to
pound tourmalines so that she could look down into the
cauldron. "Right. Okay. Here I go."

Carefully, in a separate bowl, she combined the sulfur
and black mugwort until they became an even, dull ochre
color. Then she poured the mineral oil into the cauldron.
Petunia reached for the stirring spoon and smacked herself
on the forehead. She'd left it at the sink. She ran and
hopped over to the sink, grabbed the spoon, and ran back,
by which time the oil was starting to smoke, giving off a
nasty odor.

"Oh, slugs and bugs," Petunia said. "*Halvene,*" she told
the brazier coals, causing them to go out. Using a pinch
of pixie dust, she floated the cauldron over to the sink and
proceeded to clean it out with the last of the purified water.

CRACK. The cauldron split along one side.

"Oh, no," Petunia moaned. "Cold water in a hot
cauldron. I'm an idiot. Can I fix it with magic?" She
considered the iron pot and shook her head. "Better not
take the chance. Oh, horns and thorns, Bogdana is NOT
going to be happy about that."

Fortunately, when they were really humming along
yesterday, Bogdana had started swapping cauldrons so that
she could keep brewing in one cauldron while the other
cauldron cooled enough for Petunia to clean it. Petunia
purified some more water, rinsed out the second cauldron,
and brought it back to the worktable.

"Second try," she said, measuring out more mineral oil.
"*Syty!*" she told the brazier, and it lit again. Spoon at the
ready, she poured in the mineral oil. Then, taking up the

bowl of sulfur-mugwort powder, she slowly sprinkled it in, stirring all the while, as she recited the first phrase of High Mystery as near to Bogdana's intonation as she could. "*Vahvista terveyttä ja elinvoimaa.*"

The spoon began to shake in her hand, fighting her. The harder Petunia pushed it through the liquid, the more it pushed back, until finally it shot right out of the cauldron and over Petunia's head. She heard a **CRASH** and then a *tinkle* behind her. "Halvene!" she told the brazier, and it went out again with a little puff of smoke.

Turning around, Petunia surveyed the damage. The spoon had speared one side of the scorpion tank, and the glass had shattered, releasing the scorpions, which were now skittering loose all over the floor.

"Argh!" cried Petunia, clutching her hair. "How in the Realm am I going to catch all those scorpions? I don't have time for this!"

She leaped down off the worktable and chased after a scorpion, trying to grab it by the tail so it wouldn't sting her—not that it had much venom left after all the recent milking. But it skittered away under a cabinet, and Petunia didn't want to risk crawling under there where she couldn't really see the stinger coming. She glanced around the room. All the scorpions had disappeared, finding small nooks and crannies in which to hide themselves.

"Oh, DARKNESS!" Petunia yelled. "Come on, you scorpions! Come back out here right now." She stamped her foot in frustration.

Okay, calm down, she told herself. *How would Bogdana deal with this?*

Bogdana's voice came back to her. "Scorpions are highly susceptible to illusions," the witch had told her.

Right, Petunia thought. *I'll cast an illusion spell to draw them out, something they like: some nice fat crickets to eat.*

She searched around for a substitute tank and came up with a large glass bottle with a wide mouth. It would be a bit cramped, but it would do for now. Shoving it out into the middle of the floor, Petunia leaped back up to the worktable. She pointed to a spot on the floor next to the bottles, then concentrated hard and said, "*Näytä.*"

A hazy image of crickets flickered into being on the floor. Petunia frown and pushed more magical energy into it, imagining the crickets moving and hopping around. But none of the scorpions emerged from hiding. *Scent,* she thought. *I need the illusion of scent, too,* so she added the musty, slightly oily smell of crickets, breaking into a sweat. Just as she thought she would have to release the spell, a scorpion darted out, striking at an illusory cricket. And then another scorpion, and another. In a few moments, she had a writhing mass of overexcited scorpions.

Grabbing a handful of pixie dust, she dumped it on them and yelled, "*Nouse!*" The scorpions all rose, thrashing, into the air. Petunia let go of the illusion and directed them over to the bottle, dumping them in. "Whew!" she cried, sitting hard on the worktable and mopping her forehead with her sleeve. "Now what did I do wrong?"

It had to be related to the spoon. Had she forgotten to clean it? No, she'd been very careful, after cracking the cauldron, to make sure the spoon was clean. Added the powder too quickly? No, it seemed to have something to do with how she was stirring. Abruptly, Petunia slapped herself on the forehead. "Clockwise! Bogdana always stirs clockwise." Petunia had been stirring awkwardly with her left hand, and without thinking, she'd stirred counterclockwise. "Okay, third time's the charm, right?"

Selecting a new spoon, she dumped the now-cooled

contents of the cauldron, cleaned it out, and started again. This time, she got as far as adding the orange juice, which curdled before she could add in the lunar eclipse dew. "Slugs and bugs! Forgot to reduce the heat to a simmer," she muttered, disgusted with herself.

She started over. Mispronounced the second phrase of High Mystery, and the whole batch turned an ugly grey, smelling of rot. And she started over.

And on the fifth try, she got it right. The brew turned a pale orange—not as robust as Bogdana's cures, but otherwise it looked and smelled just right. "*Halvene.* Finally," Petunia gasped, collapsing on the canister lid. "I did it." She blinked. "I did it. I DID IT! WOO HOO!!!" She had made a batch of cures. She had mastered a terribly complex potion, and she'd done it on her own. Petunia wanted to run up and tell Thea, to scry Quercius and tell him, to run straight home and crow to her mother.

Her mother, who was deathly ill.

Petunia sagged. "Right. Time to sell some potions." She used pixie dust to load a basket with vials and float it over to her, and then she carefully ladled out the cure into each vial. Jumping down to the worktable, she corked each vial and set it back in the basket. Then, lifting the basket over her head, she hopped down to the floor and headed for the door.

A scorpion darted out, its poison stinger arcing toward her. Without even thinking, Petunia yelled, "*NOUSE!*" The poor scorpion levitated so fast, it hit the ceiling, disturbing a couple of nearby bats. "Stupid scorpion, what were you thinking?" she muttered, floating it over to the bottle and dropping it in.

"Right," she said with grim satisfaction. "I have definitely earned my lunch."

Petunia brought the basket upstairs, set it down in

the parlor, then went and fetched the Second Foursday lunch package and floated it over to the kitchen table, still littered with breakfast. She shoved that aside and opened her lunch. The aroma of toasted bread and melted cheese and something just slightly spicy washed over her. Petunia picked up Millie's note.

Dear Millie and Horace,

This is the last lunch I've prepared for you. I'm planning to bring back lunch from the Logical Realm to share with you, though I'm not sure you'll be able to eat it, Horace. I'm hoping that reheating it on my good old stove will do the trick. We'll see.

For now, I've made you one of my favorites from the Logical Realm: Quesadillas. That's a sort of stuffed flatbread, tortillas and cheese and whatever else you like in them. I've made two kinds: chicken with grilled bell peppers and onions, and beef with spicy peppers. In case you run out, you can easily make more.

QUESADILLAS
Tortillas
Grated cheddar, jack, or chihuahua cheese, or a
  combination of these
Whatever other fillings you like: onions, peppers,
  tomatoes, ham, bacon, chicken, etc.

Heat a skillet on the stove, not too hot. Add just a little oil and tilt the skillet so that its bottom is completely covered. Place a tortilla in the skillet. Cover it with cheese and let it slowly melt. As it's melting, add in any other ingredients you like. With a spatula, fold the tortilla in half. The bottom of the tortilla should be lightly browned. If it isn't, wait a bit, then flip it over to brown on both sides. Remove it from the skillet and cut into four wedges. Serve with salsa and guacamole, if available. If you prefer, you can bake multiple tortillas in the oven, though then you don't get the lovely crispy texture.

I'll be home tomorrow. Seems weird to think about when I haven't even left yet. I hope things have gone smoothly for you and that Mother hasn't given you too hard a time. Just one more day.

See you soon,
Millie

Petunia glanced over the unfamiliar food. Two piles of half-moon flatbreads with cheese oozing out of them, a bowl of something made with chopped tomatoes, onions, garlic, peppers, and herbs, and a crock full of a mashed green vegetable—avocado, she discovered upon tasting—and generous bowls of rice and beans. Different, but delicious. She grabbed herself a wedge of quesadilla and munched on it as she went to open the front door.

"We are open for business," she mumbled through a full mouth.

Patients began filing in. Most were new, but some were old patients: the leaf sprite, a brownie, and several fairies. Just like Berto, they seemed drained, too tired to move. Not knowing what else to do, Petunia offered them wedges of Millie's quesadillas, which they happily chewed as she administered cures to the new patients. To her great relief and private delight, her cures worked just as well as Bogdana's had. By the time she had cured them all, the leaf sprite was apologizing, saying that she felt much better and could go home now. The brownie and fairies followed soon after, the fairies complaining loudly that this was all the fault of the goblins, and they shouldn't be allowed in the village.

"Stupid," Petunia muttered. "As though getting rid of goblins would prevent anyone from getting sick." To her surprise, the parlor emptied of patients, and she still had three cures left. Maybe the epidemic was finally letting up. Petunia began preparing two plates of quesadillas. She'd take a tray up to Millie's room for Bogdana and Horace, take the scrying bowl out to Thea, and then go back to brewing cures.

The doorbell rang, and Petunia sighed. She knew it was too good to be true.

She opened the door to a goblin collapsed on her doorstep. It was Grumpkin.

 Chapter 15

The Problem with Pixie Dust

"Please," he rasped. "Please, we're dying." He looked it. His pox had turned into open running sores, and his normally chubby frame had turned woefully thin. "No one will treat goblins. Please. I can pay."

"Slugs and bugs!" Petunia said. "Stay right there."

She grabbed a vial and brought it to him, but she hesitated, knowing Bogdana would count every feather and scale. "I'm sorry, but you do have to pay. Bogdana said I can't give away potions."

Grumpkin dug in his pocket and retrieved some crumpled roc feathers, dropping them on the ground at her feet.

"Good enough," she said, handing him the vial. "Here, drink."

Grumpkin took the vial and chugged down its contents, then closed his eyes, sighing with relief. "Water," he whispered.

"I can do better than that," Petunia said. She ran back to the table and made him up a plate of quesadilla with rice and beans, plus leftover breakfast tea which she heated with a bit of pixie dust. Setting it down beside Grumpkin, whose sores were already healing, she told him, "You're lucky Bogdana's not around. She probably would have

forbidden me to treat you, but she hasn't made me Promise
not to serve goblins, so I still can."

Grumpkin drained the teacup and stared at her over the
rim. "So you're helping Bogdana?"

"As it happens, I made the potion you just drank." At
Grumpkin's gaping disbelief, she grinned and said, "I
have two cures left. Do you want them for your mother
and sister?"

"Oh, yes, please," he replied, prodding at his skin. "I
haven't found my sister yet, but I want the cure for when
I do. You really did this? You cured me? Then why am I
paying Bogdana?"

"Her materials," Petunia said.

Grumpkin nodded. He counted out more roc feathers as
she fetched the last two vials.

A young gryphon glided in to land on the Path at
Bogdana's door. Petunia recognized him from her Potions
class. He didn't look sick as he trotted up to the door.
"Message from school," he said, pulling a scroll from a
satchel slung across his back.

Petunia took the scroll from him. "Thanks, Terrence.
Oh!" she exclaimed, unrolling the scroll. "School's
cancelled?"

"Yup, for at least a week," Terrence said cheerfully.
"Master Quercius and the Headmistress have turned it into
a hospital for spickle pox victims."

Petunia clapped her hands. "That's wonderful! No
wonder we've been getting fewer patients."

"Maybe my sister is there," Grumpkin said, levering
himself up. He had devoured several wedges of quesadilla.

"I can fly you over if you like," Terrance offered.

"No, I need to get the cure to my mother," Grumpkin
replied. "Thanks anyway." Shoving in the final bite of

toasted tortilla, he stood up. "Thanks, Petunia. I really appreciate it."

"Just don't tell anyone you got the cures here," Petunia said. "It might get back to Bogdana."

Grumpkin gave her a wicked wink and started the journey back to Pixamitchie.

"Huh," said Terrence, staring after the goblin. "He recovered super fast."

"Good," Petunia said, then slapped her forehead. "Horns and thorns, I'm out of cures again. I'll have to go make more. Hey, Terrence, would it be all right if I put up a sign telling people to go to the hospital until I've made more?"

The gryphon shrugged. "Don't see why not," he said. "See you at school, whenever that is."

"Thanks, Terrence. Bye!" she waved as the gryphon took flight and soared off over the treetops.

Petunia took down the "We're out of potions" sign and added in her own, far less fancy handwriting, "You can also go to the Enchanted Forest School for help," then tacked the sign back up.

"Okay, take the scrying bowl to Thea," she said to herself, "and then back to work."

✦ ✦ ✦

As hard as she'd worked until then, Petunia had never worked so hard before in her entire life. She used pixie dust more and more—to clean up, to float the tray of food up to Horace and Bogdana, to send up pots of tea, which was all that Bogdana seemed to want. And even though Bogdana had told her not to use pixie dust to make potions, Petunia simply couldn't keep up without it.

When they'd worked as a team, Petunia and Bogdana could make twenty cures every half hour. Now that Petunia had to do everything, it took her closer to two hours. So she cheated. She used pixie dust to enchant the pestle to grind the tourmalines and mugwort. She considered just sprinkling it right on the tourmalines and telling them to become powder, but she worried that dust residue might get into the potion. Petunia also used pixie dust to pump water, swirl the ewer, and then rinse out the cauldron. It cut her time in half, not having to run around all the time. The pestle kept pounding as she brewed the potion, so she always had plenty of ingredients handy, though she was starting to run low on scorpion venom, and Petunia had no desire whatsoever to try getting them out of their bottle for milking.

At dinnertime (leg of lamb with mint sauce), she realized that the majority of the patients she was getting were patients she'd already seen earlier in the week who, like Berto and the leaf sprite, just weren't quite recovering. When Petunia took the dinner plate upstairs, she asked Bogdana whether a second dose of the cure would help, but the witch insisted between sneezes that one cure should be enough for anyone, and two cures might have unexpected results.

She came back down to find a family of fairies had arrived, all limp as wilted daisies, insisting that Bogdana's cure hadn't worked and she still owed them a Favor. Petunia apologized and invited them to dinner, by the end of which they were all feeling much better.

"You must not be eating enough," Petunia told them. "That's why you had no energy."

A young fairy with iridescent purple wings shrugged. "We had no appetite before. But no one can resist Millie's food."

Petunia rolled her eyes. "Well, no wonder. Now go home and make sure you eat a good solid breakfast in the morning." She floated the remains of dinner out to the parlor and told all the other returning customers to eat up. Within an hour, they were all gone. As she sold cures to new patients, she admonished them to eat heartily to build their strength back up and sent them on their way.

She ran out of cures, and there were still six patients left: a gargoyle, two imps, two fauns, and Mr. Pricklesnout, whose tender nose and belly and paws were covered with pox. "Don't worry," she told him. "I'll brew a new batch as fast as I can."

"I've a message for you," he rasped. "Your family has moved to the hospital at the school. Clover's recovering well, but some of them... they look like those others who were here earlier, the ones who were so tired."

A chill went up Petunia's spine. "What about Peaty? Has he woken up yet?"

"Not when I last saw him," Mr. Pricklesnout said. "But then, I was a little distracted by the protests."

"What protests?"

Mr. Pricklesnout sniffed. "Folks insisting the goblins be turned out of Pixamitchie, that the pox is all their fault since they got it first."

"That's ridiculous," Petunia said. "If pixies had come down with spickle pox first, would anyone be trying to run us out?"

The hedgehog rolled himself into a protective ball. "Folks is frightened," his muffled voice informed her. "And when folks is frightened, they go looking for someone to blame."

Petunia trudged down to the basement with her heart in her stomach. What if the cure had come too late? What if Peaty never woke up? And what would happen to the goblins?

She was so distracted that she almost didn't notice when she reached into her pouch for a pinch of pixie dust that the pouch was empty. Petunia had run out completely.

Her shoulders slumped. She wanted to roll into a ball, just like Mr. Pricklesnout, and go to sleep right there on the worktable. But Mr. Pricklesnout was counting on her. So she got back to work. *Good thing I know how to do this without pixie dust,* she thought, feeling an odd twinge of gratitude to Bogdana.

The first batch without pixie dust wasn't so bad. She had enough ingredients prepared already to make the twenty cures, no problem, and she took them up, cured Mr. Pricklesnout and the other waiting customers, then sold the remainder to the gargoyle, who had family back in Pixamitchie. The next batch, she had to pound tourmalines again. And for the next batch, she needed more mugwort and purified mineral oil. By midnight, the sulfur was starting to run low, and she'd used up the last drop of scorpion venom.

Well, then, she thought. *That's all I can do.*

Taking the last batch upstairs, Petunia found she was too tired to go up to bed. She curled up on the sofa and went right to sleep. Her last thought was, *Millie will be home tomorrow, and then everything will be all right.*

Someone was shaking her.

"Petunia. Petunia! Wake up!"

Slowly, Petunia pried her eyes open. "Millie?" she rasped out. "Oh, Millie, you're home! Slugs and bugs, am I glad to see you!" She reached out to hug Millie's finger, just missing the end of a long blonde braid.

"What happened?" Millie asked, her eyes wide with concern. "Where's Mother?"

"Why are all those people waiting outside?" Max put in.

"And what's wrong with them?" Sagara asked with a shiver.

Max's father sniffed. "This place is a mess."

"Sorry," Petunia mumbled. "I ran out of pixie dust."

Millie's eyes went wide. "What has Mother been doing to you?"

Horace zipped into the room. "Oh, thank darkness! Millie, you need to come up and look at Bogdana. I think she's dying."

Millie's mouth fell open in a large "O," and then she took off, up the stairs to Bogdana's room, with Max and his father right behind her, leaving Sagara behind. "Sheesh," said the elf, trying to look disgusted rather than scared, "I leave for two weeks, and everything falls apart."

At this, Petunia burst into tears. Sagara pulled a handkerchief from her pocket and awkwardly rubbed Petunia's back with one finger as Petunia told her everything she could: playing with Thea, running in the walls with Horace, the spickle pox, helping Bogdana in the workshop, and finally how Bogdana had forced her to make a Promise, though she couldn't say what she'd Promised.

Sagara frowned, and her frown grew deeper as Petunia finished. When Petunia choked to a stop, Sagara stood up. "There's a lot you're not telling me, but maybe Thea can fill me in."

Petunia slapped a hand to her forehead. "Thea! I haven't watered her yet this morning."

Sagara held out a hand, and Petunia gratefully climbed into it so that Sagara could lift her up to her left shoulder. "Ouch, not the hair," Sagara said.

"Sorry," Petunia replied, letting go of a hank of ash blonde hair and grabbing onto Sagara's robes instead. The elf girl took them out the kitchen door, pausing to fill the watering can with the last of the compost tea, and brought it over to Thea. The scrying bowl still lay on the ground at Thea's roots, its water half-gone and quite still.

Both Thea and the elm were rustling frantically. Sagara stopped, "Slow down, I can't understand you when you talk that fast. Mx. Elm, why don't you tell me while I water Thea?" She began pouring.

The elm rustled and clicked together branches in a complicated pattern which apparently meant something to Sagara, who frowned even more, then nodded. "Yes, of course, I'll scry Master Quercius right away."

"What is it? Is Thea sick? I gave her a cure," Petunia said, scanning the little tree for signs of spickle pox.

"Thea's fine," Sagara told her, kneeling carefully beside the scrying bowl. "Some weird guy has been coming and staring at her and trying to get through the wards. Mx. Elm said he was tall and sort of elf-looking but with horns."

"Oh, him!" Petunia said. "That's Ospak. He's some minister from Vanaheim. He ordered a batch of spickle pox cures from Bogdana, and when she didn't deliver, he came to get them himself. He was pretty mad when Bogdana wouldn't see him."

Petunia felt Sagara go rigid. "A Vanir? Here, in person? That's..."

The kitchen door banged open. "Petunia, where's the scrying bowl?" Millie cried. "Mother is terribly sick! I need to scry Baba Luci immediately." Distantly, Petunia noticed that Millie was dressed in Logical Realm fashion: a T-shirt that read "Kiss the Cook" in English, with a pink skirt and some complicated sandals. "Oh, there it is. Thea! Hi, it's so good to see you. Have you been watered?"

Thea nodded, waving at Millie happily.

"Baba Luci's a good idea," Sagara said. "I have some things to tell her, too."

Millie knelt beside the scrying bowl and swiftly called up Baba Luci. The witch appeared, her magic scarf askew on her head, with dark circles under her eyes. "Oh, Millie, dear. I'm so sorry, I don't have time to talk. All the dryads of Dimry Vale have come down with spickle pox, and the usual cure doesn't seem to be working completely. I've been trying to figure out why..."

"Baba, Mother is terribly sick!" Millie interrupted.

"Not with spickle pox, she had the cure. This is something different. She looks awful, Baba, and I don't know what to do. If Mother couldn't cure herself..."

The Baba straightened her scarf. "I'll be right there." She broke the connection.

"Bother," Sagara said. "I didn't get to talk to her."

"You'll get your chance soon enough," Millie said. "Meanwhile, why don't you scry home and check in on your family."

"Oh," murmured Sagara, "yes, I should do that." Once the water in the bowl stilled, she began the incantation.

Millie turned to Petunia. "I don't understand," she said. "Why didn't you call Baba Luci when Mother got sick?"

"She wouldn't let me," Petunia said miserably. "She made me Promise..."

Max burst out of the kitchen with a handful of vials. "Mother says you need to take this right now," he said, handing a vial of cure to Millie and Sagara.

Millie uncorked hers and drank it down, grimacing. "Ew, extra nasty."

"Sorry," Petunia said, "I was running low on oranges."

Millie looked shocked. "You made these?"

Sagara began shouting in Elvish. The ancient elf woman in the scrying bowl yelled back. Sagara uncorked the vial and drank it pointedly, but the elf woman continued yelling. Sagara said two or three more words, then smacked the water, breaking the connection. "She never listens,"

Sagara said, switching back to Canto. "Grandmother thinks I could be a carrier. I'm not allowed to come home until this outbreak is over. Honestly, I probably couldn't anyway. The entire Sylvan Vale is sealed off, and the three or four infected elves have been quarantined."

"You can stay with us," Millie and Max said simultaneously.

Sagara grinned. "Thanks, both of you. I think I'll keep away from your mom. She's likely to be twice as cranky when she's sick."

"You have no idea," Petunia murmured.

Millie looked at her. "About that..."

A dull thudding sounded in the distance, growing louder. They could hear the groaning and thrashing of trees.

"Look out, Baba Luci brought the house!" Max said.

Mx. Elm hastily leaned far to one side as an enormous chicken leg emerged from the Forest and planted its foot firmly in the middle of the Path, joined shortly by a second leg. Atop them both, towering as high as the elm, was a neat little cottage with a front porch and a cheerful red front door, wide open so that Baba Luci could lean out.

"I don't have time for this. *KATOA!*"

Bogdana's wards didn't go down so much as shatter, making Max flinch. The chicken-legged hut stepped into the backyard and settled itself like a roosting hen.

"Baba!" Millie cried, running up to hug her. Max came after her, nearly tackling them both.

"Now tell me everything," Baba Luci said. "Weren't you off on vacation visiting your father?"

Millie nodded. "And Petunia here was staying to take care of Thea when I was gone."

"Petunia?" the Baba said. "The pixie? Where is she?"

Petunia jumped down from Sagara's shoulder and walked over. "Here," she said.

Baba Luci frowned down on her. "You've been staying here for two weeks?"

Petunia nodded.

"And in that time, did you use any pixie dust?"

"Any?" Petunia said in disbelief. "I used ALL of it. I scrubbed my scalp raw. I probably won't have more for days."

"Well, that would explain it," Baba Luci said, her mouth set in a grim line. "Fool girl, she'd lose her head if it weren't attached. It so happens that I am allergic to pixie dust. Bogdana must have forgotten that, and she's had little exposure until now. My guess is that she's having a massive allergic reaction. You," said the Baba, looking down her long hooked nose at Petunia, "will have to leave. Now."

Petunia's jaw hung open. It was all her fault. She'd made Bogdana sick. She had messed everything up. "Yes," she said. "Yes, of course I'll leave."

Petunia turned on her heel, marched to the kitchen gate, and jumped through the slats. She started up the Path.

Chapter 16

Nothing Like Home Cooking

"Hey, wait!" Sagara jumped over the gate and came after her. "Where are you going?"

"To the hospital," Petunia said. "My family is there."

"What hospital?" Sagara asked.

Petunia explained that the Enchanted Forest School had been turned into a hospital.

"Wait a minute, and I'll come with you," Sagara told her. "I'll just fetch my stuff and yours."

"Why?" Petunia asked, surprised.

Sagara shrugged. "I'm not sticking around here, and I can't go home. I may as well go be useful. Third precept, you know."

Third precept? "No, I don't know."

Sagara sighed. "The third precept of the Guardians of the Sylvan Vale: Serve the common good." She headed back to the kitchen gate. "Just wait here, okay?"

The elf consulted with Millie a moment, then went inside. A few minutes later, she emerged with her rucksack and Petunia's basket of possessions, into which she had stuffed a few stale rolls leftover from dinner. "Here you go," Sagara said, handing her the basket.

"Thanks for coming with me," Petunia said. They

headed up the Path, just exactly as though they were going to school. "Do you think... do you think Millie hates me?"

"Why in the Realm would she hate you?"

Petunia stared at the Path. "Because I almost killed Bogdana."

"Ha, good riddance if you did," Sagara said, but she winked. "Nah, Millie's not that stupid. She should be mad at her mother for not letting you call for help, not the other way around."

"Huh," Petunia said. "You can actually be pretty nice sometimes."

Sagara frowned. "You smell, do you know that? When's the last time you changed your clothes or had a bath?"

"Twosday," Petunia admitted, looking down at her bruised and battered tulip dress. "I've just been too busy."

"Well, come on," Sagara said. "I'm sure there are baths at the school."

The Path was eerily empty. Normally, when Petunia walked to school, she passed dozens of Forest folk strolling or hopping or gliding or trotting or slithering along, enjoying the magical protection the Path provided as they moved through the Enchanted Forest. Fairies and sparrowkin would flit alongside the Path, gathering nectar and pollen from whichever flowers were in bloom, singing and chattering to each other. Children would make their way to school against the tide of merchants and shoppers making their way to market in Pixamitchie. Today, she and Sagara walked alone up the Path with only the uneasy rustling of the trees to break the silence.

Halfway along the Path to the school, they ran into a family of pox-ridden sparrowkin making their way to the hospital. The poor things seemed to be molting, scattering the Path with feathers, so in addition to being sick, they

were all shivering with cold. Sagara scooped them up
gently and carried them in the crook of her arm, where
they snuggled gratefully.

Before long they reached the wide, spreading branches
of an enormous oak tree: Master Quercius, also known
as the Enchanted Forest School. The grassy glade beneath
his branches, which would be full of playing children on a
normal school day, lay woefully still. As they approached
the school, they were surprised to find a desk at the base
of the spiral staircase winding its way up the massive trunk
as wide as Millie's house. A faun in a teacher's green cap
sat there, looking a bit thin and pale but otherwise well,
carefully reviewing several scrolls. Master Augustus looked
up and smiled at them.

"Well, here's a nice change! Healthy visitors instead of
sick patients," he said. "You two know there's no school
tomorrow, right?"

"We know," Petunia piped up. "Terrence came by."

"And we are bringing you some patients," Sagara said,
setting the sparrowkin down on the desk, gently so as not
to ruffle their feathers.

Master Augustus sighed. "Of course. Names, please?"

One of the sparrowkin twittered out their names, and
Petunia recognized them from the northern end of the
briar hedge. Had everyone in Pixamitchie caught spickle
pox? Master Augustus recorded their names. "Sagara,
would you be so kind as to take them up to Mistress Pym's
classroom?" Sagara nodded, gathering them up again.

"Excuse me, Master," Petunia said. "Do you know where
I might find my family?"

"Pixies are in Master Bertemious's classroom." At her
look, he laughed. "Not to worry, Master Bertemious is
at home, recovering." Petunia sighed in relief. Master

Bertemious still hadn't forgiven her for the mud fight she'd started in his Thaumaturgy class.

"Thank you, Master," she said and set her foot on the stairs. To her great surprise, she stayed the same size. Ordinarily, Master Quercius used an enchantment to make everyone the same height, even the teachers. Master Augustus noted her confusion and said, "Even Master Quercius wouldn't have room for all the pixies and fairies and goblins and imps who've come to us if they didn't remain small, though he has been shrinking the ogres, trolls, and giants as needed."

"Oh, sure," Petunia said. "That makes sense."

"Come on, I'll give you a ride, too," said Sagara, holding out her free hand. Petunia leapt into it and climbed wearily up her sleeve to her shoulder.

"Thanks, Master Augustus!" Petunia called down to the faun.

He waved absently, already reabsorbed in his paperwork.

Sagara climbed the great winding staircase. They paused at the first classroom, usually reserved for the youngest students. All the desks had been pushed against the walls, and pallets had been laid out, where about three dozen dwarves lay, attended by family members and a few brownies in pink-and-white striped smocks. *Odd*, Petunia thought. *None of them have pox anymore. They're just lying there, exhausted.* The next classroom was full of gnomes, also without pox. And the third and fourth classrooms were jammed, wall to wall, with goblins, all just lying there. Most seemed to be sleeping.

"Something's not right," Petunia said. "If their pox are gone, they should be getting better."

"Did any of your patients have this problem?" Sagara asked.

"A few came back, complaining of weariness," Petunia admitted, "but they just weren't eating enough. Once I fed them up, they were fine." She frowned. Nearly all of the goblins' pallets had bowls of porridge lying next to them, untouched.

Sagara came to Mistress Pym's classroom. The unicorn Enchantments teacher in her green school cap was nowhere to be seen, but a brownie met them at the door and directed them to a row of empty baskets lined with soft flannel. Carefully, Sagara put the sparrowkin family into basket. Another brownie in the pink-and-white striped smock bustled up with a bottle of livid orange cure and an eyedropper. She eyed Sagara and Petunia. "Have you two had the cure yet?" she asked sharply.

"Yes, of course," Petunia answered.

"Petunia made mine," Sagara added.

The brownie's eyebrows shot up. "A potioneer? Mistress Pym and Mallow will be right glad to see you."

"I'd like to see my family first," Petunia replied.

The brownie nodded. "O' course, but when you're done with that, head up to the potions laboratory, please. We need all the help we can get." She turned and began administering drops of cure to the open, beaky mouths of the sparrowkin.

Sagara turned and left the room, passing a classroom full of fairies before she reached Master Bertemious's classroom, every bit as packed as the goblin rooms with multicolored pixies. All unmoving.

"Can you find your family yourself?" Sagara asked. "I need to speak with Master Quercius, and I'd rather not disturb the patients. I'll be up in Headmistress Pteria's office."

"Sure, Sagara," said Petunia, hopping down with her basket. "Thanks for bringing me."

The elf looked down at her gravely. "Good luck," she said, then turned and continued up the staircase.

Petunia began hunting through the room, asking the brownies for directions, until she spied Clover pacing back and forth under a desk next to the book corner. Petunia rushed over.

"Clover!" she cried, hugging him.

"Tunie! You got away from that witch!" He hugged her back fiercely. "What happened?"

She wanted to tell him, but the Promise squeezed, preventing her from mentioning Bogdana's allergy to pixie dust. "I'll tell you later," she said. "How's everyone else doing? How's Peaty?"

Clover looked grim. "See for yourself." He led her over to a throw pillow, where Peaty lay curled up beside their mother and the twins. The rest of her family—Thorn, Holly, Primrose, Vetch, Cowslip, Daisy, Birch, Alder, and Rosemary—lay on more pillows. Uncle Ash and Aunt Clematis and their family occupied several more pillows under the next desk over. All were sleeping, but at their approach, Cherry pried open her eyes.

"Ah, Primrose," she whispered.

Petunia sank to her knees beside the pillow. "It's Petunia, Mum," she said and began to cry. "I'm sorry! I'm so sorry. I left you, and now you're all sick. I abandoned you!"

"Ah, Petunia. Now, now," Cherry said. "None o' that. It's well you did. We were right worried about you when we couldn't find you, but that's my fault for not listening. You were trying to tell me something that Endsday morning." Her mother sighed deeply, closing her eyes. "It's just, there are so many of you, always chattering on about something. I can't keep it all in my head, no matter how hard I try, especially not with the twins keeping me up nights and

your father nattering on about his bacon, the greedy beast."
She managed to pop open one eye again. "You were the
only one of us with any sense. You escaped the pox, being
with that witch. And from what Clover says, you saved this
family, no mistake. Have you really been helping her?"

"I have. I even learned to make the cure myself. But it
didn't work!" Petunia wailed. "Look at you! You're all still
sick. I sold her my pixie dust for nothing."

Clover sat cross-legged beside her. "That's not true. Look
at me, I'm fine! If you hadn't cured me, I wouldn't have
been able to bring everyone here." He scratched his head
under his acorn cap. "There must have been something
wrong with the cures you gave me for the family. You just
need to make new ones."

Petunia shook her head. "Your cure came from the same
batch. If you're fine, they should be fine. None of this
makes sense!"

"No, it doesn't," said a voice behind her. Petunia turned
and found Mistress Mallow and a smocked brownie
standing behind them. It was weird, having to look up
at Mistress Mallow, who was about three times as tall as
Petunia. In school, they were usually the same size. "I'm
right puzzled by this pox, and by how you've managed to
cure Clover here all the way up. In fact, I've had reports
that most of Bogdana's patients have made a full recovery.
Near as I can tell, no one who broke out in pox before they
had one of our cures has recovered. Now, what have you
been doing differently than we have?"

"I don't know," Petunia said, glancing back at her family.
"Clearly not all that different. Look at them! What's wrong
with them?"

Mistress Mallow sighed. "I dearly wish I knew," she said.
"It's a puzzle to us all. The standard cure seems to work on

the spickle pox, but then the patients are left with this... lassitude, as though all their energy is somehow being drained. I've never seen anything like it." She looked keenly at Petunia. "Something you did was working, at least part of the time. Tell me, what was your process?"

Petunia opened her mouth and choked. She coughed hard, shaking her head. "I'm sorry," she gasped out. "I Promised Bogdana I wouldn't tell anyone what she taught me."

Mistress Mallow covered her eyes with one hand. "Yes, of course she would. Well, can you watch our process and tell me if you did anything different?"

Petunia bit her lip. "I don't want to leave my mum."

"Go on," Cherry whispered. "Do what you can. We need you. All of us." She raised a hand weakly, waving it at the room full of prone, dozing pixies. "We're not going anywhere."

Clover gave her a hug. "It's all right. I'll stay with them."

"All right," Petunia said. "Can I leave my basket here?"

Clover eyed Millie's rolls. "Sure you can."

Petunia leaned over to kiss her mother, then Peaty, who stirred fitfully. "I'll be right back," she told them.

She followed Mistress Mallow out of the classroom and up the stairs, which were much more even and easier to jump than the stairs in Millie's house, until they reached the laboratory. Mistress Pym was there, busily brewing potions.

"Oh, another recovery?" the unicorn said. "Good, we can experiment on her."

"Now, Pym, be nice," Mistress Mallow chided. "Petunia's not a recovery, she's been cooking up potions with Councilor Noctmartis."

Mistress Pym whinnied like a silvery stream of pure

laughter. "Is that so? Apprenticed a pixie? Mallow, you're too gullible."

"I'm not her apprentice. I was just helping Bogdana out," Petunia retorted.

Mistress Mallow nodded. "Not only that, but some of those Petunia treated have made a full recovery. We're trying to find out why. She's sworn not to tell of her process, and you know what that means for a pixie, but I thought she could watch us and let us know if we do anything different."

"We're being supervised by a student?" Mistress Pym retorted.

Mistress Mallow shrugged. "Do you have any better ideas?"

The unicorn's head drooped. "Not one. Fine," she said, jabbing her horn at a stool. "Sit there and stay out of the way."

Petunia climbed up onto the stool and watched as they made a batch of cures. They went very quickly, the two of them working together as easily and gracefully as a pair of dancers. Watching them, Petunia began to better understand how the elements of the potion fitted together, how the mugwort counterbalanced the sulfur and helped it to bind with the tourmaline powder. When they finished, she sighed happily. "That was lovely!"

Both teachers looked up at her in surprise. "Well!" Mistress Pym said. "Of course it was."

"Anything different?" Mistress Mallow asked, a thoughtful look on her face.

Petunia shook her head. "Mistress Pym purifies the water and the mineral oil with her horn, but aside from that, no. As far as I can tell, it's all the same."

Mistress Mallow slumped in her chair. "What are we missing?"

"I tell you, it must be a lingering magical drain,"

Mistress Pym said. "Something the pox sets up that just keeps running even after the pox is eradicated."

"We've run tests," Mistress Mallow pointed out. "All but the very worst of our patients have recovered their magical abilities. They just haven't the energy or the will to use them. And if it's a magical drain, why are dragons the most affected?"

Petunia sat up. "Dragons?" she asked. "What happens to dragons?" A sudden thought struck her. "Where's Headmistress Pteria?"

The teachers looked grave. "She's the worst of all, in a deep coma. We haven't been able to rouse her, no matter what we do," said Mistress Mallow.

Mistress Pym shook her mane, pawing at the floor. "It's so frustratingly mysterious. Dragons should be least affected because they don't rely on magic for their strength or power."

That was news to Petunia. "I thought they had tremendous magical power."

"Oh, they do," Mistress Mallow agreed. "But they don't rely on it the way, say, pixies or fairies do. Instead, they have immensely strong spirits, which powers their magic."

"Spirit," Petunia repeated, thinking furiously. There was something important about spirit, something she'd learned recently.

Clover appeared at the door. "Tunie! Come quick! Mum's feeling better!"

"What?" Petunia and Mistress Mallow cried together.

"Come and see," he insisted.

Petunia leaped down from her stool and followed him down the stairs and into Master Bertemious's classroom, with Mistress Mallow right behind them. Petunia saw her mother instantly, sticking out like a bright pink thumb among all the pixies because she was actually sitting up, chatting with two brownie attendants.

"Mum!" Petunia cried. "Mum, you're better!"

Cherry gave her a big smile and held out her arms for a hug, which Petunia gave her gladly.

"What happened?" Mistress Mallow asked. "What made you better?"

"I don't rightly know," Cherry replied. "I was just lying here, with Clover chattering at me and making me eat some of that delicious dinner roll, and then, just like that, I felt life flowing back into me."

Petunia glanced down at Millie's dinner roll, half-eaten. "You ate the roll?"

"Aye, that Millie's a fine cook," Cherry said. "I could learn a thing or two from her, I think."

And then Petunia got it. "Millie's more than a cook, she's a witch!" She turned to Mistress Mallow. "Millie's food isn't just food. It's also spirit food, so her house ghost can eat it, too. No one has ever been able to figure out how she does it, but it's true. Clover, did you eat anything when you came to Bogdana's house for the cures?"

Clover smiled. "Yup, delicious stuffed french toast."

"Of course," Petunia said, feeling stupid. "I remember thinking that the patients who came back just weren't eating enough because once I fed them, they all seemed fine."

"Spirit food," Mistress Mallow whispered. "The pox isn't just affecting magical ability—it's also suppressing the spirit! But how can we be sure?"

"Let's try it on Peaty," Clover urged.

Petunia broke off a piece of dinner roll and climbed onto the pillow next to her mother. "Peaty," she said, shaking him gently. "Peaty, wake up, it's Tunie."

Peaty stirred a bit but did not wake.

"Let me," said Cherry. Taking a few crumbs of the roll, she opened Peaty's mouth and sprinkled them on his tongue, then closed his mouth again. "Now we'll see."

After a moment, Peaty swallowed. His eyes fluttered, and then he opened them, just a crack. "Tunie?" he said wonderingly. "I was having this weird dream that you were gone."

"It's okay, Peaty," Petunia said soothingly. "Here, have some more roll." She pressed another piece into his mouth, and he chewed solemnly and swallowed.

"Wow," he said, opening his eyes all the way. "I'm really thirsty."

"Spirit food," Mistress Mallow said. "Petunia, you've done it!"

"Quick," Petunia said. "Take some roll to Headmistress Pteria. Clover and I will start feeding the others."

"We'll need more than two rolls," Mistress Mallow said. "Fortunately, Mistress Pym makes an excellent spirit tonic. We'll put it into production right away. Meanwhile, this will have to do." Tearing off a hunk of roll, she rushed off.

"And tell Millie!" Petunia called after her. "She can bake cookies for all of Bogdana's patients. What am I saying? She probably is anyway."

Suddenly, Petunia's stomach growled, and she realized she hadn't eaten all day. Clover shoved a bowl of porridge at her. "You eat. I'll start feeding everyone else."

"I'll eat later," Petunia said. "Let's get everyone up."

They tore the remains of the rolls into the smallest portions possible and went from pixie to pixie, feeding them Millie's spirit food. Gradually, the pixies began to stir and sit up, calling for water. The brownie attendants were only too happy to help, ladling out water into thimbles and bottle caps. But even torn into tiny pieces, the rolls were only enough for a third of the room, let alone the rest of the hospital.

Finally, Petunia sat and ate her porridge, wishing there were more she could do. And then she felt it: a lightening, a deep release. Petunia took a deep breath for the first time in days, and she knew for one joyful moment that her Promises were lifted. She was free.

"Oh," she said aloud. "Oh, no."

Clover glanced at her. "What is it now?"

"I think... I think Bogdana just died."

Chapter 17

A Boon from the Baba

Petunia ran back up to the laboratory to see if they had a scrying bowl. She needed to call Millie, to tell her she was so, so very sorry, but Mistress Pym immediately drafted her into helping make the spirit tonic.

"It's not so complicated as the spickle pox cure, thank the light!" Pym told her. "Just five ingredients. The trick is in the timing. We need dawn light condensed from dewdrops, smoke of sage and cedar, unicorn breath," she whinnied mirthfully, "and an amethyst to bind them all into purified spring water. Tell me, have you ever infused gaseous components into a liquid suspension?"

Petunia found herself helping Mistress Pym setup up complicated tubing that would funnel smoke from the brazier into bubbling liquid in which a large amethyst crystal was suspended. "It's very important that the crystal be placed in the exact center of the fluid to properly align the spirit matrix."

Mistress Mallow burst in. "It worked! It worked! The Headmistress has regained consciousness!" She did a merry jig around the laboratory, her bark-like limbs creaking noisily.

"Mallow, stop that at once! You'll upset the alignment of my equipment!" Pym cried.

The brownie stopped and grabbed up Petunia in a great hug. "Thank you, Petunia! You have no idea how many people you've saved today, besides the Headmistress."

"Oh," Petunia gasped out, "um, you're welcome, I guess."

Mistress Mallow stopped and set Petunia back down on the workbench. "Why, whatever is the matter? You should be celebrating. Instead, you look like someone died."

Petunia burst into tears. "Bogdana's dead! I know it!"

"Why would you think that?" Mistress Mallow gasped.

"My Promises are gone. They all stopped, just like that. There are only three ways that a Promise ends."

"You fulfill the Promise," said Mistress Pym.

Petunia nodded. "And I had nothing to fulfill other than not telling about potion-making and Bogdana being sick. That kind of Promise never ends."

"Unless the person you Promised releases you from the Promise," said Mistress Mallow.

"Can you imagine Bogdana doing that?" Petunia asked. "Not likely."

"Which leaves... death of the Promised?" said Mistress Pym.

Petunia resumed wailing. "It's all my fault! She was allergic to pixie dust, and I didn't know! I killed my best friend's mother!"

Mistress Mallow gathered Petunia up into her arms, patting her back. "There, there, it wasn't your fault. You couldn't possibly have known. And Councilor Noctmartis was... is a perfectly capable witch and knew what she was doing. I'm sure it's all right."

"Please," Petunia begged. "Let me scry Millie. I need to know."

"No need," said a voice from the doorway. Mistress Mallow turned, and there stood Baba Luci, leaning wearily on her knobby cane. "I assure you, Bogdana is very much alive."

Petunia sagged in Mistress Mallow's arms. "Oh, thank goodness. Is she all right?"

"She is recovering well. I have moved her to my hut while I have her house thoroughly cleansed of pixie dust." Baba Luci shifted her feet uncomfortably, then said, "Petunia, may I have a word with you?"

Petunia gulped. "Of course."

The Baba cleared her throat. "In private?"

"You can use the teacher's lounge, Baba," Mistress Mallow offered, bowing to the ancient witch. "I don't think anyone's napping in there right now, and most of the teachers are at home, recovering." She led them up the stairs to a door to a small room just up from the Headmistress's office. It was cozy, filled with comfy couches and overstuffed armchairs, rather like the one in Bogdana's workshop, which nearly made Petunia start crying again. A small kitchen occupied one wall, with an icebox, a sink, and a small brazier, currently unlit, with a teakettle and a coal hod nearby.

Mistress Mallow set Petunia down on a sofa. "I'll be just downstairs if you need me," she told Petunia.

The pixie nodded tearfully. "Thanks, Mistress Mallow."

The brownie glanced at Baba Luci, who also nodded, then the teacher left the room.

Baba Luci sat down opposite Petunia, leaning her cane against her chair. She spent a moment adjusting her magical head scarf and arranging her woven red skirt, her leather boots just peeking out. "First, I should say that Bogdana should be the one speaking to you now, but she's still much too weak. As the leader of her coven, and as her mother, I also bear some responsibility, but the fault is hers." Baba Luci sighed. "I have come to offer you a sincere apology on Bogdana's behalf."

Petunia gasped. "But... but I nearly killed her!"

"As Mistress Mallow pointed out, that was hardly your fault. Bogdana willfully ignored all the signs of her allergy. She always thought my allergy was an affectation." The Baba snorted. "Well, she knows better now. No, I'm apologizing because she forced you into a Promise, just to salve her bruised ego. It not only endangered her own life, it put you in an impossible situation, in danger of breaking your Promise. I insisted that she release you from both Promises immediately. It was the least she could do."

"Ah, that explains it," Petunia said. "I knew she'd never do it voluntarily."

Baba Luci raised her eyebrows at this. "Indeed. And knowing this, you made the Promises anyway. You must be terribly angry at her."

Petunia clenched her fists, but then she sighed and released them. "I was pretty mad at first," she said. "But I think Bogdana wasn't really thinking straight. I think she was sick and scared and desperate."

"That doesn't make what she did right," Baba Luci said.

"Oh, if she ever tries something like that again," said Petunia, "I'm going to kick her into next week. But I don't intend to ever give her the chance."

"Ah," said Baba Luci, looking sad. "Then there is no chance of repairing your relationship with her?"

"Relationship?" Petunia squealed. "What relationship?"

Baba Luci sat forward. "Potion-making. She was teaching you, wasn't she?"

"Grudgingly," Petunia said. "Only because she really needed the help. There were so many sick people, she just couldn't keep up with the demand."

"Tell me what you did with her," Baba Luci requested.

Petunia hesitated, automatically waiting for the Promise to stop her, but it was gone, just a memory. She took a deep breath and began recounting everything Bogdana had taught her.

"And when Bogdana became too ill to continue," said Baba Luci, "you began making potions on your own."

Petunia squirmed. "It wasn't as easy as she made it look. I, um, messed up a few times."

"I saw," said Baba Luci with an ironic smile. "Fortunately, no lasting damage. I repaired the scorpion tank, and the cauldron may be recast. At worst, you wasted some components."

In a small voice, Petunia asked, "Was Bogdana very angry?"

"Angry?" Baba Luci started laughing. "Petunia, she was ecstatic."

Petunia blinked. "What?"

Baba Luci smiled, showing her crooked teeth. The ancient witch grasped her cane, levered herself to her feet, and began pacing. "Ever since it became clear that Millie would not be Bogdana's apprentice, we have been trying to find an apprentice for her. It is required that every witch pass on her knowledge to at least one apprentice. But so far, given Bogdana's, er, poor judgement in training Millie, none of the young witches have wanted to apprentice themselves to her."

"Oh," said Petunia. "Oh, well, that serves her right. She was horrible to Millie, binding her magic in the kitchen like that. I can see why no one would want to be her apprentice."

"Exactly. You presented a solution," Baba Luci explained. "If Bogdana could train a pixie, notoriously the laziest, most ineffectual magic users in the Enchanted Forest..."

"Hey!" Petunia yelled, balling her fists.

Baba Luci raised a hand. "I'm just expressing the stereotype, not the reality. I have known many talented and powerful pixies in my day. Still, it would be quite a coup for Bogdana. And she did desperately need your help just then. Her own power was waning fast, drained by the allergy. She knew the epidemic was serious, and she had to maintain the illusion that she was still as productive as ever. So when you offered to help, you were handing her the solution to more than one problem."

Petunia gaped. "Are you saying that Bogdana wants me to be her apprentice?"

"She does," Baba Luci confirmed. Leaning close, she confided, "Badly."

"Oh," said Petunia. "Oh." A whole world of possibilities opened up before Petunia. Apprenticed to Bogdana, she'd get to work in that marvelous workshop every day. She would learn to make *all* potions, not just the cure. She'd gain a valuable trade. And she'd move in with her mistress. She would live with Millie! It seemed too good to be true, and after a moment, Petunia realized it was.

"No," she said.

Baba Luci rocked back on her heels. "No? But..."

"No," said Petunia. "I appreciate the offer, I really do. But," she bit her lip for a moment, "but I just can't trust Bogdana. Just when you think you're getting along with her, she does something horrible. I can't serve an apprenticeship where I constantly have to watch my back."

Baba Luci nodded, then sat down on the couch next to her. "You've learned a lot in the past two weeks, haven't you?" When Petunia didn't respond, she sighed.

"The essence of witchcraft is balance—balance between good and evil, between service and profit, between need and greed. An apprenticeship must also be a balance, a partnership in which each party gains from the experience, and it must be freely entered. Your entry to potion-making began on a terrible imbalance, Bogdana holding power over you. It could have ended disastrously... and nearly did. I am the keeper of the balance within the Enchanted Forest Realm. It is my duty to set things right. You may demand reparations, but I had hoped the apprenticeship would satisfy that requirement."

Petunia shook her head. "I don't want anything."

Baba Luci held up a hand. "Don't decide now. Something may yet be arranged. There's one more thing I need to know," she added. "Do you have any real interest in potions?" The Baba's eyes bored into her, and Petunia remembered Millie telling her that you could never lie to the Baba. She always saw the truth deep within you.

Petunia stared back at her, and then she started laughing. "I think it's the most wonderful thing in the Realm, and I want to keep learning about potions, as much as I possibly can. I want my own potions shop one day."

"Then, is there anything I can do to persuade you? Anything that would make you trust Bogdana again?"

Petunia shook her head ruefully. "If Bogdana were a pixie, I'd just ask her to make me a Promise, and it would all be fine. But she's not. She can break her promises."

"Hmm..." said the Baba. "That gives me an idea. Let me think on it."

"Oh, come on," Petunia said. "The whole idea is ridiculous. There's never been a pixie witch before." And then, at that moment, the joke came to her. "I'd be the pixie-witchy from Pixamitchie."

Baba Luci looked at her sharply. "Why do you do that?"

"Do what?" Petunia countered.

"Tell those atrocious jokes?"

Petunia giggled, "Well, it's fun." But the Baba was staring into her again, and Petunia knew that wasn't the full answer. "It's... it's who I am. I'm the one who tells bad jokes. That's how people remember me, how my parents can tell me apart from everyone else, even if they can't remember my name."

"So," said the Baba. "It's an identity you've created for yourself."

Petunia shrugged. "I guess so."

"You might consider whether that's really the identity you want," Baba Luci said. "I think you'll find you have other options available to you now, and pixie-witchy barely begins to describe them."

"Oh," said Petunia. Millie had warned about this, too: Baba Luci likes making mysterious pronouncements.

"Well, I must get to the real reason I came. It's lucky you were here as well," said the Baba, pushing to her feet again.

"Lucky? You didn't come to see me?" Petunia asked.

"No, I came to collect my granddaughter, Cretacia."

Chapter 18

Waffles to the Rescue

"Cretacia's here?" Petunia exclaimed. "Frogs, hogs, and bogs! Grumpkin told me she might be back in the Enchanted Forest."

Baba Luci folded her arms. "Did he, now? I'd like to talk to Grumpkin, too, once I've seen to Cretacia."

Petunia jumped to her feet. "I want to see Cretacia, too."

"I don't know if that's wise," Baba Luci said. "Quercius told me that she had a rather advanced case of spickle pox, and she was not recovering well."

Petunia rolled her eyes. "I know how to fix that. Millie's cooking!" Briefly, she explained about the spirit-draining effect of the pox and how Millie's spirit food counteracted it.

Baba Luci looked thoroughly surprised. "Well, that explains it. This must be an entirely new strain. Spickle pox has never had that effect before. How odd." She got a faraway look in her eye. "Bogdana mentioned an outbreak in Vanaheim. She said the outbreak there happened first." The Baba's face turned grim. "I think we had better scry Millie right away, and then we need to have a long talk with Cretacia."

"What?" Petunia said, confused. "How does Cretacia have anything to do with Vanaheim?"

"Cretacia's father is Ljot, Master of Arms for Her Majesty Queen Vidgis of Vanaheim." Baba Luci gave Petunia a very wicked smile. "I think perhaps I should scry him and Cretacia's mother, Hepsibat, as well. But Millie first." From a large pocket hidden in the folds of her skirt, Baba Luci produced a silver mirror, about as wide as Petunia was tall. She seated herself again on the sofa and set the mirror on the coffee table. Stroking the frame of the mirror, she intoned, "*Anna minun puhua Millie.*"

The mirror frosted over, as though someone had breathed on it, and then it cleared, showing Millie's startled face. "Baba! What's wrong? Did you find Cretacia?" She looked sweaty, and there were suds in her hair.

"Not yet, but I think I will need your assistance. Your friend Petunia has discovered that this strain of spickle pox also drains spirit energy, and your food counteracts the effect." The Baba nudged Petunia gently, and she leaned into the frame.

"It's true," Petunia told her, cringing. "That's why some of Bogdana's patients got better—I was feeding them your food." And then she couldn't stand it anymore. "Millie, I'm so sorry!"

"You're sorry?" Millie cried. "Sorry for what? This is all my fault! I convinced you to come stay at my house, and I knew my mother could be awful, but I had no idea how awful, really, and I can't believe she made you Promise, twice! And as for being allergic, that's her own fault. She should have let you call Baba Luci when you asked! Of all the stupid, stuffed up, obnoxious idiots!"

Petunia started laughing. She couldn't help it. Millie didn't often get angry, but when she did, her skin turned a red almost as bright as Cherry's. Even her ears turned bright red. She looked like a small blonde volcano. "Stop,

Millie!" Petunia cried. "You'll explode!"

The Baba was trying unsuccessfully to suppress a smile. "Calm down, Millie. I have formally apologized to your friend, and she is perfectly all right now."

"What about your family?" Millie asked anxiously.

"All recovering, thanks to your dinner rolls from last night," Petunia replied. "And how's Bogdana?"

"Twice as cranky as usual but otherwise doing much better in Baba's hut. Max and I have been busy cleaning the whole house. Horace insists there's pixie dust inside the walls, too, and I have no idea how to get that out."

"Oops," Petunia said.

"I have an excellent fumigation spell that I will teach you," Baba Luci said. "After I return with Cretacia. Right now, I need you to send some of your delicious food over and start making more, as much as you can. What can you make quickly?"

"Cookies!" Millie said. "They bake up faster than anything, and they store well, too."

The Baba nodded. "Perfect. Now, what do you have on hand?"

"We have some pizza we brought from the Logical Realm, but that won't work of course. Oh! Petunia overslept and never ate breakfast. It's still sitting in the pantry, waiting to be opened. Will waffles do?"

Petunia started to drool. "Oh, I think that will work just fine."

Max popped up behind Millie. "Did you say waffles?" he asked.

"Not for you, Max," the Baba drawled. "Do you have your magic carpet handy?"

"Of course."

"Then kindly load Millie's breakfast onto it and bring it

to the Enchanted Forest School," Baba Luci told him.

Max grinned. "Right away, Baba!"

"Oh, you just want to get out of cleaning," Millie said, swatting at him with a rag.

"Absolutely," he agreed, dashing out of sight.

"Millie, you should also stop cleaning and concentrate on those cookies," the Baba told her. "We may have to distribute them widely, especially in Goblintown and the Dragon Vale."

Millie nodded vigorously. "Bazillions of cookies, coming right up. Send Max back after he drops off that breakfast. I should have a few dozen ready by then."

"Good thinking," Baba Luci said. "All my love, sweetling."

"Love you, too, Baba," Millie replied. "See you later, Petunia!"

"Later, Millie." Petunia waved, feeling much better. She still had a best friend.

The Baba waved a hand over the mirror, breaking the connection. "Now, let's go find Cretacia."

They found her in room set aside for advanced cases, along with Grumpkin, Sagara, and a trio of hovering brownies. When Grumpkin caught sight of Petunia, he launched himself at her. Petunia put up her fists to defend herself, but Grumpkin grabbed her in bone-crushing hug. "Thankyouthankyouthankyou!" he cried. "You saved my family!"

Petunia hesitated, glancing up at Baba Luci, but the ancient witch smiled in approval, so Petunia hugged him back and said, "You're welcome, and you're looking better!" The terrible sores he'd had when she last saw him— yesterday, was it really only yesterday?—had scabbed over nicely and were well on their way to healing completely.

"My mum's doing better, too," he told her, putting her down. "And I would never have found my sister in time if you hadn't sold me the cures." Setting Petunia down, he led her over to a group of pallets. Two female goblins lay there, one an adult Petunia had never seen before, and one she recognized from school, Pucilla, both covered with healing scabs like Grumpkin's, both sleeping. Beside them, on a larger pallet, lay a human girl dressed in robes similar to those Petunia had seen on Ospak.

"Oh, Cretacia," murmured the Baba, who sank to her knees beside the pallet. Cretacia had by far the worst case of spickle pox Petunia had ever seen. Despite receiving the cure, her sores had not healed over at all, and a webwork of red lines spread over her skin. Where the other patients Petunia had seen were all pale, she was flushed, and Petunia could feel the heat radiating from Cretacia's skin, even at a distance. Where Grumpkin's family were sleeping peacefully, Cretacia was terribly still, barely breathing.

"Secondary infection," Sagara told them.

A brownie laid a cold compress over Cretacia's forehead, then began dabbing salve on the open sores. "It's a miracle she's still alive. Most of the other patients who arrived in this stage of the illness have died. She was lucky to have been brought to us in time."

Grumpkin's face twisted, looking down on the young witch. "I almost didn't bring her, you know. I'm sure she's the one who infected us. And after everything she's done to us, I thought she deserved it." He glanced at Petunia. "But then I thought about how you helped us when no one else would."

Petunia blinked back tears.

Baba Luci took Cretacia's hand. "Where did you find her?" she asked.

"Bogswaddle Hollow," he said. "Pucilla and Cretacia were holed up in an abandoned burrow we knew."

"That's a dangerous area," Baba Luci said. "It's full of wights, ghasts, and werewolves."

"Not anymore," Grumpkin told her. "It was weirdly quiet when I found them. I snuck in like I usually do, but then I started coming across wights, just lying there among the dead leaves, covered with pox sores, and pretty soon I realized there was no one left who was well enough to stop me. I don't think I could have gotten them out otherwise. I had to put together a stretcher to drag them here." He looked down at his gnarled toes. "My magic isn't working so well yet."

Baba Luci sighed. "We will have to send a contingent out with cures straight away."

"Cures!" cried Petunia. "But they're wights and ghasts! They eat people! They're horrible!"

"They *are* people, the same as you or me," the Baba said firmly. "If they all perish of the pox, it will leave a great imbalance in the Enchanted Forest. Whether you like it or not, they serve an important purpose here." She addressed the attending brownie. "Do you have any more cures available?"

The brownie turned pale but nodded. "I'll consult Mistress Mallow," she said and hurried away.

The Baba turned back to Cretacia. "Oh, child," she whispered. "What have you done?" Closing her eyes, Baba Luci began muttering under her breath, and Petunia felt the backwash of powerful magic. Every brownie in the room paused in their work and turned to stare as the Baba worked her magic. Petunia thought she saw the pattern woven into the Baba's headscarf shift, as though small, strange creatures were peeping out from behind the brightly colored woven flowers. Sagara stared, half in fascination and half in terror. Then the Baba fell silent, and the tide of magic through the room ebbed again. The red lines began to fade from Cretacia's skin, and she broke out in a sweat.

"Well," said the Baba, "that's a start."

Max swooped into the room on his magic carpet, looking utterly delighted, and Petunia had to suppress a giggle. He'd probably always wanted to fly his carpet inside the school, and now he finally had an excuse. In his lap, he cradled the last of Millie's meal packages. He landed the carpet between the rows of pallets.

"Wow, Baba, that was some powerful magic," Max said. "I could feel it all the way down the stairs, and I knew it had to be you, so I just followed it."

The Baba turned to him, looking terribly tired. "Well done, Max. Let's open that up, shall we?"

Max reached for the twine knot tying it together, but his fingers slid off. "Um, not sure how," he said. "Millie forgot to tell me."

"I know how," Petunia said, running up to him. She took the packet from his lap and set it a little farther away, where it would have room to spread. "Open sesame seeds!" she cried.

The twine untied itself and the parcel fell open, revealing a plate piled high with steaming hot waffles, sweet and slightly crispy, a dish full of fat, sizzling sausages, a crock of whipped cream, fresh strawberries and blueberries, and a bottle of Sylvan Vale maple syrup, along with a pitcher of fresh orange juice. As the aroma of breakfast filled the room, every patient stirred, turning their heads towards the smell. Every patient except Cretacia.

The Baba chuckled to herself. "And we thought Millie

had no magic all those years." She broke off a corner of waffle, then turned to Cretacia, gently opened her mouth, and popped the morsel in. For a few long moments, nothing happened. Then slowly, so slowly, Cretacia's head shifted. Her jaw began to work, and Petunia saw her swallow. Her eyelids fluttered, then cracked open. "Where?" she croaked.

"It's all right," said the Baba soothingly. "You're going to be fine."

"Baba?" Cretacia whispered. "Am I home?"

"No, dear, you're in the hospital," her grandmother replied. "You've been terribly sick."

Cretacia grimaced. "Ospak," she said. "He infected me."

"Ospak?" Petunia exclaimed. "That puffed-up Vanaheim jerk?"

"Yes," Cretacia whispered. "I didn't know. I'm sorry. I didn't know until I got here." She sniffed and her face crumpled as though she might cry, but no tears formed.

"She's dehydrated," Petunia said. "Get her some juice."

"No glasses," Max said, but a brownie hurried over with a cup, and Max poured the orange juice into it, handing the cup to Baba Luci. She held the cup to Cretacia's lips, holding up her head to help her sip.

Cretacia drank only a few swallows, then sighed and slumped back, asleep. But this time, her sleep seemed restful. Already, her sores were beginning to crust over and heal.

"Well, thank darkness for that," said the Baba. "I want to know a great deal more about this Ospak, but I think she needs to rest now." To the brownies now hovering anxiously around the breakfast, she gave a nod, and they rushed in, grabbing food and then doling out to the neediest patients. Grumpkin himself grabbed a hunk of waffle and fed bits of it to his mother and sister.

Sagara cleared her throat. "I can tell you more about Ospak. That's why I came here, to tell Master Quercius about him," she said. She related to Baba Luci what Thea and Mx. Elm had told her, and then Petunia recounted her own encounter with Ospak.

"Master of the Hunt," Baba Luci frowned. "That's a pretty high official within the Queen's Court."

Sagara nodded. "I know."

Baba Luci raised her eyebrows. "You've been to Vanaheim?"

"No," Sagara said in a bored tone. "But my grandmother has been stuffing court protocol down my throat almost before I could walk. As I recall, the Master of the Hunt is usually a highly skilled biomancer who captures and trains wild animals, even enhancing or transforming them with his magic."

"Those Vanir kinda look like elves," Petunia put in.

Sagara nodded. "We're distantly related. Very distantly. The Vanir consider elves as sort of backward cousins."

"Backward? In what way?" Petunia asked.

"Well, we don't insist that everyone treats us like gods." At their blank looks, Sagara added, "No, I mean it. The Vanir think they're gods, and they don't understand why we elves haven't made the same claim within our Realm."

Petunia's mouth fell open. "Gods? Really?" She pondered. "How do you tell if someone's a god, actually?"

Baba Luci snorted. "Depends on who you ask."

"Well, if you ask the Vanir, it's because they're the most powerful magic users in Vanaheim, which gives them the right to use that power any way they see fit."

The Baba frowned. "That's rather dangerous."

"Tell them that. Then maybe they'll stop being at war with every other sentient race in Vanaheim." Sagara rolled her eyes. "Gods, sheesh."

All around them, patients were beginning to wake, sit up, drink water, and chatter among themselves. Petunia was surprised to spy Aspen a couple of rows over from them. He spied them, too.

"You!" he croaked hoarsely, pointing at Grumpkin. "You're the one who infected me! This is all your fault, you filthy goblin." Grumpkin flinched as other pixies began grumbling around him.

Petunia put her fists on her hips. "Aspen, you idiot! You infected yourself. If you hadn't decided to pick on a poor, sickly goblin you caught all alone in an alley, you wouldn't have gotten sick in the first place."

Aspen shot her a dirty look. "Traitor. Taking sides with goblins against your own kind. You're the one who should be in this sickbed."

"*Enough,*" said the Baba, her voice ringing through the room, and everyone fell silent as effectively as if they'd been enchanted. "Sickness goes where it goes, mindlessly passing from one to another, destroying indiscriminately. If you hadn't been infected by Grumpkin, you'd have caught it from someone else, perhaps a brother or a cousin. Would you blame them for your woes?"

"No," Aspen sneered. "I'd blame the stinking goblin who infected them."

"Aspen, you can't blame goblins for everything," Petunia said.

Aspen stood up shakily. "Watch me."

A brownie attendant hurried up. "Where are you going? You're not recovered yet. You need to rest."

"I can't rest anywhere that serves goblins," Aspen growled, "and neither can any of my family. Come on, we're leaving."

Limping and weak, leaning on each other, about a dozen

pixies walked out. Several gnomes, fairies, and sparrowkin joined them.

Petunia shook her head. "Not even a thank you."

"We're going to have to watch them," Baba Luci said, frowning. "Max, you need to go back to Bogdana's house to pick up cookies. Those added to the current batch of spirit tonics Pym and Mallow are brewing will treat the remainder of the patients here. The next batch must go to Pixamitchie."

Petunia nodded. "The sooner things get back to normal the better."

Chapter 19

Dealing with Dragons

After Max went back to Millie's house for the cookies,
Petunia returned to the laboratory to help make spirit
tonics, but Mistress Mallow took one look at her and sent
her to the teacher's lounge for a nap. Three brownies were
asleep on the couch, and if they hadn't still been wearing
smocks or snoring like saws, Petunia would have mistaken
them for a pile of firewood. Petunia curled up on a chair,
but despite being bone-tired, she tossed and turned,
worrying about Bogdana, worrying about her family, and
worrying about Aspen and the other goblin-hating citizens
of Pixamitchie. Finally, she gave up and snuck down to the
pixie room to check on her family.

She found a room full of familiar chaos. Max had
arrived with a vast batch of snickerdoodles, and even
though the brownies had broken them into fourths, just a
mouthful had been enough to revive all but the worst-off
patients. Petunia found Peaty jumping up and down on the
pillow, bouncing the delighted twins all over, while Cherry,
Thorn, and Clover tried to round up all their children and
possessions to head home.

"Tunie!" Peaty shrieked as she approached. He leaped
into Petunia's arms.

She hugged him close. "Feeling better, Peaty?"

"All better," Peaty said. "Where were you? I missed you."

Guilt tugged at her stomach, but she told him, "I was busy making cures to get you better."

"That's what Mum said. Did you really work with Bogdana?" he asked incredulously.

"I really did." *Wow, I really did.* "Which reminds me... Mum, can I talk to you for a second?"

"Primrose, stop tickling Cornflower!" Cherry roared.

Petunia sighed. "That's Holly, Mum."

"Look!" Thorn strode up to Petunia and stuck out his foot for inspection. It looked perfectly normal. "That cure got rid of my gout, too!" He danced a little jig around her.

"That's great, Da," Petunia said. "Can I talk to you for a second?"

"Just a minute. Pick up your cap, my lad! We're going home!"

Petunia sighed. "I guess it can wait." She put Peaty down and turned to leave.

"Petunia? Wait a moment," Cherry called out.

Petunia turned around and goggled. Her mother had not remembered her name since she was two years old and Vetch was born. "Um, sure, Mum," she said.

Cherry handed Lilac to Clover and hurried over. "We're going home now. You could come with us."

"I'd like to, Mum," and to Petunia's surprise, this was true, "but I really should stay and help brew spirit tonics for everyone who still needs them. Before you go, there's something I wanted to talk to you about."

"Oh?" Cherry said, peeling Cowslip from her knees. "Poppy, don't cling."

Poppy's not even one of your children, Petunia thought.

"Mum, Baba Luci's here. She made Bogdana release me from all my Promises."

Cherry raised an eyebrow at the plural, but all she said was, "Good."

Petunia twisted her hands in her rumpled lily skirt. "Only, Baba Luci wants me to be Bogdana's apprentice for real, without Promises. A standard apprenticeship."

"Oh." Cherry looked confused. "I didn't know witches took pixies for apprentices."

"They usually don't," Petunia said. "It's sort of an honor."

Petunia had Cherry's full attention for perhaps the first time in her entire life. "Well, I can't say I like that witch, but if it's something you want to do…" She looked closer at Petunia's face. "Do you want to?"

"I don't know!" Petunia blurted out. "I loved the potion-making, and I love Bogdana's workshop, and I want to do more of it. I want the apprenticeship. I just… I don't want to work with Bogdana. I don't think I can trust her."

Cherry gave her a slow smile. "You have learned something, then. Look, if this is something you really want, then go ahead. But remember, Bogdana isn't the only potion-maker in the Enchanted Forest. You could find someone else to study with."

Petunia's mouth fell open. Somehow, she'd forgotten this. Of course! She could find someone else, such as Rosmerta the apothecary. She could ask Mistress Mallow who would be good to study with. Slowly, she nodded. "You're right. I'll think about it."

"Good," Cherry said. "Come on home with us. You've done your part, you've saved everyone. You deserve a little quiet time at home." Then Lily began screaming because Peaty had made a scary face at her.

"I should stay and help," Petunia said, "but I'll walk you out."

Cherry gave her a big hug. "I'm so proud of you, Primrose."

Petunia sighed. "It's Petunia, Mum." But she hugged her back.

"Yes, yes," Cherry said, letting her go. "Come on, you lot! Time to go home!"

Every one of her brothers and sisters, plus her father, Uncle Ash, Aunt Clematis, several cousins, and a few neighbors hugged her as they all filed their way out of the classroom and down the spiral stairs.

There was a dragon waiting at the bottom.

It was enormous, taking up at least half of the glade, a slender, multicolored dragon with a neatly trimmed horn on his nose and a sash across his chest as some insignia of office. He crouched uncomfortably under Master Quercius's branches, chatting with Master Augustus. "Is it true you've found a complete cure?" the dragon was asking.

"Eek!" Cherry cried. "Back up the stairs!"

Master Augustus turned. "It's all right, madam. This is Sir Ochidian, the chief alchemist of Dragon Vale. He has just come to take the Headmistress home to the Vale."

Behind them, Petunia heard a mild commotion. She turned and saw four brownies making their way down the stairs bearing a large basket between them, Sagara following behind. "Make way, down there," Sagara called out.

The pixies all pressed against Master Quercius's warm trunk, letting the brownies pass. As they reached the bottom of the stairs, Petunia peeped in and saw the Headmistress, curled up in the basket. She was so small, not much larger than a goblin, and she looked terrible. Many of her scales had fallen off, and the lavender tone of the remaining scales had faded almost to grey. But Pteria's eyes were open and gleaming. "Petunia, is that you?" she called.

Petunia rushed down the stairs to join Sagara as the brownies carried the basket out into the glade, depositing it before Sir Ochidian.

"Yes, this will do nicely," said Sir Ochidian. "Lady Pteria, are you ready to go home?"

"Just a moment," said the Headmistress. "I need to thank Petunia."

Petunia ran up and jumped onto the rim of the basket. "Here I am, Headmistress. How are you feeling?"

The dragonet smiled. "Much better, thanks to you."

"Oh?" said Sir Ochidian. "This absurd little creature helped you?"

"According to Mistress Mallow, it was Petunia who discovered the spirit component of the pox. Without her help, I would likely be dead now, and there would be no hope for the other dragons in the Dragon Vale."

Sir Ochidian's great blue-green face took on a thoughtful expression. "Is that so?"

"Petunia, on behalf of myself and all my people, you have my deepest thanks," said the Headmistress.

Petunia blushed a deep purple. "Aw, I was just trying to help."

"Hmm, well," said Sir Ochidian. "I think we should make you comfortable for our journey. *Nuku.*"

Petunia abruptly felt terribly sleepy. Her eyes closed, and she tumbled into the basket with Pteria. Struggling against the sleep spell, she could hear the cries of her family, the angry voices of Sagara, Master Augustus, Master Quercius, and the thunderous response from Sir Ochidian:

"In the name of the Duchess of Dragon Vale, I claim this pixie as treasure."

Oh, not again, Petunia thought, and she drifted off into a deep and dreamless sleep.

✦ ✦ ✦

Petunia awoke uncomfortably in the bottom of a large bottle. *Ugh*, she thought, *so this is how the scorpions felt.* She felt sore all over, as thought she'd been dropped into the bottle, and her head itched fiercely. Groaning, she got to her feet and rubbed her eyes. Opening them, she nearly stopped breathing.

She was in an enormous cavern, at least twice as tall as Sir Ochidian and twenty times as wide. It held a workshop, much like Bogdana's, but on a far grander scale. The workbench, a solid slab of basalt, came up to the alchemist's elbow, a good fifteen feet off the ground. Instead of a brazier, there was a fire pit hollowed from its center, with a neat little chute on one side for emptying the ashes. The cauldron resting on a tripod above the firepit could have contained the entire parlor of Millie's house. On the left wall, spring water cascaded down, collecting in a small pool. To the right, the cavern wall was lined with neat shelving packed with jars and crocks and vials and other containers, some as small as one of Millie's jelly jars, and others the size of the Millie's stove. Through the cavern entrance, Petunia could see a great green valley stretching away in which enormous beasts grazed.

"Slugs and bugs!" Petunia exclaimed. "I'm in the Dragon Vale!"

"You are indeed," said Sir Ochidian behind her. "Welcome to my laboratory."

Petunia spun around. "You! You kidnapped me."

Sir Ochidian looked offended. "I did no such thing. I claimed you as treasure, which is permitted within dragon law."

Petunia stamped her foot. "Do I look like a dragon to you?"

Sir Ochidian burst out laughing. "No one would claim a dragon as treasure. Only lesser beings."

"*Lesser beings?*" Petunia fumed. "If I'm so *lesser,* why would you want me anyway?"

Sir Ochidian wandered over to her, looking pleased. "Well, you solved a rather tricky problem for me. You see, the Duke and Duchess are terribly ill, but they won't allow me to cure them."

"Well, that's stupid of them," Petunia retorted.

Sir Ochidian snorted a puff of smoke. "Not from their point of view. Dragon politics are rather complicated. Usually, problems are resolved through complex negotiation, but in times of stress, we tend to use more, ah, direct methods."

"Such as?" Petunia asked.

Sir Ochidian shrugged. "Oh, the usual. Duels, ambushes, poisonings. In short, assassination."

Petunia's mouth fell open. "Oh. Then... they don't trust you?"

"Well, of course not," Sir Ochidian said as though it were obvious. "I'm an alchemist. I have hundreds of poisons and maladies at my disposal. I wouldn't trust me either. So the Duke and Duchess charged me to not only retrieve the Lady Pteria but also to acquire a potion-maker to make their cures under my careful supervision. An outside alchemist would have no reason to harm the Duke and Duchess, and every reason to assist in order to gain their freedom." He gave Petunia a wide, toothy smile. "Imagine my delight when you literally fell into my hands."

"Soooo, you need my help," she said.

"I require it, yes."

Petunia kicked the bottle. "Well, why didn't you just ask instead of kidnapping me?"

"You might have refused," Sir Ochidian pointed out. "You might have run away. I didn't have the time to go chasing alchemists, and I didn't dare invade Quercius's branches—he's terribly powerful, you know. Really, you were an opportunity I couldn't pass up."

Petunia sat down with a huff. "Well, too bad. I refuse. Your Duke and Duchess can die, for all I care."

"Ah, but then you'd never leave here alive," said Sir Ochidian. "The chaos of succession will tear the Dragon Vale apart, all the children of the Duchess vying for power, not to mention several of the more ambitious nobles. It will take decades to settle."

Petunia imagined what her siblings would be like if their parents were royalty. Would they be so horrible, tearing apart their home just to be in charge? She knew they wouldn't. Pixies supported each other. Family was family, and just then she missed her family so much, she wanted to weep. But she couldn't let Sir Ochidian know that, so she crossed her arms stubbornly and shook her head. "Not my problem," she said.

Sir Ochidian picked up the bottle, raising Petunia up to his great, gleaming, golden eye. "Well, if you won't help, I'll just eat you. Hmph, you're hardly even a snack."

"You will not! *Nouse!*" Petunia cried, and she levitated herself right up and out of the bottle to land on the tip of Sir Ochidian's nose horn. "I may be small, but I'm not stupid or lazy or helpless. You want to eat me? You'll have to catch me first!" She jumped to the bridge of his nose and kicked him as hard as she could right between the eyes. Her toes smarted as he roared in pain, but Petunia kept moving, running over his head and down his back, leaping off his lashing tail and diving under a cupboard, where she hid herself behind a jar of enormous pickled things like logs.

"Good heavens, what a nuisance," said Sir Ochidian, rubbing his head. "Come on out of there. I wasn't going to eat you. Pixies get stuck in my teeth. I was just trying to make a point."

"You're a jerk," said Petunia. "Point taken."

"Ah," the dragon said. "Behind the ogre's toes, are you?" Petunia slipped away as he reached for the jar.

"Hey, you know the problem with dragons?" she yelled to him from behind a large oak barrel. "They always flame out."

Sir Ochidian groaned. "That was terrible," he said, turning to the barrel.

By then, Petunia had scrambled to the shelf above.

"For you," she replied, "only the best. What's the problem with dragon fights? They drag-on forever."

"Argh," he groaned, plucking jars off the shelf, but Petunia had already moved away.

"What do dragons call knights? Canned food!"

Sir Ochidian sighed. "That one was old when I was in kindergarten."

"Why is it easy to figure out a dragon's weight? They come with scales!" Petunia called out, climbing higher and higher. "Why do dragons sleep during the day? So they can fight knights! Why are dragons such good storytellers? They have impressive tails! Why did the dragon cross the road...?"

"ENOUGH!" cried Sir Ochidian, clapping his hands over his ears. "Foul pixie! I wish I'd never laid eyes on you."

"Well, I'm happy to lay eyes on you!" Petunia cried, and she pushed a jar of eyes off the top shelf onto Sir Ochidian's head. He collapsed in a heap on the cavern floor, surrounded by shards of glass and rolling eyes.

A smaller red dragon with a brass badge around his neck flew in and landed at the cavern entrance. Saluting, he said, "Sir Ochidian, there's someone here to see you. Um, do you need help, sir?"

A flying carpet swooped in beside the dragon. "On behalf of the Enchanted Forest Council, we have come to demand the release of Petunia," said Sagara as Millie yelled, "Where's Petunia? Give her back!"

"You can have her!" roared Sir Ochidian. "Just get her out of my laboratory."

Petunia waved frantically from the top shelf. "Millie! Max! Sagara! I'm up here!"

Millie sagged with relief as Max zoomed his carpet up to her, which was sagging a bit in the middle under the weight of a pile of Millie's cooking gear. "Hiya, Petunia!" Max said as she hopped onto the carpet, taking care not to land in a ladle. "You okay?"

"Bruised my toes kicking that dragon, but otherwise I'm fine. Pretty well rested, actually," Petunia said. "Kinda ravenous, though."

"Oh! I have cookies!" Millie said, handing her one.

Petunia giggled. "Of course you do."

"Good," said Sagara. "Let's go."

"No, wait," Petunia replied, her mouth full of cookie. "There are some sick dragons here."

Max's mouth fell open. "You want to help them? After they kidnapped you?"

"Well, from what I understand," said Petunia, "things here will totally fall apart if the Duke and Duchess die. Shouldn't we try to prevent that?"

Sagara rolled her eyes, but she said, "Yes, probably."

Sir Ochidian paused in picking glass and eyes from his head scales. "You mean you'll actually help, after all that I did? You're more altruistic than I thought."

"Oh, no," Petunia said, waggling a finger at him. "You are going to PAY for our services. I'd say an umbre wyrm's egg would suffice."

The color drained from Sir Ochidian's face scales. "But I have only one! And it took me months to acquire. You have no idea how protective umbre wyrms are."

"Well, that's too bad," said Petunia. "I guess we'll be going, then."

Sir Ochidian shot to his feet. "No, wait!" He hung his head. "You can have the egg. Just save the Duke and Duchess."

"One more thing," said Petunia. "I want an apology from you, right now."

Sir Ochidian rolled his eyes, but then said, "I apologize."

"For what?" Petunia prompted.

He sighed. "I apologize for kidnapping you and bring you here against your will and inconveniencing your friends. I apologize most humbly."

"That's more like it." Petunia turned to the others. "Okay, I can do this, but I need your help, especially yours, Millie. Will you help me save the dragons?"

"Of course," said Max, and Millie chimed in, "Mistress Mallow told us we might have to pitch in. The dragons will need spirit food. I was planning to barter my cooking in exchange for your release, Petunia."

"Oh, that explains why you brought half your kitchen with you," Petunia said. "What about you Sagara? Wanna help?"

Sagara's face was shining like she'd just received the best present ever. "Oh, just wait until I tell my grandmother about this. She's been wanting to get some hold over the dragons for ages."

"And just who is your grandmother?" asked Sir Ochidian.

"Lobelia ap Arela," Sagara replied.

All of the alchemist's scales turned pale, and he swallowed hard. "Your Highness! I apologize! Had I known this pixie was your friend..."

Sagara waved off his apology. "We have work to do, yes?"

Sir Ochidian bowed his head. "We do. If you would care to land your vehicle, I will provide whatever you require."

Chapter 20

Mastodon Stew

Sir Ochidian dismissed the red guardian dragon as Max landed the carpet by the workbench and stared up at it. "How are we going to do this? Everything is so huge."

"I'd use pixie dust," Petunia said, "but I'm all out."

"Wait," Millie said. "I have a better idea. I've been studying transformations with Baba Luci." Millie put her chin on her fist, frowning. "Okay," she said. "I think I've got it. I'm going to grow you to giant size, kind of the way Master Quercius does when you enter the school. His spell is much more complicated and precise than what I'm going to use. Is that all right with you?"

"That's a great idea!" said Max.

"Wait, the last time you did a transformation on me, you needed a potion," Petunia pointed out, a little nervous.

Millie nodded. "That's because I was turning you into a human, which is changing your fundamental makeup— very tricky. This time, I'm just changing your size. Nothing fundamental, no essential change. You'll still be you, just bigger. You do this every day at school," she pointed out.

Petunia frowned but nodded. "Okay, try it."

Millie stood up, pointed at Petunia, and said, "*Kasva jättiläismäiseksi.*"

A tingling sensation rushed over Petunia's skin. For a moment, she felt as though she were dissolving. Then it seemed as though Millie were shrinking, and the ceiling was rushing down at her head, and just when she was sure it was going to hit her, it stopped. She looked around, and it took forever just to turn her head. Petunia had grown to just below Sir Ochidian's height. Fortunately, so had her dress and acorn cap. "Wow," she said, and her voice boomed in the cabin, making the bottles shake. "Oh, sorry!" she whispered.

Sir Ochidian's head reared back on his long, sinuous neck. "Good heavens!" he exclaimed, glancing back and forth between Petunia and Millie. "Well, I see now that I have underestimated you."

Sagara rolled her eyes. "Hey, Mega-Petunia, I've got something for you." She fished around in her robes and drew out a long spiral horn, holding it up.

Delicately, Petunia took it. Twice Petunia's normal height, it was now about the right size to serve as a toothpick.

"Is that...?" cried the alchemist, startled.

"A unicorn horn?" Sagara finished. "Yup, bequeathed to Mistress Pym by her Great-Aunt Morven. We were told that one of the reasons you stole Petunia was to ensure the Duke and Duchess weren't poisoned. Well, this will detect and neutralize any poisons."

"Alas, this is true," said Sir Ochidian. "There have been several, ah, incidents of late. When the spickle pox outbreak reached us, they even became convinced that this was an attack aimed at them."

"Hardly," Millie said. "It's all over the Enchanted Forest. It actually appeared in Pixamitchie several days before it got to you."

Sir Ochidian bobbed his head in agreement. "I know, I know, but, well, when you are a leader of dragons, it pays to be paranoid."

Millie repeated the transformation spell for Max, Sagara, and herself. "Okay, how can we help?"

"We'll need your spirit food," Petunia said. To Sir Ochidian, she explained, "This new strain of spickle pox drains spirit. Millie has the unique ability to make food that strengthens the spirit."

The alchemist smacked himself on the forehead, then winced. "Of course, it all makes sense now. I didn't understand why I recovered fully when others I'd given the cure didn't. It's because I take a spirit tonic every day."

"I brought cookies, but I'm not sure they'll be enough for two large dragons," Millie said.

"And all their children," Sir Ochidian pointed out.

Millie nodded. "Definitely not. Is there someplace where I can cook? Probably something in a large batch, such as soup or stew."

"Certainly," said Sir Ochidian. "Miss, er, Millie, may I escort you to my cooking hearth?" He led Millie farther back in the cavern to a bubble in the volcanic rock with a natural chimney leading up through the ceiling. Within the bubble, a brick hearth had been built. A fire already crackled within it. As with the work table, a huge cauldron hung on a cast iron hook, currently swung away from the fire. "You may produce your spirit food here."

Millie glanced ruefully at all her cooking implements, which would be useless unless she transformed them as well. "We'll need ingredients," Millie said to Sir Ochidian. "Something fit for the Duke and Duchess."

"Yes, over here." He led her to a small side cave and, with a word of High Mystery, withdrew the ward. A blast of cold air came out.

"Oh," said Millie. "Oh, my. That's a lot of meat."

Sir Ochidian chuckled. "Well, we are dragons."

"Is... is that a mastodon? And that looks, um, reptilian."

"Haunch of brachiosaurus," said the alchemist.

"What?" Max cried, racing over. "You hunt the dinosaurs?"

Sagara rolled her eyes. "Again, dragons."

"I'm afraid the Dragon Vale's space is limited," said Sir Ochidian, "and with all the endangered species we've rescued from the Logical Realm, we have a problem with overpopulation."

Millie tapped her nose. "How do dragons feel about root vegetables?"

"We eat them only when absolutely necessary," said Sir Ochidian.

"What about red wine?"

Sir Ochidian smiled. "The duke is quite fond of it and keeps an excellent wine cellar."

Millie smiled back. "I'm thinking boeuf bourguignon, a delicacy from the Logical Realm."

"How exotic!" exclaimed Sir Ochidian. "I regret, however, that we have no beef at present."

"I can substitute the mastodon. I will also require potatoes, carrots, onions, flour, and," eyeing the cauldron, "a full barrel of aged red wine. What do you have in the way of herbs?"

Sir Ochidian gestured to a shelf full of dried and powdered herbs. "Help yourself. I shall summon a servant to fetch the wine and other ingredients."

"Thank you," said Millie.

"Can I help?" said Max.

"Sure," said Millie. "Sagara, what about you?"

"I could use your help mixing the cure," said Petunia. Sagara shrugged. "That should be interesting."

So they rolled up their sleeves and got to work. Petunia had already pulled the ingredients for the cure from the shelves. Now she waved the unicorn horn over the various components arrayed on the workbench. The horn gave no sign of poison. Just to be sure, she checked the cauldron, the fire pit, and the spring water as well. The horn remained still in her hand. "Everything looks fine," Petunia said.

She found a mortar and pestle and set Sagara to grinding the tourmalines, which Sagara grumbled about but seemed to enjoy. Petunia purified some of the spring water and cleansed the cauldron, then took several logs from one corner of the cavern and set them ablaze in the fire pit. Meanwhile, Millie and Max wrestled the mastodon out of the cold room and tested it with the unicorn horn, then Millie transformed her knives, using her best filet knife to remove the furry hide, section the carcass, remove the meat from the bones, and chop it into nice dragon-bite-size chunks.

"Oh, wow! Utaraptors!" Max exclaimed as two huge, feathered dinosaur servants dragged in several burlap bags containing vegetables, a canvas sack of flour, and a barrel of wine. And this was where they began to run into trouble. As Millie waved the unicorn horn over the potatoes, it began to quiver, vibrating violently, until it sprang out of her hand and impaled a potato right through the sack. Millie extracted it and found it oozing a green, noxious substance.

"Oh, dear," said Sir Ochidian. "That looks like basilisk venom." He produced a cast iron box lined with strong enchantments, and Millie gratefully deposited the potato in it, then used a bit of Petunia's purified water to cleanse the horn. Checking the sack again, she said, "It looks like that was the only one. The rest seem safe."

However, all of the onions were poisoned with a rusty red powder that blended into the orange onion skins. Sir Ochidian's scales clattered nervously, and he backed away hastily. "Dragonscale rot," he said. "A very nasty fungus. Could you please dispose of them?" Millie dumped the whole thing in the box as Sir Ochidian sent a servant for more onions.

Meanwhile, Petunia reached for the stirring spoon Sir Ochidian had set out for her and stopped. She could feel the tingle of magic before her fingers even touched it. Not poison, but something else. A charm, to make her foul up the cure? Or worse, something to kill her outright? *No,* she thought, *it'll be something that would look like an accident, an easy mistake a "lesser being" could make.* Petunia backed away, then rummaged among the various implements hanging from one of the shelves and chose a set of tongs with magically insulated grips. "Sagara," she murmured, "stand back a moment."

Sagara caught her look and stopped pounding tourmalines, then stepped back and pretended to stretch her back.

Once the elf was well back, Petunia gingerly picked up the spoon with the tongs, then carried it over to the spring. With her left hand, she poured purified water over the spoon, which crackled and sent up shooting sparks. Max and Millie stopped dredging the mastodon chunks in flour to stare.

"I think you forgot to wash this spoon after your last batch, Sir Ochidian," Petunia said. "It had a rather large magical buildup on it. Good thing I noticed. It could have caused the cure potion to explode."

Sir Ochidian flushed pink right to the tip of his tail. "Oh, my! What an embarrassing oversight. Thank you for catching it."

Millie glanced at the cooking implements hanging by the hearth, and Petunia was suddenly grateful Millie had brought her own equipment.

Sagara let out her breath and went back to pounding.

"It's okay, Sagara. I think we have enough now. Could you measure out a cup for me? Um, I mean a gallon?"

"Have you taken into account the square-cube law?" Sagara asked her.

"The what?"

Sagara rolled her eyes. "The area of a circle is pi times the radius squared, but the volume is four-thirds times the radius cubed." At Petunia's glazed look, she simplified. "It means that when volumes grow, you may need more than double the amount of energy or time. And you may need more of the magically potent ingredients."

"Oh, that makes sense." Petunia thought about it. "The tourmaline acts as a matrix, not a magically active ingredient, so I think sticking to the same proportions will be fine. But I'll probably need more mugwort, venom, and dewdrops." She frowned. "And I'll need to increase the proportion of mineral oil to have enough substrate for them. But I'm not sure how much more."

"I can do the conversions for you," Sagara said, "if you'll give me the proportions."

Petunia smiled at her gratefully. "Thanks!" She scribbled out the components and their proportions on the worktable surface with the end of a charred log. Sagara took the log and calculated the adjusted amounts.

Petunia began making the cure, painfully aware of

everyone's eyes on her, especially Millie's. Fortunately, Millie began browning the meat and stopped paying attention. At each step, Petunia remembered Bogdana's instructions and followed them exactly. *It's too bad*, she thought for the thousandth time. *When she's not being obnoxious, Bogdana is actually a pretty good teacher.*

Steam billowed up from the hearth. Millie had added the red wine to deglaze the cauldron. Millie had peeled all the vegetables instantly with magic, telling Max, "Dad would be so jealous if he saw that," and added them whole into the stew cauldron. She fetched a large ladle from the carpet, transformed it to the proper size, and began stirring in various herbs, then added small amounts of water until the mixture looked just right. Selecting a lid, she tested with the horn and rinsed it with purified water, just to be sure, then covered the cauldron. "Now it just needs to simmer," she told Sir Ochidian.

Petunia reached for the orange juice, already measured out by Sagara, and poured it into the potion very, very slowly, letting it come up to temperature more gradually than usual, and she was rewarded by the usual vinegary fizz. *Square-cube law,* she thought. I'll have to remember that. To Sir Ochidian, she called out, "Done. It just needs to cool. Do you have some flasks ready?"

"Right here," said the alchemist, reaching for a row of bottles on a high shelf. As he picked one up, the entire shelf came down on him. Instinctively, Petunia hunched over the cauldron, protecting the potion, as bottles and equipment rained down on her and Sagara. Behind her, she heard Max shout out, putting up a ward around the hearth. Something hit Petunia hard on the back of the head, and she nearly pitched headfirst into the cauldron, but Sagara sang out, "*Jäädy!*" and Petunia froze in place.

The last of the equipment clattered to the floor. Max took down his ward, and he and Millie rushed over to help. Max pulled out his handkerchief and tied it around a nasty gash on Sagara's arm, while Millie grabbed hold of Petunia and said, "*Katoa.*" Petunia sagged forward, and Millie pulled her back, away from the potion.

"Are you all right?" Millie cried.

Petunia reached up to feel her head. Her acorn cap was gone, shattered on the floor beyond the worktable, and she had a bit of a lump rising where it had been. "I'm okay," she said. "I think my acorn cap saved me."

"Oh, thank darkness," Millie said. "Let me get you some ice for your head."

"I think we'd better tend to Sir Ochidian first," Sagara said.

The dragon lay sprawled out on the floor, his shoulder impaled by an iron rod. It looked like one of the supports for the shelf, but this one had to have been sharpened and tipped with magic to penetrate the alchemist's scales.

"A simple mechanical trap," Sir Ochidian murmured. "How ingenious."

"Yeah, spiffy," Petunia drawled. "Where do you keep your healing salves?"

"They were on that shelf," he said. "Oh, but I do keep a small pot by the hearth. My servants occasionally get burns."

Millie ran back and found it. "Small pot," she muttered. "It's the size of a watermelon." She brought it over. "I'm sorry, but we'll have to remove the weapon first. It will likely be quite painful."

"I have not yet recovered my fire breath," he admitted, "but I might nip one of you. If you could bring me a large log to bite?"

Max fetched the largest log he could find, which had once been a mature pine tree. Gently, he placed it in the dragon's mouth. Sir Ochidian nodded, and Petunia and Max tugged out the rod. The dragon's claws dug gouges out of the stone floor, and his tail thrashed as bright green blood spurted from the wound. Millie smeared the salve onto it, and the bleeding slowed, then stopped. Sagara peeled off her robes, hissing as Max's bandage came off her arm, revealing a T-shirt that said, in English, "Pi makes the world go round." She used her robes to bind the dragon's shoulder. Sir Ochidian bit the log in half like it was a twig, then passed out.

"Let me see that arm," Millie said to Sagara. She applied salve to Sagara's cut, and Max bound the handkerchief on again.

The two guardian dragons bustled into the room, yelling, "Alert! Alert! Foes!" Seeing Sir Ochidian on the floor, they bellowed and came for the kids. Max threw up another ward.

"Wow, you're fast," Petunia said.

"Try living with Cretacia," he replied. "It'll make you fast."

The dragons clawed at the ward. "We shall destroy you!" they said.

Petunia stood up, hands on her hips. "Now stop that!" she said. "We didn't hurt your master. In fact, we just patched him up."

"Lies!" they roared. "We know this is a plot!"

"So do we," said Sagara, getting to her feet and glaring at them. "You two got here awfully fast."

"An alarm sounded," the red dragon said. "It alerts us should Sir Ochidian ever lose consciousness."

Sagara sniffed. "Convenient. Whoever planted this

trap would have needed regular access to this room. The servants we've seen are all too small and weak to have messed with the shelf. Unless Sir Ochidian has an apprentice or assistant?"

The red dragon roared, "You're just trying to draw the blame away from yourself," but the green dragon looked rather thoughtfully at the shelf, then back at the red dragon.

"Georg," said the green dragon, "you recovered from the pox before I did. You would have had time. And isn't your uncle a blacksmith?"

The red dragon began to say, "Preposterous," but seeing the look on his companion's face, he chose to turn and flee instead.

Sir Ochidian sighed. "I had so hoped it wasn't Georg. This will break his mother's heart."

"You knew?" Millie cried.

The alchemist slowly sat up. "I suspected, but I had no proof. Thank you for helping me to find the traitor in our midst."

"Then this was all an elaborate set-up?" Petunia said.

"Oh, my, no," Sir Ochidian said weakly. "The Duke and Duchess really are terribly ill. Say, rather, that this was an opportunity. Now I must follow the trail Georg has left to determine who managed to bribe him."

Sagara sighed. "I hate court intrigues."

Sir Ochidian smiled. "Me, too."

Max took down his ward, they found suitable replacement flasks, and as soon as the stew was done cooking, they brought bowls of it and flasks of cure up through tunnels in the volcanic rock to the ducal suite.

"Oh, my," Millie gasped.

"Slugs and bugs," said Petunia. Max just whistled.

Two gigantic dragons, at least fifty feet long and more

than twice the size of Sir Ochidian, were curled up on an enormous pile of gold, gems, and jewelry. Beside them lay several young dragons ranging in size from six to twelve feet. Headmistress Pteria's basket had been nestled in gold coins beside the Duchess's head. Against one elaborately carved wall, locked cupboards displayed rare and valuable items: crowns, cut crystals, statuettes, vases, tomes, scrolls, and things Petunia couldn't even identify. Another wall was decorated with magnificent weapons, all far too small for a dragon to use.

"Quickly," said Sir Ochidian, clutching his shoulder. "They're fading fast."

Petunia peeled her gaze away from all the treasure and gasped again. These dragons had lost most of their scales, and open sores covered their vulnerable skin. They were deathly still, with only the barest of exhalations indicating that they still clung to life. Only the Headmistress seemed to be sleeping easily.

"The youngest first," Petunia said.

"The Duke first," Sir Ochidian insisted.

"Both. Sagara, help me with the Duke. Max and Millie, start on the kids."

It took both Sagara and Sir Ochidian to pry Duke Malfalchion's mouth open. Petunia poured in a flask of cure and followed it with a spoonful of stew. Then she stroked the Duke's neck until he swallowed. Not waiting for the results, she hurried over to the Duchess, and they repeated the procedure. Behind her, Petunia heard a young dragon mew. Then the Duke twitched and opened one massive eye. "What?" he muttered. "Where?"

"You have been ill, Your Ferocity," Sir Ochidian said soothingly. "A new strain of spickle pox, but you have been cured."

Beside him, the Duchess stirred. "Mmm, mastodon?" she murmured. Sir Ochidian began soothing her as well, explaining the details of their illness. Petunia and Sagara moved on to the next dragon child, and then they ran out of cures. Max and Millie had used the rest on the remaining children, who were all starting to show signs of life.

"Nonsense," the Duchess rumbled. "Cured by a pixie. What rubbish."

Sir Ochidian bowed to her. "I assure you it is true. Petunia, Millie, could you come over here?"

Petunia left the stirring dragonling to Sagara and trotted over to the Duke and Duchess. Both eyed her dubiously as Millie joined her.

"That," said the Duke, "is too big to be a pixie."

Millie curtsied. "I cast a giant spell on us both," she explained, "so that we could use Sir Ochidian's equipment."

"Hmm," said the Duchess. "How do I know you're not a sorceress in disguise, trying to make me look foolish, you great blue creature?"

Headmistress Pteria stirred and lifted her head from the basket. "Blue? Petunia, whatever are you doing here?"

Petunia smiled at her. "It's a long story, Headmistress, but we're here to help your family."

The Duchess glanced at Pteria. "You know this creature?"

"She is one of my students. They all are," she said, noticing Max, Millie, and Sagara. "It was Petunia who discovered the correct cure for this strain of spickle pox. She cured me, and it looks as though she's cured all of you."

The Duchess eyed her appraisingly. "Is that so? Perhaps we should claim her as treasure, then."

"Regina, you know that sentient beings may not be claimed as treasure," Headmistress Pteria chided.

"Is that so?" Petunia said, glaring at Sir Ochidian.

The Headmistress followed her gaze. "Ochidian, you brought them here? Did you assist in the preparation?"

Sir Ochidian bowed. "I merely observed," he said. Turning to Petunia, he handed her a small box. "Your payment, Petunia. One umbre wyrm's egg, as requested."

The Headmistress blinked at this, then smiled at Petunia. "Ah, a business arrangement, I see."

"I'm tired," said the Duchess. "Begone and let me rest."

The Duke opened his mouth in an enormous yawn. "I want more of that stew. It was quite delicious." The young dragons began demanding more stew.

"Thank you," Headmistress Pteria told her students pointedly.

"Yes, yes, thank you," said the Duchess. "You may go."

Sir Ochidian bowed to them as they passed. "Indeed, thank you," he murmured. "What an enlightening experience."

Chapter 21

Where There's Smoke...

Once Millie shrank them all back to normal size, along with her knives and ladle, they settled on the magic carpet, and Max launched them out of the cave and into the Dragon Vale. Petunia gasped. Spread before them was a huge, bowl-shaped depression, filled with vast woodlands broken by occasional open fields, with several rivers and a large central lake. Petunia thought several mountains could have fit in that space.

"Holes and bowls," Petunia gasped. "That looks like the most giantish giant ever stomped on the Forest."

"It's the crater of an extinct supervolcano," Max told them, "and it's protected by very strong wards to keep the dinosaurs from wandering into other parts of the Enchanted Forest."

Petunia peered over the edge of the carpet. "Look at all the dinosaurs!"

"Did you know that there are over a thousand species of non-avian dinosaurs alone? And that a brachiosaurus eats a ton of foliage every day? And that people in the Logical Realm think dinosaurs went extinct 65 million years ago?"

"Do tell," said Sagara in her most bored voice.

Petunia had to giggle. "I've never seen Max so excited

about anything before," she whispered to Millie.

"He was always like this when we were younger," Millie replied. "He'd get totally obsessed with something, like stars or rocks or species of frog."

"Huh. Well, you're a little like that, too, except that you concentrated all of your obsession on food."

Millie blushed. "Yeah, I guess so."

"I've never been obsessed about anything," Petunia said. "Well, until now."

They zipped along over the crater, racing for a distant depression in the blanket of greenery. Millie's hair streamed out behind her, occasionally whipping across her face. Petunia shivered a little. She usually rode in Millie's apron pocket, but somehow, she felt uncomfortable doing that just now.

"Is that really what it's like?" Millie said in a tight voice, not looking at Petunia. "An obsession?"

Petunia swallowed. "Sort of. I think so. Ever since I first peeked into Bogdana's workshop and saw her working, I just knew I had to do it myself."

"Wait," said Millie, glancing at Petunia. "How did you do that? Mother took extraordinary steps to make sure no one could see in. Believe me, I tried when I was little."

Petunia told her about playing in the walls with Horace, startling Millie into laughter. "I never thought of that! So Horace is just a little boy, and a lonely one at that. I'll have to shrink myself and go play with him every once in a while."

Petunia nodded. "I think he'd like that."

"So, then, how did you manage to get Mother to teach you potions?" Millie asked.

Slowly, haltingly, Petunia told the whole story. She was shaking by the time she finished, and not just from the cold.

Millie reached up and wiped away a tear.

"Oh, Millie, I'm sorry," Petunia said. "I never thought about how you'd feel if I worked with your mother. "

"I know," Millie said. "It's not your fault. I'm really glad you found something you love to do. It just reminds me how badly I've failed Mother."

Petunia sat up. "But you didn't fail Bogdana. You know that, right? She just had ridiculous expectations. Did you know she never wanted to be a potions witch?"

Millie stared at her. "Really?"

Petunia nodded. "She wanted to be something much flashier, like her sisters. Baba Luci basically forced her to stop being ridiculous and learn her potions." Petunia left out the necromancy, which might be too disturbing for Millie. She realized suddenly that Bogdana had told her all of that believing that Petunia would never be able to tell anyone because of the Promise she'd made.

"Well," Millie said slowly. "That explains a lot. Maybe I'll ask Baba Luci about it."

"Maybe ask your mum instead?" Petunia suggested.

"Maybe." Millie wiped her face. "So what will you do now?"

Petunia shrugged. "I don't know. I haven't had much of a chance to think about it. But I do want to continue studying potions. Baba Luci came and tried to convince me to become Bogdana's apprentice. I told her no."

Millie's jaw fell. "She did? Really? Do you have any idea how unusual that is?"

"Um, no," Petunia said. "I mean, witches take apprentices all the time, don't they?"

"Witches generally only take humans as apprentices," Millie told her. "The Coven would have to make a huge exception for you. Just being asked is a great honor."

"Oh," Petunia said, surprised. She hadn't thought of it that way.

"It's too bad," Millie went on. "I understand you not wanting to work with Mother. She can be horrible sometimes. But she's an excellent potions witch, and you probably won't find a better teacher in our part of the Forest. You'd have to go away to apprentice, and I would really, really miss you. But if you apprenticed with Mother, I'd see you every day." Millie looked at her shyly. "I've always wanted a sister."

Petunia thought about it, how much she'd missed Millie during vacation, how wonderful it would be to stay in the house with her. "I'd like that, too! I'd love to study with your mum. I want to learn everything about potions, and someday, I'd like to have my own shop." She clenched her fists. "Argh! Stupid Bogdana! She messed up everything! I can't work for someone I can't trust."

"Hmm..." Millie said, looking thoughtful. "If I could work something out with Mother, something that would let you trust her again, would you do it?"

"Maybe," Petunia said dubiously. "It would take a lot of convincing, though."

Millie looked sort of sad, so Petunia said, "Look at me, yapping about myself the whole time. What about you? What did you do in the Logical Realm?"

Millie blushed. "Oh, darkness, there's so much to tell you!"

"All right, then start with your new favorite recipe."

Millie's eyes began to sparkle, and she grinned from ear to ear. "Macarons. No, donuts. No, gumbo. No, wait, sushi!"

"Is she doing that again?" chorused Max and Sagara.

"Well, I haven't heard it before," said Petunia. "Tell me everything, Millie."

So Millie told her every recipe she learned from her father and all the restaurants they ate at. Millie grinned. "I want to open a restaurant someday! There really aren't any in the Enchanted Forest. We have bakeries and butchers and taverns, but no place that just serves really good food, that makes an art of it the way my dad does."

"Wow!" Petunia said. "I would eat there every day!"

"Really?"

"Of course!" Petunia exploded. "You're the best cook I've ever known, besides being my best friend. I bet you're even better after your vacation with your dad."

Then Max told them about New York City and explained that trains were like big mechanical wagons, and when they moved in tunnels under all the buildings, it was called a subway. He told them all about flying in an airplane and about his family in Puerto Rico. "My cousin Santiago would be so jealous if he knew I'd been to the Dragon Vale," Max chortled. "Of course, I can never tell him. Dad made me promise never to tell any of them about the Enchanted Forest or the other Realms. He said they'd think I was crazy. Dad told them we live in Portugal."

Sagara refused to tell them anything about her vacation on the grounds that it was the most boring ten days ever.

Max was quiet for a moment, then said, "Actually, something kinda weird happened while I was in Puerto Rico... oh, but that will have to wait. We're coming up on the Dragon Vale ward."

They came to a halt before a ward like a shimmering bubble that extended over the entire crater.

"Does this keep all the dinosaurs in?"

"Yup," said Max. "Good thing, too. Sagara?"

The elf pulled a scrap of parchment from the pocket

of her jeans and read off something in snarling Dragon. An opening appeared in the ward, and Max slipped them through.

"You speak Dragon?" Petunia asked.

"I'm just learning," Sagara replied. "I had to scry my grandmother for the pass phrase, told her I was going off to practice with actual dragons. The funny thing is, most dragons in the Enchanted Forest don't speak Dragon anymore. They all use Canto, like everyone else."

"Want me to take you home first?" Max asked. "The Sylvan Vale is pretty nearby." He pointed off in the distance, where Petunia spied the trunk of a tree so enormous, it made Master Quercius look like a sapling. She couldn't even see its branches or leaves; they disappeared in the clouds above.

"What is that?" she asked.

"The World Tree," Sagara said. "A transcendental being, the connection between all Realms with magic. We elves guard and tend it."

"That does not look like something that needs tending," Max said, awed.

"But that does," Millie cried. "Look over there!"

Petunia turned to where Millie was pointing. In the distance, she could see an ugly smudge of smoke rising from the forest.

"Looks like a forest fire. Where is it, Max?"

Max had turned pale. "Pixamitchie."

"No," whispered Petunia, then she wailed. "My family! They were going home!"

"Go, Max, go!" Millie urged.

Max leaned forward and twisted a tassel. The magic carpet hurtled across the canopy of the Enchanted Forest, racing for Pixamitchie. Petunia stole a glance at Millie;

she was looking distinctly green but determined, leaning into the wind, her eyes streaming. Long before they reached Pixamitchie, they could smell the smoke. As they approached, they could see live embers rising on the wind generated by the blaze.

"Oh, no," Petunia said. "It's Goblintown. Aspen said he'd drive out the goblins. What if he and his gang set it on fire?"

"They'll burn down the whole Forest!" Max yelled angrily. "What were they thinking?"

Sagara clenched her fists. "They weren't thinking at all!" she replied.

Max had to circle to the west to avoid the column of smoke, ash, and embers as they burst out of the Forest over Pixamitchie. Petunia gasped. All of Goblintown was in flames. Villagers were streaming out of the buildings, running over the bridges and out to the Dryad Grove and the Centaur Flats.

"Where's the Water Guard?" Petunia cried. "They're supposed to put out any fires."

"Aren't they all naiads?" Sagara asked. "Has anyone checked on them to see if they're infected? It's not like they can leave the river and go visit Bogdana."

Petunia's face fell. "Oh, no, they're probably all sick." *Or worse*, she thought.

"Without Millie's spirit food, most people are probably too sick to fight the fire," Max pointed out.

Millie peered over to one side. "It's starting to spread to the rest of Pixamitchie."

"Look, there's Baba Luci!" Sagara yelled. They saw the chicken-legged hut emerge from the Forest and settle in the Centaur Flats, where it was mobbed by refugees.

"We've got to do something!" Petunia cried. "We've got to help!"

"I'll put up a ward," Max said, "try to keep it contained."
He set them down in the market square. A few of the
leaves of the great spreading silver maple had caught fire,
and two imps and a gryphon were hauling buckets of water
up and dumping them over the branches. Other villagers
were setting up magical pumps, trying to spray down the
homes to keep them from catching, too. But there were too
few villagers, and they all looked pale and thin.

Max ran down a side street, looking for the leading edge
of the fire. When he spotted it, he stopped and put out his
hands. "*Muodosta energiakupla*," he cried. A shimmering
wall much like the bubble over the Dragon Vale snapped
into being, but this one immediately turned bright red.
"The fire's too strong," he called back to the others. "I'm
going to have to stay here and hold it, but I won't be able
to do that for very long. You've got to find a way to put
out the fire." Max had already broken out in a sweat. He
turned back to the ward and started chanting the spell over
and over, strengthening the ward, holding back the flames.

Chapter 22

The Battle for Pixamitchie

"How can we put something like that out?" Millie asked.

"The river!" Petunia yelled. "We need to use the river water."

Sagara's forehead wrinkled. "Maybe we could divert it and flood Goblintown."

"That might drown people!" Millie said. "What we need is a good downpour."

"Levitation!" Petunia told her. "You've gotten good at it. Can you levitate the river?"

Millie looked shocked, then she nodded. "I think so. I can certainly try. But how do we get there?" She gestured at the ward.

"Follow me," said Petunia, and she dashed off down another side street, the others not far behind. They pelted right out of Pixamitchie onto a bridge over the River Twiddle. Goblins, imps, and other panicking villagers streamed over the bridge, heading for the Centaur Flats where it was safe. The river formed a natural barrier that the fire could not cross. For the moment, it looked as though the fire was contained between Max's ward and the water, but they could see the ward rippling and buckling under the strain.

"Hurry, Millie," Petunia urged.

Millie nodded and closed her eyes. Petunia could see her lips moving silently. Then she opened them. Holding her hands out over the river, she spoke the words of High Mystery in rolling tones. " *Tänne*."

For a moment, the river seemed to stop flowing. Then, gradually, its course began to shift, rising into the air. Millie turned and pointed it toward Goblintown, and it began to cascade over the burning homes.

A rotten tomato sailed through the air and smashed into Millie's left shoulder, breaking her concentration. The river fell apart, sending a small wave of water over the southernmost homes, extinguishing them but leaving the rest of Goblintown to burn.

"Stop, you witch!" Aspen darted up the bridge, along with a large gang of smallfolk—not just pixies and fairies and sparrowkin, but also some gnomes, imps, a couple of dwarves, even a few brownies. "You let them burn, all of them. They brought the pox to the Enchanted Forest."

"Aspen, you idiot!" Petunia yelled. "It wasn't them! The epidemic came from a different Realm, from Vanaheim. A traveler brought it over. The goblins were just unlucky enough to catch it first."

Aspen sneered. "Why should we believe you, goblin-lover?"

"Sheesh, ungrateful much?" said Sagara. "Petunia saved all your lives, do you know that? She made hundreds of cures herself, and she figured out why the standard cure wasn't working and how to fix it. You wouldn't be standing here if it weren't for her."

A murmur ran through the crowd. "It's true," a brownie piped up. "My Aunt Myrtle works at the hospital, and she said it was a blue pixie girl who figured it out."

"And did you know that she gave the new cure to the goblins first?" Aspen called out.

Petunia growled, "No, I didn't. I gave it to my family first. Family first, that's the pixie way, isn't it?"

The pixies in the crowd nodded, chattering to each other in approval.

"But these people—Millie, Sagara—they're my family too. And so are you." She jumped up to grab hold of Millie's dress, then climbed up to her shoulder. "You're my friends and neighbors, you're family. So are all the students I go to school with. And so are the goblins."

"Goblins are NOT my family!" Aspen cried. "They're scum! They're filthy, stupid, and disease-ridden. We should have run them out of Pixamitchie long ago." A rumble of agreement rippled across the crowd.

"They're different, yes," Petunia said, "but they're still people. Did you know that most people won't sell to goblins? If they'd been able to buy cures early on, the pox might not have spread. And you, Aspen, you attacked Grumpkin, alone and sick in an alley. That's how you got infected, and you probably spread that infection all over the Hedge. You can't treat them like dirt and then blame them for the results of your own mistakes."

"They're the mistake!" Aspen said. "This fire will clean them out for good."

Sagara said. "It'll clean you out just as thoroughly. Look!" She pointed downriver.

The southern end of the Hedge had caught fire. As they watched, more embers fell into the briars, sparking new flames. Pixies, fairies, and sparrowkin began pouring out of the Hedge.

"My family lives there," shrieked a purple pixie. A fairy cried, "Mine, too! We've got to put it out!"

"We have to put out Goblintown first," Petunia yelled. "Otherwise, the fire will spread and destroy the whole village. It may even spread into the Forest."

"What can we do?" asked the fairy.

"How many of you know levitation spells?" Sagara asked. Three or four hands went up. "Okay, Millie's going to show you how to do it. Then you can move to another bridge and do the same."

"The rest of you can help get those people still too sick to move out of their homes," Petunia called.

"Mum!" cried a pale orange pixie girl. "I'm coming!" She dashed for the Hedge, and the gang broke, just like that, everyone running either toward the Hedge to help or away and out onto the Flats.

Aspen had fallen to his knees, clutching his head. "No, no, no," he moaned. "The fire was only supposed to burn Goblintown."

Petunia jumped down and kicked him. "You messed up, Aspen," she told him. "You probably just burned down your own home and mine."

He looked up at her, tears making twin streaks through the ash smeared on his cheeks. "It's not my fault," he whispered. "The goblins made me do it."

"Ignore him," Sagara said. "Let the Council deal with him later. We have people to save."

Millie had raised up the river again. A brownie, three fairies, and an imp imitated her, raising small streams of their own. "Good," she said through gritted teeth. "Now spread out, two to a bridge, and start putting out this fire." The imp remained, and Petunia recognized him: Grumpkin's friend, Titchy. Who'd have guessed he'd be good at levitation spells? He flew up above the stream Millie created and began directing it to fan out over

Goblintown. The fires sputtered and began going out.

Petunia yelled, "Go, Millie! Go, Titchy!"

"Come on!" Sagara told her.

They dashed back into the village, down the twisting alleyways of Goblintown, now drenched with river water. They checked each ramshackle, half-burnt home for survivors. Fortunately, the homes seemed to be mostly deserted. They found an elderly goblin lady in one, still covered with pox and with a few slight burns, so Sagara hauled her out and carried her to the bridge. Petunia kept checking house after house.

She came to an onion-shaped house that had caved in on one side. Was that crying she heard? Petunia darted in among the fallen timbers and broken chunks of mud plaster. A goblin lay unconscious beneath the rubble, but the faint crying came from inside an overturned washtub. Summoning all her strength, Petunia used a piece of broken chair to push the still-smoking timbers off both the tub and the injured goblin. Under the tub, she found a goblin baby in a stinking diaper.

"Shh, baby, it's okay," Petunia said. "You're going to be all right. Let's get you out of here."

"Nooooo," groaned the injured goblin. "You horrible, evil pixie! You won't get my baby!" Despite an obviously broken leg, the goblin began dragging herself toward Petunia.

"It's okay, I'm a friend," Petunia replied. "I'm here to help get you out."

"Lies," hissed the goblin. "Pixies hate goblins, always have."

Petunia couldn't blame her. How many times had she ganged up on goblins before. "Well, that's going to change," she told the injured goblin, "starting with me."

Automatically, she reached for her pouch of pixie dust, then swore. It was empty, of course. *Well,* she thought, *if I can make potions without pixie dust, I ought to be able to float a few things.* Pointing at the baby, she said, "*Nouse!*"

She felt the magic flow out of her, wrapping around the baby, raising it into the air. It was hard, so hard, and Petunia was so tired. She could feel the spell starting to wobble out of control. Petunia gritted her teeth and concentrated, willing the baby to float through the rubble and out into the street.

"Thief!" wailed the baby's mother. "Thieving pixies!"

"Whoa!" came a surprised voice from the street. "Gotcha." Grumpkin poked his head through broken wall, the baby in his arms. "Petunia? Is that you?"

"Hiya, Grumpkin! I'm glad you're okay," Petunia told him. "How're your mum and Pucilla?"

"Fine, I got them out as soon as Aspen and his mob started waving around torches. They're hiding nearby in the Underforest."

"Grumpkin, save me!" wailed the baby's mother. "This pixie is trying to steal my Otto."

"It's okay, Mrs. Stinkweed," Grumpkin said. "Petunia's a friend of mine. She's just trying to help."

The injured goblin gaped at him. "Friends? With a pixie?" She turned back to look at Petunia. "You weren't lying."

"Petunia saved half the village," Grumpkin told her. "She's the one who figured out how to cure the spickle pox. Remember that cookie I gave you and Otto? Our friend Millie made it, and it made you better, didn't it?"

"Nobody," Mrs. Stinkweed began, then broke off, coughing wretchedly. "Nobody has ever cared about us goblins before."

"Can you help me get her out?" Petunia asked him. "I'm all out of pixie dust."

Grumpkin nodded. "I'll get her. You keep an eye on Otto." He bent over, out of sight.

Petunia clambered out of the house and found Grumpkin setting Otto down in the street. He gurgled and splashed in a puddle, then turned his face up to drink river water sprinkling down. The water trickled to a halt, and Petunia glanced around. Some of the homes were still smoking, but she couldn't see any active fires burning. Off above their roofs, she saw that Max's ward had also come down.

A crash behind her made Petunia jump. She turned and saw Grumpkin carrying Mrs. Stinkweed over a newly collapsed wall. He shrugged. "It was easier than trying to thread her through all those beams."

Glancing around, Petunia saw other people searching homes, with more arriving every moment, mostly goblins, but also fairies, imps, brownies, sparrowkin, and even a hedgehog.

"Mr. Pricklesnout!" Petunia shouted.

He turned. "Ah, Petunia. What're you doing here? I thought you were working for that witch."

"Nope, released from her service," Petunia said. "What's going on at the Hedge?"

The hedgehog shook his head. "It was a close thing, but your pops started using his plant taming to snap off the burning briar canes and toss 'em in the street, where the folks with hooves and heavy boots stomped them out. Some elf girl came out and started helping him, and between them they kept the fire from spreading until the rain came. My burrow's flooded, o' course, but it'll drain in time. I figured I may as well come help." He scratched his nose. "Oh, I passed that young wizard you're friends with along the way. Seems he got himself in some trouble."

"Max?" Petunia cried.

"Aye, that's him. Never seen the like, not here."

"I've got to find him," she said. "Can you get someone to carry Otto out of here?"

The hedgehog nodded, and Petunia dashed off to the junction where she'd left Max with his ward. She found him there, lying on the ground, flopping around awkwardly. Max spotted her and waved her back.

"No," he cried. "Don't come any closer!"

"Is that... is that a tail?" Petunia asked.

Max slumped and stopped trying to shoo her away. In place of his legs, he now had a long, scaly fish tail poking out from under his wizard's robes. The shreds of his pants lay scattered on the ground. "I've been having this problem whenever I get too wet. I, um, I haven't really gotten the knack of changing back yet."

Petunia stared at him. "You're a merman?"

He sighed. "When I went to Puerto Rico, I found a portal buried in sand on the beach near my cousin's house. I cleared it and went through it to Atlantis, and when I did, I, um, changed. Turns out my family has mer blood. Who knew?"

"So, how do you change back?"

"My friend Iulia told me I'll eventually learn to do it whenever I like," Max told her, "but right now, basically, I have to wait until I'm dry."

"Huh," Petunia said. "Well, I could go find you some towels." She turned to go.

"Wait!" he called. "You're not going to laugh at me, or make some stupid joke about mermaids?"

Petunia considered. "I do know a really terrible joke about a mermaid and a walrus. But I'll let you off the hook, this time." She grinned at him.

"Argh," Max said. He glanced up at the sky, which had turned a soft orange in the west. "Oh, no, did the fire spread to the Forest?"

Petunia shook her head. "Nope, that's sundown." Above her, a magelight lamppost flickered on.

"Oh, right." Max sighed with relief. "I can't believe all that happened in one day."

Petunia spied the magic carpet. "Hey, Max, can you fly a carpet with a fish tail?"

He smiled. "Only one way to find out."

It was just as easy, they discovered, as the carpet lifted them up above the village. Petunia surveyed the damage. Most of Goblintown north of the river was damaged or completely destroyed, along with two homes and several rooftops in the village proper. Several sections of the briar hedge were singed, but there didn't appear to be any serious damage. Everything was sopping wet.

"I see Sagara," Max called out.

Petunia spotted her by the briar hedge with an orange-skinned pixie. "She's with my da. I bet she helped him save the hedge. Where's Millie?"

"Over in the Centaur Flats by Baba Luci's hut," said Max. "I think they're setting up a field hospital."

"Let's go there," she said.

As they approached, Petunia could see the Baba herself, rushing back and forth, directing the injured brought in from Goblintown into triage areas. Mistress Mallow had arrived, bringing her clan of helpers and supplies of burn salve and bandages. Dwarves were erecting portable magelights. Centaurs had begun loading the worst injured into wagons, to be taken up to the hospital. Millie, being Millie, had set up a camp kitchen with the supplies she'd brought for the Dragon Vale, with a teakettle just starting to sing over a brazier. Even Bogdana moved slowly through the injured, distributing cures to those still infected with spickle pox. As Petunia passed, she called out, "Pixie!"

Petunia paused. "You're looking better," she said.

Color had returned to Bogdana's face, though it was pink like Millie's rather than her usual witchy green. Her hair was still matted, but she wore her pointy witch's hat and stood straight, if a bit shakily.

"You ruined my second-favorite cauldron," Bogdana said.

"Sorry," said Petunia. "I made a few mistakes. I'll try to get it fixed for you."

Bogdana waved off the offer. "Millie turned my favorite cauldron into a pumpkin, which exploded all over my workshop. It took her days to clean up properly. At least the cauldron you broke can be salvaged." She jiggled the basket hanging from the crook of her arm. "And you made these. A bit weak, but they work. Well done."

A warm glow grew inside Petunia, making her cheeks flush purple. "Thanks." She started to walk away, but Bogdana called out to her, "Wait!" Then the witch looked flustered. "I, er, well... I'm sorry. I was a poor hostess and ungrateful besides." She actually blushed a bit herself, then stamped her foot in irritation. "That's how witches are, you know. We're always trying to get the best of each other. But I forgot," she said, wringing her hands now, "I forgot you're not a witch. I should have been more, er, gracious."

Max's jaw dropped, and he stared at his mother, then at Petunia. Petunia had been struck speechless. The only person Bogdana had ever apologized to was Millie. Apologizing to a lowly pixie? Unheard of. Not knowing what to say, she nodded. "Okay, um, thanks. I want to go check on Millie and Cretacia."

"Fine. Good." Bogdana harrumphed and hurried over to the next pox-ridden goblin.

Beside the Baba's hut, a ward bubble shimmered. As they approached, Petunia saw that it contained Aspen and his cronies, currently being questioned by Max's father and the salamander Councilor who represented Pixamitchie and the surrounding Underforest. On a couch on the porch lay Cretacia, awake but lying tucked under a tattered black quilt.

Millie spotted them and ran up. "Max, Petunia! Thank darkness you're all right. Um, *are* you all right? What happened to your pants and shoes?"

Max rolled over and stared down at his bare feet poking out from his robes. "Oh, good, I dried out." He stood up. "Long story, which I will tell another time. I'm beat, aren't you?"

"I'm pretty tired," Millie admitted. "What a day!"

"Millie," Cretacia croaked from Baba Luci's porch. "Come here. I need to tell you something."

Millie swiveled to look at her. "Hey, you're doing better!" She went over to the hut, and Max and Petunia followed.

"I am better," Cretacia said. "Thanks to you and Petunia. Still really tired, though."

"You're lucky to be alive," Petunia said.

Cretacia grimaced. "You have no idea."

Chapter 23

Cretacia's Tale

Cretacia spoke slowly, pausing frequently to take sips from her cup of tea, but she told them everything.

✦✦✦

I know you all think I'm this amazing witch, powerful and scary. That's because I work really, really hard to make you think so. The truth is that I'm stupid. So very, very stupid. I'm so stupid that I can't read.

Hey, that open-mouth fish face you're making is really appealing, Millie. You should do that more often.

Seriously, though. I can't read Canto or High Mystery. I've tried and tried, but when I look at words, the letters get jumbled up, and I can't tell what they're trying to say. I can figure it out if I have enough context and if I recognize enough other words. When I was little, and the spells were simpler, I could do that.

As I got older, they got more and more complicated, and I understood them less and less. Instead, I watched my mother and other witches very carefully, and I memorized what they said and did. Then I'd experiment with the spells to make them do what I want. You know that wart curse I've used on you so many times? The spell I use is actually a cosmetic spell my mum uses because she has trouble growing warts herself. I just made it a little more powerful and something I can cast at people instead of on myself.

But I can't learn spells from books or scrolls. One time, I actually burned down a wing of our old manor house that way. I'd put together a spell that reads scrolls aloud, and I wasn't paying attention while it read the scroll to me. It started the spell, and everything caught on fire. Then it got to my stash of magical components, and they exploded. Yeah, that was *not* good. I burned down my secret hideaway, damaged one of my favorite golems, and nearly died. Not that I would have let it burn me, but I used too much magic, and I was sick for a week after that. I know you remember, Millie. My mum bragged to everyone about how I was too powerful for my own good.

That was the problem, really. Mum was so proud of me; she loved bragging to everyone about how talented I am, so I couldn't bear to tell her I'm stupid.

By the way, Max, that's why I hate you. Oh, wipe that shocked expression off your face, you annoying know-it-all. You're always reading things and learning things, and it's so, so easy for you that I can't stand it. I had to put spiders in your bed after that. Really, you asked for it, flaunting your reading around me all the time.

I was starting to get desperate because my journeywitch year is coming up. That's when I go away for a year to train with a different witch in a discipline other than Mum's. Did you know that you have to write an essay to pass the journeywitch exam? Hmph, I guess no one told you because no one thought Millie the Magicless would ever take the exam. Well, if reading is hard, writing is even harder. I can barely write a sentence, let alone an entire essay. It's impossible! I thought I was going to have to tell

Mum and break her heart.

Then Baba Luci told us about the Enchanted Forest School, and I thought, hey, maybe they can teach me to read, and no one in the Coven will ever know, and I can make everyone think I was going there to trash the place. But no! Baba Luci sends you, Millie. The one person even more stupid than me. I guess that sort of made sense, actually, but I was so mad. My one chance at learning to read, and you snatched it right out of my hands. You and your horrible, delicious cookies, charming everyone to do your bidding.

That's why I sent Grumpkin to make your life miserable. I was trying to make you quit so that I could go to school. Later, I realized that we could both go to school, though then you might learn my secret. So I visited the school to find some way to get you tossed out, and that's why I tried to steal Thea. I was so sure you had cheated somehow, because you'd never shown the slightest shred of talent before, and now suddenly you're doing incredibly powerful transformations? I just didn't believe it. I didn't want to believe it. That would make me the worst witch of all.

So, yes, I'm stupid that way, too. I didn't know what a dodonas was. It's not like I could have read about the dodonoi in a book. I really didn't understand what you'd created or how bad it was for me to threaten Thea until I ran away to my father in Vanaheim. Well, where else could I go? The Enchanted Forest Council was going to bind my power, and you had all gone into the Logical Realm, which is even worse, so I went to visit Papa.

I told him about being stupid, and he laughed. At first, I thought he was laughing at me, but then he hugged me and said no, it was just that I'm a Vanir. It turns out that all Vanir have trouble reading languages like Canto. The

Vanir language is so much easier to read. Have you ever really looked at Vanir runes? They're the same backwards and forwards, and each one is unique, so you can't get them mixed up. Papa also says that the runes have an enchantment in them so that Vanir can read them easily.

He started to teach me, and he was right! I can read Vanir sooooo much better. It's hard at first because you have to memorize everything. They don't really have letters like in Canto, just a symbol for each word, and sometimes you can tell that similar symbols have similar meanings, like the runes for tree and forest are almost the same. Finally, I started being able to read.

Then Papa invited Ospak over and everything went sideways on me. Again. I should have known. I should have seen it coming. I'm so stupid!

Papa and Ospak live in the same building, the Annex, which is where the Menagerie and the prison are and where Papa keeps and maintains the golem army. Along with Aud, the Prison Mistress, they're the only Vanir who live in the Annex, so they tend to meet and invite each other to dinner a lot. The thing you should know about Ospak is that he's terribly bitter. He hides it really well, but I can tell. He hates being stuck as Master of the Hunt. Once, this was a great honor. The Hunt was made up of really powerful creatures: dire wolves and tame giants and stuff. But then my grandfather introduced the idea of a golem army. Now Papa is the Armsmaster, directing and maintaining the army, and the Hunt has become a sort of genteel pastime. The Vanir take them out when they want to hunt down game for a feast or to harass the dwarves or the troglodytes.

Ospak hates being sidelined. What he really wants is power. Papa's power. He experiments on his creatures,

trying to make them bigger and nastier. He wants to be
the Armsmaster with his monstrous troops. He once said
something that made me shiver all over. He said, "What
good are servants who neither fear you nor feel pain?" Oh,
he wants to rise in court, and he wants it badly.

Well, duh, Max, Ospak is obviously a biomancer. You
can tell by his antlers. He grew them himself, and he's very
proud of them. He can change living things, like this dire
wolf that he gave wings. I kinda befriended him. What a
sweetie he is, not at all the way Ospak wanted him to be.
He wanted an army of flying dire wolves to counter the
valkyries, but Fenwing was a dismal failure, too friendly
and afraid of flying. Ospak tried growing scales on humans
to make them into armored warriors, but humans are
too fragile and age too quickly. Experiments on giants
completely failed because they're already too crazy full
of magic, and they generally die. He has one captured
valkyrie, but valkyries are immune to Vanir magic. That's
what makes them so dangerous. The Hunt is full of Ospak's
failures.

Argh, no! I didn't know any of this at first. The first time
I met Ospak, he actually sneered at me, the nerve! And
whenever he met Papa or came to dinner, he would just
pretend I didn't exist. Even if I spoke to him, he wouldn't
respond, though he could tell it made Papa unhappy. Vanir
are very snooty about bloodlines, you see, and I'm only
half-Vanir. I'm never invited to the Queen's feasts.

But one day, when we were in Aud's apartments for
dinner, I started complaining about you and your stupid
baby tree, and Ospak got interested. He started being
sympathetic and giving me advice on getting my revenge on
you. He told me that I'm much better off among the Vanir
anyway. He smiled and flattered me, which was the first time

any Vanir other than Papa had said anything nice to me.

After that, he kept coming to see me. Ospak told Papa how marvelous I was, how intelligent, constantly pointing out that I must get my strong magical ability from Papa. Actually, Papa does this a lot, too. He only wants to see the Vanir in me, and sometimes he kind of winces when I tell him stories about the Coven. But Ospak never did that. He just flattered me, made me feel clever and important.

I'm so stupid, I ate it all up. It made Papa happy, too, and he started encouraging me to spend time with Ospak in the kennels, which is where I met Fenwing. I used to feed him, saving tidbits from Papa's kitchen.

The whole time, though, Ospak was asking me questions about the Enchanted Forest, and you, Millie, and especially Thea. Was I sure she was a dodonas? How big was she? Had she started talking yet? Those kinds of things. I learned a lot about Thea from him, actually. Like I said, I hadn't really understood what she was before, but the more he told me, the more I realized what an awful, horrible thing I'd done. Look, I don't mind being horrible to people when it serves my purposes, but I actually don't hurt anyone in any permanent way. That's unsubtle and tends to backfire on you. So when he explained how rare dodonoi are, and how powerful Thea could become, I started to feel really, really bad about what I'd done.

Did you know that a single dodonas can balance the life magic of an entire forest? That they can help channel energies between Realms? Did you realize that Quercius is much, much more than a school? He regulates the flow of magic between the World Tree and all the trees of the Enchanted Forest. He's the reason that all the trees can speak to each other. He's incredibly powerful, and someday, Thea will be, too.

Gradually, Ospak began convincing me that I needed to go back to the Enchanted Forest to check on Thea. That I should go apologize to her, because it never hurts to have a really powerful being on your side. I didn't need to make amends or face the Coven or the Enchanted Forest Council because I was Vanir, but I could start reestablishing my influence there. So I finally decided to go back, just to make sure Thea was okay and maybe apologize. I told Papa I was going to visit Mum for a few days, just to let her know I was okay and to get a few things I wanted.

I sort of didn't want to go because Fenwing and most of the other creatures of the Hunt had gotten sick. Yup, you guessed it: spickle pox. Ospak was tending them, taking careful notes on their response to the illness and to various medicines he gave them. He told me not to worry, that all Vanir are immune to spickle pox. But I think Ospak must have infected me with spickle pox before I left. I was feeling a little tired the day I came back through the Portal, but I thought it was just that I hadn't flown my broom in so long. I found Grumpkin's sister, Pucilla, and got her to tell me everything that was going on in the Enchanted Forest. She told me Thea was at your house, Millie, and that you were spending a lot of time in the Logical Realm with your father. Seriously? Your dad has no magic at all? No wonder you were so hopeless all those years.

Stop glaring at me, you miserable pixie. I'd give you warts, but I don't have my magic back yet. Otherwise, you'd be covered from head to toe. Just you wait until I'm better. Oh, fine, fine, I nearly died, and I've lost my magic, but you want to hear about the stupid baby tree.

When I found out that school vacation was coming up in a week, I thought that was the perfect time to go talk to Thea, because none of you would be around. I went and hid out in an abandoned goblin hut that Pucilla found for me on the edge of the Salivary Swamp, and I waited for you to leave so I could talk to Thea.

That night, I broke out in pox, all over. They itched so much! I got a terrible fever, and I was thirsty all the time. Pucilla tried to help, but then she got sick, too. We needed help, so I tried to fly to the Vanaheim Portal, but we only made it halfway there before I had to land, and in Bogswaddle Hollow! Fortunately, Pucilla knew about this abandoned burrow, and we holed up there, hoping to get better.

I thought I was going to die. I had run out of water, and I couldn't get up to get more. I couldn't do any magic, and I lost feeling in my legs. I don't think I would have lasted another day if Grumpkin hadn't come and rescued us.

But here's the important thing: Baba Luci told me you've seen Ospak here, in the Enchanted Forest, that he's been visiting Thea and trying to get past Aunt Bogdana's wards. You need to watch her very, very carefully. I think Ospak wants her, and there's nothing he won't do to get her.

I know I've done a lot of bad things, but I'm trying to make up for it. I'm not good at it, okay? But I'm learning. Please, believe me. Thea is in danger.

↯ ↯ ↯

Petunia tugged at Millie's ankle. "Didn't Baba Luci take down all of Bogdana's wards when she came to help? Did she ever put them back up?"

Millie looked shaken. "I think we had better go and check. Max, can you take us?"

"Climb aboard," he replied.

"Thank you, Cretacia," Millie said gravely. "I know we haven't been friends in the past, but I think maybe we could be, if you want to try."

Cretacia started to roll her eyes, saying, "Friends? With you?" But then she stopped herself. "Well, maybe. I can try, anyway. It's not like I have anything better to do."

They hopped aboard the magic carpet and zoomed off into the dusk, the sky like a bruise above them. It took just a minute to get to Millie's house, and Max called out, "I can feel a ward up, but it's the Baba's, not Mother's."

He flew them up to the kitchen gate and set them down on the Path, which was littered with elm branches. Mx. Elm rustled agitatedly at them.

"Darkness," Millie said. "I wish we'd brought Sagara to translate."

"I know what she's saying," Petunia said, peering through the slats of the fence around Millie's house. She peered as hard as she could into the gloom, but she couldn't find Thea.

Max lit his wand and pushed through the kitchen gate with Millie, but Petunia couldn't get through—naturally, Baba Luci hadn't wanted any more pixie dust coming in.

"Oh, no!" Millie gasped, falling to her knees.

Where Thea had stood, there was only a hole in the ground.

"He got her," Petunia whispered. "Ospak got her! How did he get through the ward?"

Max paced around the hole, frowning at the ground. "He didn't. Baba Luci was sloppy. She forgot to extend the ward underground." He kicked at the edge of the hole. "This isn't a hole, it's a tunnel. And I'll bet it comes out at the Vanaheim Portal."

 Epilogue

A Final Promise

Petunia stood where she had never in her life expected to stand: between the inner and outer circles of the Coven's standing stones. A bonfire blazed before the altar, and all the witches of the Enchanted Forest had assembled, including Baba Luci, Bogdana, Millie, Cretacia, and her mother Hepsibat. Nearby, a young willow dodonos stood, its toe roots digging at the earth. Max was there with Alfonso, and Sagara stood nearby with her grandmother, an elderly elf in elaborate robes. Petunia's parents stood uncomfortably next to her, looking ready to run at the least little thing. "It's all right," Petunia said to her mum. "No one will hurt us. I'm an important witness, remember."

Cherry nodded, clutching Petunia's arm. Thorn tried to stand tall and brave, but he kept glancing behind him to make certain they could escape if needed.

Baba Luci raised her hands, and the babble and chatter around the circle ceased. "Now," she announced, "we shall proceed with the trial of Cretacia Noctmartis-Ljotsdotter."

Hepsibat hugged her daughter fiercely, but Cretacia pulled away from her and walked to the center of the circle.

"Cretacia," said the Baba. "You have been charged

with attempted kidnapping and attempted assault upon a dodonas."

A ripple of outrage ran through the crowd. The dodonos rustled angrily.

"How do you plead?" asked the Baba, staring into Cretacia's eyes.

Cretacia raised her chin. "Guilty, grandmother."

Hepsibat buried her face in her hands.

The Baba nodded her approval. "We have discussed this case at length already, among ourselves and with the Enchanted Forest Council, and we understand that there are mitigating circumstances. First, that you have already lost your magic as a result of a severe case of spickle pox. Is that correct?"

Cretacia nodded. All the apprentice witches whispered furiously among themselves.

"Second, that you have expressed remorse for your actions and attempted to make amends by warning Thea's caretakers of the danger posed by Ospak. Is that correct?"

Millie came forward and said loudly, "That is correct."

"Very well," said the elf. "It is the judgement of this Coven that you will make amends by recovering Thea from Vanaheim. As you are half-Vanir and are familiar both with Vanaheim and with Thea's alleged kidnapper, you are the best choice for this task."

"No," Petunia murmured. "Not her!"

The Baba raised her hands. "Cretacia Noctmartis-Ljotsdottor, I place upon you this Geas: that you will go forth and retrieve Thea from her captors, and that you shall not return to the Enchanted Forest Realm until you have done so." This was one of Baba Luci's great powers. A Geas, once placed, was irresistible. A pixie could choose to break their Promise, but a person under Geas had no choice but to obey. Petunia pitied Cretacia.

Cretacia staggered and fell to one knee as Hepsibat burst into tears. Slowly, Cretacia got to her feet. "I'll need help. I can't even get through the Portal by myself now."

Baba Luci addressed the circle. "Are there any here who will assist Cretacia?"

Petunia stepped forward. "I'll help!"

"Me, too!" Millie called out. "I'm Thea's guardian. It's my duty to go."

"You're not going without me," yelled Max.

Sagara sighed and stood up. "I had better go, too, just to keep all of them out of trouble. I am well versed in Vanir court etiquette."

A surprised ripple ran through the Coven, but Sagara was looking down at her grandmother, who nodded her approval.

"Thank you," Cretacia said, visibly relieved.

"You may leave at first light," said the Baba. "You are now dismissed from this Coven."

Cretacia turned and walked out of the center, past the outer ring of stones, and into the darkness, her mother following behind.

"Now," said the Baba. "There is one more matter to consider."

A murmur of surprise rose amongst the witches.

"Bogdana Noctmartis has requested permission to take an apprentice," said Baba Luci.

"About time," said one of the witches. Another said, "What fool of a girl would study with her?"

Baba Luci smiled. "Bogdana Noctmartis and Petunia of Pixamitchie, please come forward."

"What?" "It can't be!" "A *pixie*?" "Madness!"

Petunia squeezed her mother's hand, then stepped before

the altar next to Bogdana.

"Bogdana," said the Baba. "You are requesting a pixie as your apprentice. This is rather unusual. Please explain to the Coven the reasons behind your selection."

Bogdana cleared her throat. "Petunia is highly skilled, for a pixie. She assisted me during the recent spickle pox outbreak and learned to make the cure. On her own, she discovered why the standard cure did not fully work and found a solution. She is talented and dedicated. She is also the best student I have ever had."

Several snickers erupted from the crowd, since the only student Bogdana'd had was Millie.

"Petunia," said the Baba. "I understand that you had grave misgivings about apprenticing yourself to Bogdana. Why do you still want to work with her?"

Petunia twirled a lock of hair nervously. "Well, I really like making potions. I learned a lot from Bogdana, not just about potions, either." She thought of the umbre wyrm's egg tucked away at her parents' apartment against future disasters. "Bogdana is a good teacher. But... I need to know she won't be horrible to me again."

"I believe I can provide that. Bogdana, are you willing to be placed under Geas, guaranteeing that you will not mistreat Petunia?"

Bogdana bowed her head. "I am."

The entire Coven gasped. "Really?" someone murmured. "You're that desperate?"

Bogdana looked up, then gave a wry smile. "She's that good."

"Are you prepared?" the Baba asked. When Bogdana nodded, she said. "Bogdana Noctmartis, I place upon you this Geas: that so long as Petunia of Pixamitchie serves as your apprentice, you will treat her with dignity and respect, and you will not force her to do anything against her wishes in any way."

Bogdana gasped as the Geas took hold.

Baba Luci turned to Petunia. "Does this satisfy you, Petunia?"

Petunia glanced back at her parents, who, though still terrified, nodded at her. She turned back to the Baba. "Yes," she said. "I accept. As soon as I return from helping Cretacia find Thea, I will serve as Bogdana's apprentice to the best of my ability." Taking a deep breath, she added, "I Promise."

The Enchanted Forest School Beginners' Guide to High Mystery

Anna minun puhua [person] – Scry [person]

Halvene – cease, stop

Hehku – light, glow

Kasva jättiläismäiseksi – Grow to the size of a giant

Katoa – cancel (a spell to cancel spells)

Kuunnella – listen (eavesdropping spell)

Kuten kerran olit, niin oletkin – a very formal mending spell, returns the object to its state from the past.

Lämpene – warm (reheat food, basically a microwave spell)

Muodosta energiakupla – Create an energy ward

Nopeasti - cook

Nouse – levitate

Nuku - sleep

Paikata – patch, mend

Paloittele tämä hanhi – carve this goose

Puhdista – clean

Puhdista tämä vesi – Purify this water

Siivoa – Tidy up

Sulje – close

Syty – ignite (light a fire)

Tänne – come to me

Yhdisty – mend (fix something broken)

Acknowledgments

'This was not the novel I'd intended to write. I wanted the central plot element to be Thea's disappearance, and Petunia, feeling responsible, would lead the effort to rescue her. That's the novel I first turned in. A few weeks later, Corie Weaver at Dreaming Robot Press responded to my submission.

"I got the dev edit report from Laura yesterday, and she said a couple things that made me wonder about a possible turn to take with Petunia," she wrote. "In some ways, there are almost two different stories happening in the book - Petunia finds her magical path and saves the village, and the storyline about the Vanir and the rescue of Thea."

Uh oh, I thought.

"And in the second half, there's a lot going on... I'm almost wondering if that should be a book in its own right."

Um, what?

"Which I know brings up all sorts of issues - one of which is the title, but that's a possibly minor thing. The larger issue is that leaves us with half a novel :)"

Right! Yes! This is a terrible idea!

But Corie really loved the section in Vanaheim. "The detail and action are so rich though, I'd almost love to see that all expanded out into a full novel of its own."

ARRRRGH!!!

At first, I hated the entire idea. I'd written the novel. The novel was DONE. I was already moving on to the next book, in which Max would be the protagonist. But the more I thought about it, the more I began to agree with Corie and Linda and Marti Johnson, who'd said the exact same thing in one of my critique groups. It took me a good month of wrestling with myself, but I finally admitted it: I had kitchen-sinked the novel. I had thrown in every idea that came into my head, and the result felt rushed and confusing and crazy.

Worse, I'd let Sagara take over the entire second half of the novel, leaving Petunia as a mostly helpless bystander, and that was no good at all. I'd robbed Petunia of the opportunity to really explore and expand into herself. The novel needed a new ending. On the positive side, I'd always wanted to do a novel with Sagara as the protagonist, I just hadn't come up with a plot, and now one had fallen in my lap.

I went back to Corie with a new plot outline. We did a long, complicated round of negotiations, and we ended up putting together a three-book contract for *A Pixie's Promise*, *An Elf's Equations*, and Max's book, with the title still to be determined. Wow! A multi-book contract! Now all I had to do was write a whole new ending to *A Pixie's Promise*, which I finished smack in the middle of the Kickstarter campaign to fund the initial publication run.

Thus, I find myself with a much larger number of people to thank than I'd ever expected. I apologize right now if I forget anyone. Believe me, I really do appreciate every single person who contributed to this project.

Thanks to Corie, Laura, and Amanda Coffin for all their hard editing work on *Pixie*.

Thanks to the Pathfinders critique group – Marti

Johnson, Dirk Tiede, Laura Speare, and Lauren Barbieri – for reading through two completely different versions of Pixie. Thanks also to the Cornerstone critique group – Miki Burlage, Josephine Gow, Julia Knowles, Courtney Quinn, Cary Rand, Elizabeth Stern, Jenifer Tidwell, Margaret Wachs, and Kayla Zuber – for plot rejiggering assistance and general hand-holding.

Thanks to Anahita Ayasoufi, Timothy Gwyn, Courtney Quinn, and Jenifer Tidwell for agreeing to exchange novel manuscripts with me and providing me with great feedback, even though not a single one of you has given me a manuscript to review in return. I await your novels with great anticipation.

Thanks to the members of the New England chapter of Broad Universe, especially those at the fall 2017 and winter 2018 retreats, at which I wrestled through many of the thorniest problems in A Pixie's Promise: E.C. Ambrose, Elizabeth Black, Terri Bruce, L.J. Cohen, Randee Dawn, Justine Graykin, Rona Gofstein, Angi Shearstone, Morven Westfield, and Trisha J. Wooldridge.

Thanks to my young beta readers and Facebook party participants: Alice, Dina, Erin, Julian, Katarina, Luka, Meredith, Nomi, Ruti, and William. Thanks to Aidan for bad jokes and Nyx for the inspiration for Cretacia's tale. Thanks also to Ms. Russell's entire fifth grade class at the Peabody School in Cambridge for reading the earlier version and letting me blather at them about writing.

Thanks to the New England Society for Children's Book Writers and Illustrators, whose annual conference in Springfield has given me invaluable information and advice on plot development, revision, and much, much more.

Thanks to Michael Gross of the Authors Guild for his extensive and detailed contract advice, as well as Holly

Thompson who suggested I join the Guild in the first place, and thanks to everyone who contributed advice on multi-book contracts.

Thanks to my darling, Nora, who drew the initial sketch for the cover, Nataliia Letiahina for turning a 10-year-old's artwork into a gorgeous illustration, and Sean Weaver for pulling it all together into a fantastic cover.

Thanks again to Nina Niskanen who corrected my pidgin Finnish and turned it into poetic High Mystery.

Thanks to Corie and Sean for running yet another successful Kickstarter campaign, to Bill Wolfe my Kickstarter partner, whose book *Twain's Treasure* is fabulous and makes me look good by association, and to everyone who contributed to the campaign to make this book possible. You are all marvelous and have excellent taste in books.

Finally, and most importantly, thanks to my husband, Alex, and my children, Annie and Nora, for inspiring me, supporting me, and generally putting up with me. I love you with all my heart.

About the Author

Dianna Sanchez is the not-so-secret identity of Jenise Aminoff, also known to her children as the Queen of Sarcasm. She has worked as a technical writer, electrical engineer, programmer, farmer, and preschool cooking teacher, among many other things. Her middle-grade fantasy novel, A Witch's Kitchen, debuted from Dreaming Robot Press in September 2016. A Latina geek originally from New Mexico, she now lives in the Boston area with her husband and two daughters.

CPSIA information can be obtained
at www.ICGtesting.com
Printed in the USA
FSHW01n1629290918
52509FS